218 FIRST HUGS

E. L. TODD

Hartwick Publishing

218 First Hugs

Copyright © 2017 by E. L. Todd

CONTENTS

1

Amelia

Bree and I couldn't have the conversation right there on the couch since Evan was down the hall. So she left with a terrifying look of accusation heavy on her face. I knew the second the sun was up and we had some privacy, she would drill me like she was trying to get through solid rock.

The next morning, I let Evan out before the girls woke up. I felt dirty, like I had a nasty secret that would be the death of me. Bree knew exactly what I was doing, and I was afraid she would tell Ace, not that he would care anyway.

I walked Evan to the door and hoped he would leave without further conversation.

Of course, he didn't want that. "Everything okay with Bree?"

"Why did you come into the living room?" I countered.

His face fell in confusion. "Just wanted to see if everything was okay."

"No one was yelling or screaming. Everything was under control. So you were either being nosy, or you wanted Bree to see you."

His face turned into a stone wall, completely unreadable. "What does it matter if she sees me? I know you tell her everything anyway."

"I definitely wouldn't tell her about this."

"Well, you should."

"There's nothing to tell. We aren't getting back together. We're just fooling around."

"For now."

My eyes narrowed. "Have a good day, Evan." I turned back to the couch, needing to get away from him.

He grabbed me by the arm and yanked me back. He planted a hard kiss on my mouth before he let me go. "I hope everything is alright with Bree. You know you can call me." He walked away without another word.

I got the girls ready and dropped them off at school before I walked up to Amelia's Place. There was no doubt that Bree would be there, and once everyone else left, she would turn on me.

When I walked into the office, no one was there.

Except Bree.

Damn.

She sat on her desk with her legs dangling down. She wore a black shirt and jeans, ready to head to the café as soon as this conversation was over.

I was surprised the rest of the gang wasn't there. But I guess it wasn't surprising that Cypress hadn't made an appearance. After his last conversation with my sister, he was probably laying low.

Bree started talking the second she saw me walk through the door. "You're back with Evan?" She shrieked so loudly I was certain people on the bottom floor heard every word she said. "What happened to all that talk about not getting back together with him?"

"We aren't back together." I tossed my purse on my desk and sank into the leather chair. "And would you keep it down? Everyone is going to hear you."

"So what?" she asked. "If you aren't back together with him, then what are you doing?"

"I don't know...I've just been depressed over Ace, so I wasn't thinking clearly."

"Why would you still be depressed over him? You hooked up one time."

I couldn't tell her the truth without throwing Ace under the bus, so I kept the knowledge to myself. "I don't know...it's just taken me a while."

"Amy, Evan is the biggest douchebag on the planet."

"I'm aware."

"And yet, you're sleeping with him?"

"I'm not saying it was the best decision. But I wasn't happy, so I made a dumb decision. It happens."

"It better not happen again. He doesn't deserve you, Amelia."

"I know he doesn't." I'd never been so lost in my entire life. I loved one man, but he didn't see me as more than a warm body to sleep beside. The man who betrayed me wanted me back even though he didn't deserve another chance. I was jealous of people who lived simple lives...if such people existed. "What's going on with you and Cypress?"

"What do you mean?"

"You said you broke things off. Have you spoken since?"

"No. But we aren't talking about me right now. We're talking about you. I need to know you aren't getting back together with Evan."

"I'm not."

"I need a promise, Amy." She pointed her finger right at my chest.

That was a promise I couldn't give. I had no idea what the future held. "Why do you care so much? I know you want the best for me, but you're getting really involved in my personal life. When it came to Cypress, I gave you your space."

"Because I lost my memory. Totally different situations."

"Not really. I know you don't like Evan, and neither do I. But I'm going through a hard time right now. Instead of being judged for it, I should get some slack."

Bree finally realized she was being too hard on me when she sighed and hopped off the desk. "I'm sorry. You're right."

My sister was stubborn as hell, but she came to her senses eventually. "It's okay."

She joined me and hopped on my desk so we were close together. "Why do men have to be such assholes?"

A question no woman could answer. "I don't know…"

"They're such pigs. All of them."

"Yeah."

She hopped off the desk again and grabbed her purse. "I need to get to work, but I'm glad we had this talk. I can't explain how much I hate Evan. I want to run him over with my car. Like, that's how much I hate him."

I chuckled. "I know."

"I want you to be with someone better."

That someone better didn't want me. "Me too."

"I hope we both find a happy ending someday. Right now, it doesn't seem possible."

My outlook on life was just as bleak. "Yeah…but let's keep hoping."

She sighed and headed to the door. "And dreaming."

I WAITED UNTIL WE CLOSED DOWN AMELIA'S PLACE AND ALL the employees left. Cypress didn't say more than two words to me either, so he obviously didn't want to talk about my sister.

I wanted to talk about it even less than he did.

We locked all the doors and broke down the two registers.

Cypress counted the cash and rolled it into wads, his eyes concentrating on what he was doing.

I stood at the counter and stared at him, waiting for him to acknowledge me.

He didn't.

"Cypress, we're gonna have to talk about this."

He slammed the register harder than he should, making a loud, ringing noise. He clenched his jaw as he swallowed back the cold retort he had on his tongue. After he squeezed the edge of the counter, he looked at me. "I guess we do."

"Why did you tell Bree anything?"

"Because she asked. I can't lie to her."

"But the kiss was just a stupid mistake. She doesn't need to know about it."

"Which is why I didn't tell her you were involved. If I did..." He shook his head. "She would feel betrayed. I know she would."

"But she's willing to divorce you over this, Cypress."

"I know. I was there when she told me."

"We can't let that happen." I couldn't let Cypress lose the woman he loved because of my stupid mistake. I couldn't let Bree lose the man who loved her more than anything. This was all my fault—and I should take responsibility for it.

"It's already happened. I know I can't change her mind

about this one. There's nothing that can be done. I have to let her walk away."

"Cypress, we aren't doing that. I'll tell her what happened."

"No." He looked me in the eye with his menacing gaze. "That's not an option."

"I don't like it either, but that's the only way to fix this."

He shook his head. "She'll never forgive you. She'll never forgive you for kissing me."

I knew she would be angry, heartbroken, and every emotion in between. And she would have every right to be. "She won't forgive me right away. It'll take her some time. But I know she will. Even if she doesn't, she deserves to know that you were always faithful to her, that I kissed you, and you pulled away. She's probably assuming something far worse than what actually happened."

"She'll be so hurt, Amelia. She'll be more hurt than she is now."

"When I tell her how depressed I was...how broken I was...she'll understand."

He shook his head again. "She'll never understand how her best friend, her sister, could kiss her husband. She'll never let it go, Amelia."

"She gave you a second chance, didn't she?"

"But you're her sister. It's totally different. She'll see it as a worse betrayal."

"Yeah, you're right. But we're still blood, so she'll forgive me."

He looked down at the counter between us, his eyes shifting back and forth. "Are you really willing to risk it?" His fingers dug into the wood until his knuckles turned white. When he released the edge, he grabbed the money and tossed it into the leather pouch. "I don't want her to lose you. I don't want you to lose her. I love both of you, and I can't rip you apart."

"And you think I'll let myself rip you two apart?"

He zipped up the bag full of cash and tossed it on the counter. "I love my wife more than anything in the world. That being said, she can always find another husband. She can't find another sister. You're the only family she's got in the entire world, Amelia. I can't let her lose you."

I grabbed his left wrist, the hand that held his wedding ring. "You're her family, Cypress. You are more family than I am. We have to do the right thing. And the right thing is me telling her the truth."

"There's a chance she won't take me back anyway. Her seeing Vanessa just fucked everything up." He ran his hand through his hair, sighing in irritation. "That stupid bitch fucked everything up. God, I hate her."

I hated her more. "You'll recover from that. Bree will know she's just being jealous."

"I'm not so sure."

"I am. Bree needs to know that kiss wasn't your fault. It was my doing. It's gonna suck. It's gonna hurt. But we've gotta do the right thing."

He pulled his hand away. "No. She needs you more than she needs me."

"Cypress, you're being ridiculous right now."

"I'm not gonna tell her. I'd rather divorce her and lose her forever than have her lose her sister. It's not worth it."

"And I'm not gonna let you suffer for a crime you didn't commit. I'm gonna tell her the truth, whether you like it or not."

He pinched the bridge of his nose between his thumb and forefinger. "It's a bad idea, Amelia. You're risking both of us losing her. The second you tell her, I'm still complicit in the situation. There was still a kiss. So she might still divorce me anyway. At least this way, there is only one victim, not two."

"We're gonna have to see what happens—together."

"Amelia—"

"I have to tell her, Cypress."

"You weren't gonna tell her before. So why tell her now?"

He was right. I wasn't going to tell her. I thought it would only cause harm instead of good. "Because now she's gonna lose the best thing that ever happened to her. I have to stop it."

"There's nothing you can do to stop it, Amelia," he said quietly. "This relationship is just too complicated. Now we're gonna make it more complicated. Nobody can come back from this."

"That's not true," I whispered. "We're family—and we'll come back from this."

2

BLADE

I worked at Olives with Ace that afternoon. The lunch rush was just as hectic as the evening rush, even more so because people didn't usually make reservations during the day. We had to accommodate large parties without being prepared for them.

"Any new ladies in your life?" I cycled the hot food to the front of the counter and handed the hot plates to Isabella, who rushed them to customers in the main dining room.

Ace took the clean dishes sitting on the wash counter and stacked them so the cooks could grab them easily. "Not really. Just been doing my own thing."

"Lady hasn't come back around?"

"Nope. We haven't spoken since I ended things."

"I'm surprised she wanted to be serious. She seemed pretty easygoing."

Ace shrugged and got back to work. "What about you?"

"Nothing has changed with Celeste and me. She's awesome as hell, and I'm trying not to fall for her."

"That's pretty insane considering you've never fallen for anyone in your life."

"I know. Pretty shitty." I remembered the night we slept together, and it was difficult not to get hard thinking about it. "By the way, don't call me when I'm about to get laid. Really bad timing."

"What are you talking about?"

"You called me after we left Cultura. I was literally making out with Celeste against the wall when you wouldn't stop calling me."

Ace was about to carry a batch of dirty dishes to the sink when he halted. "Dude, what are you talking about? I never called you after we met up at Cultura."

"For one, we never agreed to meet up. You just crashed my date. And two, yes, you did. Celeste answered the phone and said I was too busy getting laid to talk."

Ace still wore the same confused expression. "Dude, wasn't me."

"If it wasn't you, then who was it?"

"I don't know. Why don't you check your phone? Isn't that what the call log is for?"

Come to think of it, I'd never looked. If Bree or Cypress were the ones who called me, they probably would have mentioned by now. "Good idea."

Ace rolled his eyes then walked out to the dining room to help bus tables.

I pulled out my phone and scrolled through the log, seeing who called me at that specific date and time.

Mom.

Fuck, my mom called me.

Shit.

She was the one Celeste had been speaking to. No one

else called me that night. Actually, no one had called me that entire day.

God fucking dammit.

I didn't embarrass easily, but this had to be the most humiliating moment of my life. The woman I was seeing told my own mother I couldn't come to the phone because I was about to fuck her.

Jesus Christ.

Ace returned with a tray of dirty plates and silverware. He placed everything on the counter next to the dishwasher then turned back to me. "Why do you look so pale right now? You just ate lunch like fifteen minutes ago."

I wiped my damp forehead then held up my phone for Ace to see the name.

He squinted his eyes as he read it. "Mom? Your mom was the one on the line?"

I nodded. "Man, this is bad."

Ace tried to hide the grin that stretched over his mouth, but it made him look like he was cringing. "I think that's the funniest thing I've heard all day."

"It's not funny. This is the most embarrassing thing that's ever happened to me."

"You think your mom doesn't know you have sex?"

"I'm sure she does, but I doubt she thinks about it." I shoved my phone back into my pocket. "No wonder why she hasn't called me in a while."

"Must think you're busy," he teased. "At least you don't have to worry about your mom ever meeting Celeste."

"Why?"

"Because she's going back to Paris," Ace said. "So maybe it's good it didn't work out."

Even with the embarrassing episode, I'd still rather have

Celeste stick around and meet my parents. "That doesn't make me feel better, man."

He grabbed two plates of hot food then handed them to the waitress who stepped into the kitchen. "Look, we're all adults here. If you explain that neither one of you knew who was calling, it should be fine. You guys can have a big laugh about it."

"Not anytime soon."

"Your mom will get over it. Don't worry about it. I'm sure she's found your porn or your old condoms in the garbage can in the past. Moms know everything, I swear."

"But it's gonna be so awkward when I talk to her. Maybe I just won't talk to her ever again."

"Good luck with that." He chuckled before he walked out with two more plates of hot food.

I watched the cooks work over the blazing stoves in their white hats and jackets. The world continued on around me, but I was stuck in the haze of the past. I'd have to work this out with my mom eventually. May as well get it over with sooner rather than later.

I texted Celeste. *Can I see you later? I have a story to tell.*

Come by when you get off work. I'll cook dinner.

I loved her cooking. I loved being in that beautiful French house with a beautiful French woman. I didn't mind taking her out for a nice meal, but I would take her home-cooking any day. *I'll see you then.*

***

I'D NEVER GOTTEN A WOMAN FLOWERS BEFORE, BUT I PICKED up purple irises before I knocked on her door. Giving a woman flowers was cheesy and overdone, but anytime I came over, she had fresh flowers in vases on every table, even on the picnic table outside. It seemed like something she would genuinely want.

She answered wearing black pants, heels, and a pink blouse. Her eyes immediately moved to the flowers, and she hardly looked at me. "Are those for me?"

"I thought they would look nice on your picnic table."

"And you're right." She took them from my hand and kissed me on the mouth. "Thank you."

I'd do anything for more kisses like that. "You're welcome."

Like she'd done it a hundred times, she pulled out an empty vase from the cabinet, trimmed the stems, and then dropped the flowers inside along with some water. "They look beautiful." She set them on the picnic table outside then returned to the kitchen.

Steam was erupting from the pan, so I knew something was going on. "Need help?"

"No. Everything is finished." She turned off the burners then scooped the food onto two plates.

I had no idea what it was. Some kind of pasta.

"Gnocchi and salad. Is that okay?"

I'd eat anything she made—even snails. "Looks good."

She set the plates outside before we took our seats. She had a bottle of wine with two glasses and poured the red liquid into each one.

"This looks great. Thanks for having me."

"No problem." She took a few bites, her lips painted deep red with lipstick. "So, what's the story?"

I'd finally stopped thinking about it once I'd laid eyes on her. "Remember how you answered my phone when we were getting it on against your wall?"

"Yes." She grinned at the memory. "I definitely remember."

"Well, apparently, it was my mom."

She nearly spat out her food when she released a loud laugh. She covered her mouth then wiped her face with a napkin. "Are you serious?"

"Unfortunately."

It was the first time I'd seen her cheeks blush with embarrassment. She covered her face and laughed again. "Oh no..."

"Yeah."

"Wow."

"Yep."

"What did she say?"

"I haven't spoken to her. I was talking to Ace about it today, and we figured out she was the one on the line."

"That's gonna be the most awkward conversation in the world. I'm so sorry."

I shrugged. "I'm sure we'll get past it. Maybe one day it'll be a funny story."

"I doubt that."

I chuckled. "Yeah, probably not. I'll call her and get it over with soon."

"What will you say?"

"Not much. She already heard the entire exchange."

"What about me?" she asked. "Will you tell her about me?"

"Yeah, I guess."

She laughed before she drank her wine. "Then she's not gonna like me very much."

It's not like she would ever meet her anyway. "Whatever."

Celeste returned to eating her food, seeming to forget the entire exchange. "I'm sorry I answered the phone like that. I shouldn't have done that. I just assumed it was Ace or Cypress or something..."

"Don't apologize, baby. It was hot."

"Yeah?" The corner of her mouth rose in a smile. "It was hot that I spoke to your mother that way?"

"Well, it was hot at the time. I thought you were talking to Ace too."

"I've learned my lesson." She sipped her wine, smearing more lipstick on the glass.

"Maybe check the screen next time," I teased.

"Or silence the phone."

"Good idea."

She swirled her wine before she took another drink, a flirtatious smile on her face.

I had a feeling I was going to get laid again tonight.

"How are your friends?" she asked.

"Good-ish."

"Ish?" she asked.

"My friends Cypress and Bree are going through a rough patch. They say it's over for good this time."

"I hope not. They were cute together."

"I don't know. They've had a lot of problems, and I don't think they'll get over them this time."

"What happened?" she asked.

"Cypress kissed someone when they were married."

Her eyes popped open. "He cheated?"

"I guess. But he won't tell anyone who he kissed. He says it was short and didn't mean anything, but he won't give us the details. It's strange because I can't picture him doing that. He cheated on her a long time ago, but he's been super-loyal ever since."

"He cheated on her in the past too?" she asked incredulously.

I knew that made Cypress look like dirt. "Yeah...not his finest hour."

"If I were Bree, I wouldn't be able to trust him anymore. Sounds like he has a problem."

I used to hate Cypress, but I recognized how much he'd changed. I believed there was more to this story. "I think he had a good reason for what he did. He's just not sharing it with us."

"If he's gonna lose his wife, shouldn't he say something?"

That was a good point. "Yeah..."

"Some people just aren't meant to be in a relationship. Monogamy isn't normal anyway. Very few beings in the world are monogamous."

Did she share that belief as well? I was under the impression she was a bit of a drifter, moving from place to place. It made sense because she never seemed interested in anything more serious. She never asked if we were exclusive or if I was seeing anyone else. "Maybe. But I know Cypress loves her."

"I'm sure he does. But maybe he just needs more, physically. The guy was pretty much single for eighteen months. A little unrealistic to expect him to be alone that entire time."

"Yeah, I guess. But I still have a hard time believing that."

She set down her fork and surveyed the trees around her, her eyes filling with a gloss that was caused by the setting sun. Her hair was always thick and her makeup heavy, and I had yet to meet a more beautiful and elegant woman. I loved the way she carried herself, the way she always held a strong posture. She exuded strength and independence, not weakness and clinginess. She was the kind of woman who didn't need a man.

And I found that sexy as hell.

WE DID THE DISHES TOGETHER AND CLEANED UP THE KITCHEN, each doing a different task until the house was back to its usual cleanliness. It was sleek and cute, reminding me of a picture from a French catalog. She seemed to be strictly disciplined, always cleaning up every single spot until she was finished.

She dried her hands on the towel then looked at me with that cute smile. "You want to see my room?"

My cock came to attention. "I think I've already seen it. But I wouldn't mind seeing it again."

"That was the spare bedroom. My room is upstairs and down the hall."

"Lead the way." I didn't pay attention to the bedroom last time. I was too busy looking at the naked woman I was fucking.

She grabbed my hand and pulled me upstairs, revealing the beautiful master bedroom that was just as well decorated as downstairs. She pulled her top over her head and unclasped her bra with a simple movement, making it drop to the floor.

I stared at her tits in fascination. "Your boobs are perfect." I gripped them with both hands and squeezed them. My thumb brushed over the nipples, and I squeezed them harder, my cock harder than steel now that her ample breasts were in my hands.

Her fingers moved to my jeans and got them loose as I felt her up. She yanked them down along with my boxers, letting my cock come free. She licked her palm before she wrapped her hand around my length and stroking me, her thumb brushing across the head of my dick and swiping away the drop that formed.

Damn, she was good at that.

I got her jeans open then tugged them down, slipping her out of the denim as well as the heels she wore. Her panties came next, sliding down her soft skin until they were on the floor.

I didn't have a chance to appreciate her body last time because we got to fucking right away. But this time, I slowed things down. I guided her to the bed and positioned her on her back before I kissed her, my body pressed against her folds. I loved feeling that nub against my length as well as the arousal that was seeping at her entrance.

I'd never want to fuck a woman more in my life.

My hand was on her cheek then in her hair before I returned it to her tit. I gripped it as I kissed her harder, our bodies wrapped around one another. She looked beautiful with her dark hair stretched out across the bed, her beautiful eyes bold and confident. I loved it when a woman felt sexy. There was a distinct difference to being vain. She wasn't arrogant or coincided, just aware.

I wanted to fool around her with her all day, but this foreplay was just making me harder. I wouldn't last long with all this stimulation. Just her tits alone made me want to come.

Like an idiot, I hadn't brought a condom. I assumed she had some stashed in her nightstand. "Do you have a condom?" I asked as I kissed her.

She wrapped her legs around my waist and pulled me toward her. "I'm on the pill."

I'd only fucked bare pussy a few times—and it was fucking heaven. But I didn't know this woman that well, so it wouldn't be smart. "Maybe we should use one anyway."

"I'm clean," she said into my mouth. "Are you?"

I got tested regularly. My last result had been recent, and I hadn't slept with anyone since. "Yes."

"I want to feel you...just you." When she said those words with that French accent, I was powerless to think. I just wanted to fuck.

I pointed my cock at her entrance and slid inside, entering the tightest, warmest, and wettest pussy I'd ever known. "Fuck..." I slid all the way inside until my balls rested against her ass. "Fuck." I held myself up and looked down at her, all my senses ignited into a powerful fire. I didn't want to move because she felt so good. All I could think about was dumping all of my come deep inside her, but I had to please her first.

And I would.

I rocked into her, moving through her tight wetness as my arms flexed to keep myself above her. Every time I thrust, her tits shook, her nipples hard. The sexiest thing I looked at was her face. Her red lips were open, revealing small teeth where her tongue was pressed between them. Her eyes were bright with desire, fixed on me like I was the only man she'd ever been with. She could look so sexy without even trying. She was better than any fantasy I'd ever had. My brain couldn't even conceive of a woman this beautiful.

And right now, she was mine.

She didn't just lie there and enjoy it. She gripped my biceps, using my frame to lift her bottom up and slide down my length. She moved with me, wanting my cock as much as I wanted to give it to her. Her deep breaths turned to suppressed moans. Not much longer after that, she was saying my name. "Blade..."

This woman. Fuck.

She locked her ankles together and rested them at my

lower back. I could feel her toned thighs right against my sides. Her calves pressed into my back, also strong from walking in heels all day. Her hands slowly slid down my back, her nails teasing my skin with their sharpness, and when she reached my ass, she gave me a hard squeeze.

No woman had ever grabbed my ass before. I liked it.

She guided my hips, showing me exactly how she wanted it. She wanted long and even strokes, a slow pace. She wanted to know when every thrust was coming so she could enjoy it.

That was hot.

She rolled onto her back and bit her lip. "Just like that..." She kept one hand on my ass and dug the other into her hair, holding on as the pleasure swept through her. "Fuck me like that, Blade."

Thank god she was gonna come. I wasn't gonna last much longer.

I kissed her jawline and trailed my lips to her mouth. "I love fucking you."

Her hands gripped my back, and she held on as she came all around my dick. "Blade...god." She bit her lip and moaned at the same time, her nails ripping apart my skin.

I fucked her harder and tried to make her sensations last as long as possible. I wanted to make her come every night, and I wanted her to want me to be the man who made her come every night.

She released another moan that came out as a grunt, and she finally stopped, nearly piercing my skin with her nails. "I want you to make me come again."

"I'd love to." I was a gentleman. If a woman asked me to do something, I'd oblige.

"But I want you to come inside me first."

Damn.

With flushed cheeks, she looked me in the eye and gripped my ass with both hands. She pulled me into her, wanting my entire length. She wanted my balls to slap against her ass. "Come on, baby." She rocked with me, using her core to lift herself up and take my length.

I didn't need much incentive. She was already gorgeous underneath me, with rockin' tits and a sexy expression on her face. She was begging for my come, like I wasn't just as thrilled to give it. I ground into her harder, inserting my length deep every time. "Here it comes..."

She bit her bottom lip as she watched me. *"Donne le moi..."*

I didn't need to know what she said to appreciate the sexiness. I came with a powerful convulsion, the heat searing all the way up my spine and through my balls. I released with a loud moan, my vision blurring because all I could do was feel. I couldn't see, hear, or smell. I could only bow to the powerful explosion that brought me to my knees. "Fuck..." I gave her all of my come, wanting to make sure she had every single drop of that seed. I wanted it to sit inside her all night while she slept. I wanted it to seep from between her legs when she was in the shower so she would think about me.

"Yeah...that felt good." She locked her arms around my neck and kissed me, still slightly grinding beside me.

The sex that evening even topped the last fuck we'd had a few days ago. Every round with this woman got better and better.

"But you aren't going anywhere." She grabbed my hips and kept me in place as I started to soften. "I want more."

I kissed her slowly, giving her a gentle embrace despite how aggressive we both were just a minute ago. "More, it is."

I WALKED INTO THE OFFICE TO SEE ACE AND CYPRESS. AMELIA and Bree must already have been at work because they were nowhere in sight.

"Same clothes as yesterday..." Ace looked me up and down. "Must have had another good night, huh?"

"A very good night." I sat in my chair and looked at Cypress, who'd looked constantly grim for the past week.

"Talk to your mom?" Ace teased.

"No." I rolled my eyes. "Not yet."

"Your mom?" Cypress asked in confusion.

Ace immediately jumped at the chance to tell the story. He told it in full, not skipping over the heated words Celeste had said to me.

Cypress barely cracked a smile. "Yikes. That's bad."

"And I haven't spoken to her since," I said. "I'm sure my mom hasn't called me either for the same reason."

"Let me know how that goes," Cypress said before he turned back to his computer. His shoulders were slumped and heavy, and he nearly had a full beard on his chin.

Ace eyed him before he turned back to me.

"Cypress?" I asked.

"What's up?" Cypress didn't look away from his screen.

"So...who did you kiss?" He still hadn't told us what happened, and Ace and I were eager to get the bottom of it. The three of us told each other everything, so I didn't understand why that would change so suddenly.

Cypress ignored us. "Doesn't matter."

"You know you can talk to us," Ace said. "We won't say anything to be Bree."

Cypress ignored us altogether.

After an awkward moment of silence, Ace turned back

to me. "Glad that you've chilled out about Celeste. No reason to freak out when you're getting laid."

"Well...last night we were fooling around, and I asked for a condom. She told me she didn't want to wear one because she was on the pill...so we didn't." When I had a fling with someone, we never even discussed protection. It was always assumed we would use a condom in every instance.

"Seriously?" Ace asked. "She was the one who asked?"

"Yeah. Said she wanted to feel me." It was so hot that I didn't have any regrets. It was probably foolish, but whatever. She seemed like a smart girl who wouldn't catch anything from anyone.

Ace still stared at me in shock. Even Cypress looked at me.

"Makes me think we're more serious than a fling," I said. "Should I ask? Or should I keep saying nothing?"

"If you're fucking without a condom, I think it's perfectly okay to have the conversation," Ace said.

"You need to have the conversation," Cypress said. "Just for health reasons. If you're fucking other people, it wouldn't be smart."

"So you think I can talk to her?" I asked, hoping I would finally get to straighten things out with her.

"Definitely," Ace said. "You aren't being clingy by asking where you stand. If she's fucking other guys, you have a right to know. At least, now you do. Just don't make it sound like you're in a hurry to be serious. Just make it sound like you're concerned about your health."

"Yeah," Cypress said. "That should go over well."

I was finally going to figure out exactly how Celeste felt about me. If we weren't using condoms, then I assumed we were only seeing each other. If that were the case, I'd be happy. I wanted to keep her as my own. I didn't want to share her with anyone. And maybe we would grow closer together until she wouldn't want to leave.

It was just wishful thinking, but it was a nice dream to have.

A very nice dream.

3

BREE

Cypress must have believed I meant what I said because he didn't try to talk me out of it. He'd left me alone since that horrible conversation we had in front of our houses. In fact, he avoided me. He was never in the office when I went to work in the morning, and we never worked the same restaurant at the same time.

A part of me was relieved. Another part was heartbroken.

Just when I saw the good side of him, he revealed his true colors. I started to see him as the amazing man every person described him to be. But then he hurt me again. Just like when I caught him with Vanessa the first time, I'd caught him again.

It sucked.

The fire was roaring in my fireplace, and I threw another log on to keep it going for a few hours. It was cool that day, the sky overcast and the air chill. The second I came home, I took a hot shower to warm up and threw my sweats on.

When I stood upright, I looked out the window and saw

Amelia and Cypress standing together. Whatever they were talking about was intense because Cypress looked angry. When Amelia turned away to walk to my front door, he grabbed her by the elbow and kept her in place.

What was going on?

They exchanged a few more words before Cypress finally dropped his grasp, letting Amelia go. They shared one more look before Cypress walked back into his house. Amelia watched him go, heaving a deep sigh before she turned to my front door.

I quickly sat down out of sight so my sister wouldn't know I witnessed the whole exchange.

I couldn't figure out what was going on based on that heated exchange, but it seemed like Cypress didn't want Amelia to come to my house. Maybe she was going to try to convince me I should give him another chance, but Cypress didn't want her to bother? I didn't have a clue.

Amelia knocked.

"Come in."

She walked inside without a smile on her face. Her hair was pulled back into a bun, and she wore jeans and a baggy sweater. She seemed exhausted, like she'd been up all night taking care of one of her sick girls. "Hey."

"Hey." I was on my guard, knowing I was about to be ambushed. Amelia didn't have time to drop by for no reason anymore. If she needed to talk to me, she usually just called. If she was here without her girls, that meant she got someone to watch them. So whatever she wanted to say was serious.

She took a seat on the other couch, bringing sadness into the house. She hardly looked me in the eye. It was as if she was ignoring me, even though I was the only reason she was there in the first place.

"Everything okay, Amy?"

"Yeah...I just need to talk to you about something." She cleared her throat even though her voice hadn't cracked. She looked at the flames in my stone hearth, her eyes heavy with sorrow.

"Okay..." Now I was scared. What if there was something wrong? Mom died young, and health issues were always on my mind. "Please tell me you're okay. I need to know you're okay. If it's something else, then fine. But I need to know it's not that."

"No," she whispered. "I'm in perfect health, Bree."

Then whatever she was going to say couldn't be that bad. "Thank you. What is it?"

She clasped her hands together in her lap and stared at her fingertips. She released a quiet sigh before she looked up and met my gaze. "Before I tell you what happened, you need some background information."

"I'm listening."

"When you lost your memory, it was hard on me. Even though you were alive, I felt like I lost my sister. I couldn't call you. I couldn't see you. Every time I did and you didn't remember what happened the day before, it just hurt. My girls didn't understand what was going on, and the more they grew, the more I had to hide them from you. Then Evan left... I was in a dark place."

"I wish I could have been there for you."

"I know," she whispered. "I could deal with Evan leaving me. But losing you...that was so much harder. You're my sister."

"I know, Amy."

She looked down again, staring at her hands. "A year went by, and things didn't get much easier. Cypress was the one who was there for me the most. He helped me with groceries, picking up the girls from school, watching them so I could go to the doctor...everything. He did everything."

It softened my heart because I knew Cypress was a good man. He just didn't know how to be with one woman.

"I wouldn't have known what to do without him," she whispered. "The doctors told us repeatedly that you weren't going to get better and we should sell the house and put you in a special home for the mentally disabled. Cypress refused to do that, and I'm so glad he did. Personally, I wanted to let it happen because I wanted Cypress to move on. I wanted you to come back, but I didn't think you ever would."

"That's okay," I said. "if I hadn't hit my head, who knows what would have happened?"

"Now that I've told you all of that, I hope you go a little easier on me..."

Easier on her? "What do you mean?"

She looked at her hands again, unable to meet my gaze. "Cypress was over one night. I'd drunk a lot of wine and had put the girls to bed. We were just talking. I was lonely and sad...and I did something really stupid."

I couldn't breathe. I couldn't take a single breath until I knew what happened.

"I kissed Cypress." She closed her eyes because looking down wasn't enough to block me out. "I was the one who kissed him."

While I heard what she said perfectly clearly, I couldn't process it. Amelia was the last person in the world I expected to kiss my husband. And she was the last person I expected Cypress to kiss. There were a few people in life you could always count on to be loyal to you. Amelia had always been that for me—no matter what.

But now she'd betrayed me.

"Cypress was the one who pulled away. The kiss lasted a

few seconds at most. He ended it and left. We didn't talk for a few days until we were finally comfortable facing one another. I apologized, and he forgave me and said he never wanted to talk about it again."

I held my silence, unable to think of a single response. All I could do was picture Cypress kissing my sister, and such a rush of nausea hit me that I thought I would hurl. Imagining him kissing Amelia was somehow worse than Vanessa.

"Cypress didn't want you to know it was me because he didn't want you to push me away. But I needed you to know the truth because you shouldn't let him go. He's the best guy I know. It wasn't his fault. He's always been faithful to you."

My husband and my sister. Disgusting.

Amelia finally looked at me, terror in her gaze. "Bree?"

"You kissed my husband." My hands shook. "My own sister?"

Tears formed in her eyes. "I told you I was in a dark place—"

"What if I kissed Evan after I caught Cypress cheating on me with Vanessa?" I didn't raise my voice because I wasn't angry. I was just numb, unable to believe this had happened. Even if Cypress and I were divorced, it was still wrong of my own flesh and blood to be with him. It was wrong on so many levels.

"I know...it's wrong—"

"It's not just wrong, Amelia. It's... There are no words."

She bowed her head again.

"And he kissed you back." That made me feel even worse. Amelia didn't move on, and Cypress didn't pull away before their lips touched. He tasted her, felt her.

"For only a few seconds," she said. "And he was the one who ended the kiss."

"Who cares about who ended the kiss? The kiss still happened."

"But Cypress was depressed too. He'd been alone for so long, and every day he hoped you would come back to him. He was in just as dark of a place as I was, Bree. I don't want you to blame him for this when it was entirely my fault."

I shook my head. "And you were never going to tell me, huh?" Cypress only mentioned it because I asked him point-blank. I actually respected him for coming clean about it even though he didn't give me all the details. It was more than what Amelia had done.

"I..."

"That's what I thought."

"I knew it would do more harm than good. And it wasn't worth telling. It was the shortest and lamest kiss on the planet. I thought you were never coming back."

"So what if I didn't? Would you have slept with Cypress if I had died? How would you feel if I hooked up with Evan after you died in a car accident? Amelia, it's just wrong. Even if Cypress were just an old boyfriend, it would still be wrong."

"I know..."

"Obviously, you don't." I hopped off the couch because I couldn't sit still anymore. "How could you do that to me?"

"I'm sorry—"

"How can you be sorry when you never planned on telling me?"

"Because it was just a stupid drunken mistake." She rose to her feet, tears in her eyes. "You know I would never do anything to hurt you on purpose."

"Except steal my husband."

"Whoa, I wasn't trying to steal him. I was just looking for comfort that one night—"

"And not a single other guy on the planet was available?" I asked incredulously. "You couldn't even find someone on a dating app? The only solution to your horny loneliness was your sister's husband?"

Her eyes fell at the insult.

"Get out of my house." I didn't want to look at her face anymore. When I understood I'd lost the last three years of my life to amnesia, I knew my sister was one thing I could rely on. I knew she would be the rock to get me back on my feet. But now all that trust was gone.

I walked up the stairs without looking at her. "Now."

"Bree—"

"Get out." I moved to the foot of my bed then slid down to the floor, my arms resting on my knees. I wanted to cry, but I wasn't entirely sure why. When Cypress told me he kissed someone, I just assumed he'd been the one to instigate it. It hurt badly, but not as much as this. My sister being the culprit was a million times worse.

She was my family.

She was my everything.

And she betrayed me. Backstabbed me. Hurt me.

My father left. My mom died. Amelia was all I had left.

And she kissed my husband.

———

I DIDN'T LEAVE THE HOUSE FOR NEARLY THREE DAYS. MY PHONE died, but I didn't bother charging it. There wasn't a single person in the world I wanted to talk to right now. All my drapes were pulled closed so Cypress couldn't see me—not that he wanted to see me.

If he wanted to speak to me, he probably would have

come to the front door by now. His silence told me he still respected my wishes.

I didn't go to work or bother calling in sick. I was certain the whole gang knew exactly what went down, and they didn't need a personal explanation from me. When I was ready, I would come back.

But I was too angry right now.

Late one afternoon, someone knocked on my door.

It could be anyone. It might be Amelia, hoping we could talk again now that I had some time to calm down. It could be Ace, wanting to console me as a friend. I could be Blade, telling me Amelia and Cypress were both wrong for what they had done, but I needed to let it go. Or it could be Cypress.

I wouldn't know until I answered the door.

I opened it.

It was Cypress.

His chin was covered by a full beard, and his clothes seemed a little baggier than usual. The brightness in his eyes was gone, replaced by a matte flatness. His hands sat in his pockets, and he looked at me like he didn't want to be there.

I didn't say anything, wanting him to address the reason for this visit.

"Can I come in?"

I kept my hand on the door like I was blocking him from entering my home. I slowly lowered it before I stepped aside. It was unrealistic to expect Cypress not to come knocking eventually. He gave me three days of space. I couldn't ask for more. "Sure."

Cypress walked in and stopped in the living room. He didn't take a seat on the couch like he usually would, obviously assuming he wasn't welcome to make himself comfortable.

I faced him, my arms across my chest.

"Amelia told me what happened."

"Yeah."

He looked out the window before he turned back to me. "Amelia is pretty terrified right now...thinks she lost her sister."

I was pissed off and out of my mind. But there was nothing she could ever do to make me cut her out of my life. She was all I had, and I loved her so much. "She hasn't lost me...but I don't want to talk to her."

Cypress gave a slight nod, approving my answer. "I'll pass that along." He headed to the door.

"That's all you have to say?" I asked incredulously.

He stopped in his tracks, tightened his shoulders, and then turned around. "What else am I supposed to say?"

"Maybe you should apologize for kissing my sister."

His eyes narrowed. "I didn't kiss her. She kissed me."

"And you kissed her back."

"For two seconds," he snapped. "Not even. When her lips touched mine, I didn't think. All I knew was, the woman I loved despised me. Every day when I saw her, she wanted to rip my eyes out. I was alone, depressed, and lost. I'm sorry for giving in to comfort for two seconds," he snarled. "Misery does crazy things to people. I admit it shouldn't have happened, but I pulled away. I ended the kiss for many reasons. Obviously, I was married to you, and I kept my vow. Secondly, Amelia is like a sister to me. Yes, she's beautiful, but she's not my type. Going down that road would just be a big mistake for both of us. So I stopped it." He snapped his fingers. "Like that."

I was still angry, still livid.

"What do you want me to say?" He threw his arms down. "I know I fucked up in the past and this incident doesn't make me look much better, but you know what?" He pointed his finger into his chest. "You're always gonna get honesty from me. You wanna know something, I'll tell you. You never have to worry about me keeping something from you. I'm a man, and I own up to my mistakes. I don't make excuses for the stupid shit I do."

"If you're always honest, why didn't you tell me my sister was the one you kissed?"

"She deserved to be the one to tell you. I'm not gonna throw her under the bus."

"Wow, you're such a gentleman."

His eyes narrowed. "You're lucky I love you as much as I do."

"Lucky?" I asked. "I'm lucky that my cheating husband loves me?"

"That wasn't cheating, and you know it."

No, I didn't really classify it as that. It was still a betrayal that hurt, but it wasn't like Cypress had an affair with her. He ended the kiss and went home. If he'd slept with my sister, that would have been different.

"I still want to make this work. Despite all the odds, I believe in us."

I stared at him, at a loss for words.

"Sweetheart?"

"Seeing Vanessa changes everything..."

"Why?"

"It reminds me of what you did. I felt like shit all over again."

"I get that. I do. I'd feel like shit if I saw a man you fooled around with, even if you hadn't cheated on me with him. But Vanessa is just some woman from my past. She doesn't mean anything to me. She wanted to get married, and I didn't. Then I fell in love with you. You're the woman I married. You think that doesn't bother her? Of course, it does. So don't let her tear you down. At the end of the day, I made my choice. I picked you."

His words had the desired effect and melted right into my heart. Despite all the stupid things Cypress did, he still came out on top because of all the sweet stuff that would tumble out of his mouth.

Cypress watched my reaction, absorbing it directly into his skin. "So where do we stand? Do you still believe in us?"

If he'd asked me that question five minutes ago, I would have said no. "I don't know...I need some time."

Cypress could have been upset by that answer, but he wasn't. "I'll take it. You can have all the time you want." He walked to the door, dismissing the conversation because there was nothing left to say. He turned around before he shut the door behind him. "You're the only woman I've ever loved. And you're the only woman I ever want to love."

4

AMELIA

I paced back and forth in the kitchen, my arms across my chest. The girls just finished dinner, and now they were getting ready for bed in the bathroom. They were both brushing their teeth and giggling when they splashed water onto each other.

I hadn't been able to think about anything except Bree.

She was so angry with me.

It was like she hated me.

Cypress knocked on the door when he finally arrived.

"Come in." I walked to the entryway just as he opened the door. Before he could say a single word, I asked what was on my mind. "What did she say?"

He sighed before he shut the door. "She's still upset."

I deduced that on my own. "What did she say?"

"She feels betrayed. Even if she died, it would still be wrong for you to kiss me. It's a line that shouldn't have been crossed."

God, this was bad. I was gonna lose my sister. I covered

my face with my hands and stepped away, unprepared for the gravity of the situation.

Cypress continued. "She's mad at me too."

"You didn't do anything wrong."

"Well, she's still upset about it. But she's not as angry as she was. She finally told me she didn't consider it to be cheating. I asked if we could move on, and she said she needed some time. That's a good sign. She'll come around."

As selfish as it sounded, I didn't care about their relationship right now. "What about me? Is she just never going to talk to me again? Should I try apologizing again?"

Cypress leaned against the counter. "I talked her down. She said she doesn't want to talk to you right now, but she's not cutting you out of her life. She just needs space."

"Thank god." I finally fell into the chair at the kitchen table, relieved my little sister wasn't walking out on me. I knew our relationship would never be the same, but at least we still had one.

Cypress took the seat beside me and rested his hand on mine. "I know my wife. She'll let it go, and she'll forgive you."

"You really think so?"

He nodded. "I told her the circumstance, that we were both going through a hard time. She can't judge us too harshly. Your husband left you, your sister was gone...she'd have to be heartless to not understand."

"But you're her husband... I understand why she's mad."

"Nothing more happened. We kissed for two seconds."

"But if you hadn't pulled away..." I didn't finish the sentence.

"Doesn't matter," he whispered. "Nothing happened. That's all that matters." He pulled his hand away and gave me a sympathetic look.

"Cypress, everything is so fucked up right now..."

"Yeah, I know."

"A part of me doesn't blame her for being so upset. You're her husband..."

"You were drinking and depressed. Don't be so hard on yourself. And for what it's worth, I think you would have stopped things before they developed into something more."

"Why?"

"Because I know you," he said quietly. "I know you love your sister more than anything. She'll realize that eventually. Don't lose hope."

I reined in my tears before they could fall. "Thank you..."

"Of course."

I stared at the table between us, still out of my mind with sadness. A stupid decision I made years ago had wreaked havoc on my life. Now I was sleeping with my ex because the man I loved didn't want me. My life was so messed up. I thought I'd hit rock bottom weeks ago, but there was definitely more room for me to fall. "You think you guys will work it out?"

He nodded. "She could have said no when I asked her. But she didn't. She said she needed space. That means she wants to try again, just not right this second. I'm glad she listened to me."

"I'm happy for you. I didn't want you to lose her."

"I know," he whispered. "And I'll make sure you don't lose her either. We're all family here. We're gonna stay a family."

I'd just gotten into bed when my phone vibrated with a text message.

You awake? It was Evan.

I didn't want to deal with him right now, so I ignored it.

I'm standing outside. I want to see you.

Wow. Our relationship had already escalated to midnight booty calls. I got out of bed in just my t-shirt and walked to the front door. My hair was pulled back into a bun and I looked terrible, but I didn't care. His opinion didn't mean anything to me.

I opened the front door and looked at him with my broken gaze. "What?"

He stood in jeans and a t-shirt, his hair styled like he'd done it just before he came over. "What's wrong?"

"What's wrong? Why are you showing up on my doorstep in the middle of the night?"

His eyebrows furrowed in confusion, like he couldn't believe the question. "We've been sleeping together for over a week now. You really think this is presumptuous?"

"Damn right, it is." I shut the door, not wanting to deal with this asshole tonight.

He caught the door with his hand and stepped inside. "Amy, what's wrong?"

"There's nothing wrong. I just don't want to see you, Evan."

He locked the door behind me and stared me down. "I was married to you for eight years. I know when something is wrong."

"I was married to you for eight years, and I thought you wouldn't cheat on me. Looks like we don't know each other that well."

Evan sighed at the insult but didn't back down. "Talk to me. What is it?"

Seeing the concern in his eyes, the affection I used to live for, made me burst into tears. I'd craved that love for so long after he left. I dreamt of him loving me, holding me. When he left me, he didn't look back. He didn't care how much he hurt me. And now he was back, loving me the way he used to.

If he'd never left, I wouldn't have kissed Cypress.

I wouldn't be in this mess.

"I did something really stupid...and Bree won't talk to me." I covered my face because I didn't want Evan to see my cheeks turn blotchy and red. I was so ugly when I cried. I didn't want him to witness such a pathetic scene.

He grabbed my wrists and gently pulled my hands from my face so he could see me. "What happened?" He backed me up into the counter and dug one hand into my hair. His lips moved to the corner of my eye, and he kissed a fresh tear that rolled down my cheek. "What did you do?"

I didn't want to tell him I'd kissed Cypress. I didn't want Evan to ever treat him badly. It might make him jealous, even though he had no right to be. "It doesn't matter...but she won't talk to me."

"Families fight. I wouldn't worry about it."

"But I did something really bad...and really stupid. Cypress said she just needs some time, but I'm afraid our relationship will never be the same. She's my best friend. I lost her once, and I can't lose her again..."

He rubbed his big hands up and down my arms. "Did she find out you were sleeping with Ace?"

"No...she already knew about that." At least, that I slept with him once.

"I could give you better advice if you told me what happened, baby."

I wasn't going to tell him. "It doesn't matter now. I'm not

asking for advice anyway. I already apologized to her, and now I'm just hoping for the best."

"Then what can I do?" he asked. "If there's anything I can do for you, I'm here."

There was nothing anyone could for me. "You can leave."

He pushed his body farther into mine, telling me he wasn't going anywhere. His fingers closed around my neck, and he tilted my head up so my lips were more accessible. With a brooding gaze, he burned me from the inside out. "We both know I'm not leaving tonight."

WHEN I WALKED INTO THE OFFICE THE NEXT MORNING, ACE was the only one there. In dark slacks that made his ass look unbelievable and a black collared shirt, he looked like a million bucks. With a beautiful physique like that, he looked incredible no matter what he wore—or didn't wear.

Ace and I hadn't been alone together since he broke off our secret affair. It wasn't necessarily awkward between us, but it wasn't the same either. The friendship that I loved had dried up quicker than the desert. He never came by the house anymore or dropped off firewood. Might be a good thing since Evan popped up all the time.

I walked to my desk and didn't meet his eyes. "Hey."

Ace turned to me, and I could feel his gaze looking into the side of my face. "I heard what happened."

Either Bree or Cypress told him. I couldn't blame them. The secret was bound to come out. "It was a stupid mistake, and I'd give anything to take it back and I just—"

"Whoa, hold on." He pulled his chair across the gap between the desks so we were beside each other, his knee touching mine. "I didn't bring it up to give you a hard time about it. I just wanted to know if you're okay."

That was why I fell in love him. He was so kind and compassionate. I did something terrible, and he still gave me his concern even if I didn't deserve it. "You wanted to know if I was okay...?"

"Yeah. I haven't seen Bree this mad since Cypress hooked up with Vanessa. I know it must be killing you."

"It is..." I ran my fingers through my hair even though it did little to comfort me. "Cypress told me she just needs space right now, but I need her to forgive me. Until she forgives me, my stomach is gonna be knotted up like this."

"Bree will forgive you," he said with confidence. "But you know how she is. She's an emotional person, and she needs more time to bounce back than the average human."

I did know that. "Yeah..."

"I know you aren't gonna stop stressing out about it, but you should try to relax. Even if she didn't forgive you, Cypress, Blade, and I would set her straight and make her see reason. Alright?" He placed his hand on my back and rubbed gently.

I wanted to tell him I loved him. I wanted him to know his comfort meant the world to me. I was spending my nights with the man who broke my heart, wishing I were with Ace instead. But when Ace looked at me, he just saw an attractive friend.

That's it.

"Thanks," I finally said. "That means a lot to me."

"Of course."

"And thanks for not judging me..."

"Judging you?" His handsome smile grew on his face. "How could I judge you? We all make mistakes. And your mistake wasn't even that big of a deal. We've all gotten carried away with someone we shouldn't."

Was he referring to us? His attempt at making me feel better just made me feel worse. "Yeah."

"I'm glad you told Bree the truth. That must have been hard."

"If I didn't, she was going to leave Cypress."

"I know," he said. "You could have said nothing and saved your own ass. No one would have known. But that's not what you did." He squeezed my shoulder before he dropped his hand. "You did the right thing—and that took balls. I respect you even more now."

And just like that, he made me feel good again. "Thanks, Ace."

"No problem." He wrapped his powerful arm around me and pulled me in for a hug.

It felt so nice.

"I'll be working at Olives today." He pushed his feet against the ground and slid across the floor back to his desk. "I think you're downstairs."

"Okay. Great."

The door opened, and Bree walked inside. She obviously expected me to be at work already because she eyed me with eyes as big as golf balls. She stopped in her tracks and stared me down, just as angry as she had been when I told her I kissed Cypress.

I felt sick again.

She finally tore her gaze away, marched to her desk and snatched her laptop out of the drawer. She stormed off as a second later with the computer tucked under her arm. "Hey, Ace." She disappeared out the door.

Hearing her address Ace just to prove she was ignoring me hurt like hell.

"She'll come around," Ace said. "Let her get it out of her system."

"Get what out of her system?" I said weakly. "She hates me."

"She doesn't hate you. No matter how mad she is, she could never hate you."

I knew there was nothing she could ever do to make me hate her, so I had to believe she felt that exact same way for me.

If I didn't, I'd hit a depression worse than the last one I'd just been through.

And that was already pretty bad.

5

Blade

Cypress and Ace were already sitting at a table in the bar when I walked in. I got my beer then joined them, hopping into a conversation of silence. Cypress's beard was still wild, getting thicker with every passing day. Ace looked exactly the same, but there was a particular aura of sadness about him.

"Both of you had a bad day?" I asked before I drank my beer.

"Every day for the past eighteen months has been a bad day for me," Cypress muttered before he drank his dark beer.

Ace stared into his glass, his face a mask of stoicism.

"Bree is still shut down?" I asked.

"She hasn't talked to me," Cypress said. "She just goes to work then goes home. Wants nothing to do with me—or Amelia."

"Hopefully, it blows over soon," Ace said. "It's weird not having the girls around."

"It is weird. I said hi to Amelia yesterday, and she stared

at me like I was high." The girls lightened the atmosphere at work, bringing fresh flowers into the office and adding nice touches to the restaurants. Those were things none of us guys would think of on our own.

"This is the last time for me," Cypress said.

I didn't know what he meant, so I looked at Ace.

Ace kept his eyes on Cypress, obviously not knowing what that meant either.

I was the first one to ask. "Last time for what?"

"Last time I'm making this work with Bree. I love her, but I can't keep doing this. Every time we go ten steps forward, we go a hundred back. I want to make my marriage work, not just because I don't want to get divorced in my thirties. But this drama is wearing me out."

I didn't blame him. There was hardly a good day for the two of them.

"I didn't even do anything wrong in this situation, but Bree pushed me away anyway. The only reason why I'm still here is because she really did give me a chance. She kept an open mind and tried. Then Vanessa fucked everything up..."

"Anyone would be exhausted," Ace said. "And no guy would have stuck around this long."

"I know," Cypress said quietly. "So, this is it for me. I hope Bree comes back soon and we can move forward."

"You should tell her it's the last time for you," I said. "That way she understands the severity of the situation."

Cypress shrugged. "I don't want to make it sound like an ultimatum. Those aren't romantic..."

Some pretty women walked inside, two of them. They both wore jean shorts and tops, obviously hot after the scorching weather we had that week. They headed right to the bar and glanced at Ace and me.

I didn't know where I stood with Celeste, but I felt like I

wasn't available. Besides, if I were going to get laid that night, I'd rather be with Celeste. The sex was great because that woman was fantastic. "Ace, hot babes checking you out at the bar."

Ace didn't glance in their direction. "Yeah, I saw them."

Cypress didn't turn around to look. "Are you gonna make a move?"

"Why do you expect me to make a move every time a hot woman walks by?" Ace asked, still not looking. "If I went after every woman I saw, I wouldn't have time to do anything else—let alone drink my beer."

I thought it was an odd thing to say, and it made me wonder if calling it off with Lady bothered him more than he let on. Maybe she was the one who ended it with him, but he didn't want to admit it.

Cypress let the topic go.

I did too.

"Have you talked to Celeste about where you stand?" Ace asked.

"No, not yet," I answered. "I haven't seen her in a couple of days." I was actually avoiding the conversation as long as possible. I didn't know where the exchange would take us, and I hoped it wouldn't lead us further apart. All I wanted was to be closer. If I said the wrong thing, I could sabotage the great thing that I had.

But maybe sabotaging myself was in my best interest. If I allowed myself to fall hard for her and it didn't work out, I would just be more hurt in the end. As if she were sitting there listening to us, my phone lit up with a text message from her.

Just got home. If you aren't doing anything, you wanna come over?

I already knew my answer without thinking twice about.

Sure. I'll be there in twenty minutes. I had to finish my beer and my conversation—even though Cypress and Ace were both having an off night. Both were depressed about very different things.

"Was that her?" Ace asked.

"Yep," I said. "And don't read my phone."

"I didn't," Ace said. "I just know no one else would text you."

Cypress chuckled. "Good point."

"Lots of people text me," I said defensively. "That could have been Bree or Amelia."

"Your business partners?" Ace said sarcastically. "Doesn't count. And you know your mom prefers to call."

Cypress jolted before he laughed. "Ouch. Burn."

I rolled my eyes. "You know what?" I got out of my chair and chugged my beer. "You can pay for that." I set the empty bottle right beside Ace's hand before I walked out.

Ace called after me when I left, "It was worth it."

As soon as Celeste opened the door, she grabbed the front of my t-shirt and kissed me on the mouth.

Hard.

When no words were exchanged and she just kissed me more, it was obvious why she invited me over.

She wanted to get laid.

She wasn't interested in quiet conversation by the fire with a bottle of wine. She wanted to be naked with me, to feel my bare cock inside that warm pussy.

I could definitely put our conversation on hold until we were done.

We didn't make it up to her bedroom, settling for the

couch even with the windows wide open. One of her legs was propped over the back of the couch, and I pressed the other against my chest. I fucked her into the cushions, her dress pulled up the waist because we didn't bother undressing.

She didn't want to wait.

Her pussy was just as incredible as I remembered, and I made her come before I filled her with my seed. When I was inside her like this, I didn't think about where this relationship would go. I didn't care about how far France was. I just thought about the beautiful woman underneath me with the great tits. My jeans and boxers were pulled down to my ass, and my shoes were still on.

We fucked like animals.

When we were finished, I got off her and pulled up my boxers and jeans but left the fly open. A satisfied high rushed through me, an exhilaration that felt soothing after an orgasm like that. I could fall asleep right there, but I felt awkward doing that.

She walked into the bathroom to clean herself up, and when she returned, she was just as classy as she was when she first opened the door. In red pumps and a black dress, she looked like a model on the runway. She grabbed a bottle of wine and two glasses before she set them on the coffee table. "Wine?"

"Sure."

She poured two glasses then sat back, her legs crossed. She was back to her former self, like she hadn't just gotten pounded on her couch.

I adored her.

The longer I sat beside her, the more uneasy I became. What if she was doing this same thing with some other guy? What if she had a date in the past few days while I'd been busy collecting my thoughts. I didn't want to share her with anyone.

I'd never been good at sharing.

I didn't take a drink of my wine before I set it down on the coffee table. "Are we exclusive?" I asked the question bluntly because I lacked any form of tact. I'd never been the one to initiate this kind of conversation. The woman usually brought it up. Instead of beating around the bush, I cut right to the chase. A woman like her would probably appreciate it.

She had just finished drinking from her glass, and a mark of red paint outlined where her lips had been just a moment ago.

"We're fucking without condoms, so can I assume we're monogamous? I'd like to know, for health reasons." I kept my cards close to my chest, taking Ace's advice to navigate through the conversation. It made me wonder if Celeste would have ever brought it up if I hadn't.

"No, I'm not seeing anyone else in Carmel."

I was hoping that would be her answer, but it was nice to hear it out loud. But she phrased it strangely. She wasn't seeing anyone in Carmel? Did that mean she was seeing someone else in France? But that would be cheating, and she didn't strike me as a cheater. "And are we going to stay that way?" I did my best not to come off too strong. She was obviously attracted to me and enjoyed spending time with me, but I might just be a warm body in a bed to her.

"Yeah, I suppose." She swirled her wine before she took a drink.

Goddammit, why did she have to be so cryptic? She wasn't giving me anything to work with. Maybe she was waiting until she knew exactly how I felt because she admitted how she felt? I couldn't figure it out.

"For the time being."

And there it was—the deathblow. In just those few words, she told me this had a deadline. When the summer was over, she would return to her life in France.

I didn't mean anything to her.

I took a long drink of my wine to drown out the pain. The truth hurt even more than I anticipated. I'd never wanted to mean something to a woman before, and the one person I actually liked didn't feel the same way.

Talk about ironic.

The tension filled the room, and I knew I was responsible for causing it. I didn't know how to get out of it, so I thought I would just keep going. Now that I'd started it, I might as well finish it. "When are you going back to France?"

She looked down at her wineglass, purposely avoiding my gaze. It wasn't something she'd done before. "Late September."

I nodded even though I didn't like that answer. That was just a few months away. Not much time at all. "So, this is just a fling, then?"

She leveled her head and looked my way. "I thought that was clear when we first went out. I told you I lived in Paris for most of the time."

It was clear. She never hid anything from me. I was just the idiot who hoped something more would happen. "It was clear. I wasn't sure if anything changed since we stopped using condoms. Just curious."

She turned away.

I kept thinking about that phrase she'd used. She wasn't seeing anyone else in Carmel. Did she have a boyfriend at home? A husband? I was disgusted at the thought. "Are you seeing someone back in France?" If she was, how could she be away from him for three months straight?

She set her glass on the coffee table even though she would have drunk most of it by now. "Yes."

Yes?

Seriously?

She had a boyfriend?

I was some dirty secret?

I could deal with being a fling. I could deal with an expiration date. But I didn't like liars and cheats. I'd never been cheated on, but I knew it didn't feel good. I didn't want any part in that.

I rested my elbows on my knees and felt my hands tighten into fists. It was okay not knowing all the details of the relationship, but that was something she should have told me. "Celeste, I don't hook up with cheaters. Not my thing." I left the house and walked to the door. "I would have appreciated a heads-up." I was so pissed I couldn't think straight. I'd just fucked this woman without a condom. Did she feel any guilt? Did she think about him? I felt disgusting.

"Blade." She came after me and grabbed my arm when I reached the door. "You've got the wrong idea."

"The wrong idea?" I yanked my hand away and turned around to face her. "You're seeing someone else. There's no way I could have misinterpreted that. I'm a one-woman kind of guy. If I make a commitment to someone, I keep it. I'm not fucking some other man's woman. Not my philosophy."

"You don't understand. I'm in an open relationship."

"An open relationship?" I repeated with a raised eyebrow.

"Yes," she said. "It's mutual. We see other people, and we

know about it. It's not cheating. I'm not that kind of woman either."

Her boyfriend was okay with her sleeping with other guys? He sounded like a dumbass. "So you've told him about me?"

"Yes. He knows everything about you."

"And he's fine with me fucking you without wearing a rubber?" I found that hard to believe.

"Yes."

What kind of freak show was this? "Is this some kind of European thing?"

"Not really, but it's more common there. He travels a lot, and I'm away all summer. It's unrealistic to expect us not to be attracted to other people. And not to act on those attractions is even more unrealistic."

I still couldn't believe this. "So you're okay with him sleeping with other women?"

She nodded.

"Do you want to marry this guy someday?"

She shrugged. "We've talked about it. But it's nowhere in the near future."

I ran my hand through my hair and took a step back. "I just need a second to process this."

"I understand," she said. "I can understand why it would be weird to people who live a different lifestyle."

"It's not really a different lifestyle," I said. "I've slept around a lot in life, but not while I was committed to someone. If you ask me, when you're with someone, that's it. You're with them. There's nobody else. You obviously don't love him. If you did, you wouldn't look at me twice."

Her eyes narrowed.

"And if he loved you, he wouldn't let another man touch you. He wouldn't let you live on the other side of the earth for three months." I didn't understand why I was getting so worked up. I'd had tons of flings before. If some other woman had said this same thing to me, I wouldn't have cared. It wasn't much different than what Ace had with Lady. But it bothered me—really bothered me. "That's not love, Celeste. That's not passionate and beautiful. That's just...empty and sad. You deserve better than that."

With rosy cheeks, she only stared at me. Her beautiful eyes were a mystery to read. Only when we were in bed making love could I understand how she felt. But now, it seemed like I was talking to a concrete wall.

I'd already ruined this relationship...or whatever the hell it was...enough as it was. I should just walk away and say goodbye. I fucked her on the couch, didn't drink her wine, and then insulted her for having a philosophy that was different from my own. I was a complete ass, and I knew it.

But I wouldn't apologize for it.

I walked out the door and to her porch, knowing she wouldn't stop me from leaving this time. "Goodbye, Celeste."

When I reached the street, she stepped onto her porch and looked at me. "Blade."

I didn't know why I stopped and looked at her. I should ignore her. I should just walk away and never stare at that stunning face again. But I looked anyway, knowing that beautiful woman meant more to me than all the women in my past combined.

"I still want to be with you..."

Not in the way I wanted. She wanted to use me while she was in town for the summer. She wanted to fuck me because I made her come. With someone else, I would have been thrilled to have a no-strings-attached relationship with an alluring foreign woman. But not this time. "I want all of you or none of you at all."

———

"How'd it go with Celeste last night?" Ace asked as soon as I walked into the office.

"Fucking terrible." I dropped into my chair and threw my feet on the desk.

Bree was sitting at the other desk, wearing the same angry expression that I wore on my own face. She was still pissed at Amelia, a fight all of us had stayed out of. "What happened?" She stopped looking at her computer and turned into the concerned friend she'd always been. She dropped her own personal baggage and cleared the slate so she could hear me out.

"I asked about our situation last night," I said. "She said she wasn't seeing anyone else *in Carmel.*"

"In Carmel?" Bree asked. "What does that mean?"

"Dude, you're looking too much into it," Ace said. "Don't overanalyze her."

"Actually, I'm glad I analyzed her." I put my foot back on the floor and spun in my chair to look at him. "Because she is fucking someone else. She has a goddamn boyfriend back at home."

"What?" Bree shrieked. "You're serious?"

"And she told you that?" Ace asked incredulously. "She's a cheater? Ugh, I hate cheaters."

"Me too," Bree said bitterly. "How hard is it not to fuck someone? It's pretty simple."

Before Bree could go on a tangent about Cypress and Amelia, I continued. "She said they're in an open relationship. He sees other women, and she sees other men. It works for them because they both travel a lot."

"Ohh…" Ace nodded like he understood. "Well, that's totally different."

"Yeah, not cheating," Bree said. "If that's their agreement, as weird as it is, she's not doing anything wrong."

"How is it different?" I snapped. "She's committed to him, but she's fucking me. You don't think that's sick?"

"I think it's a little strange, but not uncommon," Ace said. "A lot of people do that."

I clenched my jaw. "Well, I don't like it. That's not love. That's… I don't even know what the hell that is. If the guy loved her, he wouldn't be able to sleep at night knowing she's been with me. So she obviously doesn't mean shit to him."

"I agree with you there," Bree said. "There's gotta be some jealousy in a relationship. If there's none, then you have a problem."

"So what happened?" Ace asked.

I shrugged. "I left."

"And that's it?" Bree asked. "You just walked out?"

"She said she wanted to keep seeing me, but I said no. I kept walking." I didn't want to settle for that arrangement. Whenever I was with her, I would think about that other guy. I didn't even want to know his name.

"What if she just wanted a fling?" Ace asked. "Would that have changed anything?"

"No, probably not." If it had been just the two of us, I had a chance to change her mind about staying.

"Then what difference does this make?" Ace asked. "The guy is on the other side of the world."

"Because she has someone waiting for her back at home," I snapped. "How do I stand a chance of getting her to stay if she already has someone she wants to be with? I'm just gonna invest all this time and get my heart broken. I've never wanted a fling since the day I met her. I've always wanted more."

Bree gave me a sad smile. "That's really sweet."

"Maybe if she knew that, it would change things," Ace said. "Tell her you don't want a fling."

"That's the dumbest thing I've ever heard." I put my feet back on the desk. "We haven't been seeing each other for long. I'll sound like a psycho."

"She's gotta feel something for you too," Bree said. "She's obviously just as passionate."

"That's just because she's French," I said. "The French are passionate."

"Keep seeing her and change her mind," Ace said.

"Forget it." I wasn't investing any more time in this twisted relationship.

Ace came over to my desk and jumped on the surface. "This is the bottom line, man. You actually like this girl. I've never seen you act this way with anyone else."

"That's true," Bree said.

"So if she means something to you, fight for her. Steal her from the other guy. Show her what it's like to be loved by a real man."

Bree gave Ace such a harsh glare that it was impossible not to notice. I watched her burn holes in his face from the savage look.

What was that about?

Ace noticed it too but ignored her. "She's not engaged to him, right?"

"No."

"Then you can do this," Ace said. "If you really like her, don't give up on her."

Bree cleared her throat loudly.

Ace ignored her again. "Just think about it. If it doesn't work out, at least you got to have incredible sex for the rest of the summer."

I didn't care if I sounded like a pussy for saying this. I could say anything to these guys. "But the more I'm with her, the more I want to be with her…"

Ace patted my shoulder. "I get it. But you have to try. You're gonna lose the only woman who's ever meant anything to you. Either way, you're gonna get hurt. You may as well try to have everything you want in the process."

"You're such a fucking hypocrite." Bree stormed out of the office and slammed the door on her way out.

Ace watched her go, an irritated look in his eyes.

"What was that about?" I asked. "How are you a hypocrite?"

He hopped off my desk. "Just think about what I said, alright?"

How could I think about that when all I could think about was what Bree said?

What did it mean?

6

BREE

Cypress knocked on my door.

We hadn't spoken in a while, and I knew his patience couldn't last forever. I opened the door and came face-to-face with him, his beard thicker than I'd ever seen it. He'd obviously given up on shaving.

I liked it when he had a shadow on his face, but now it was getting out of control. I didn't care for it, but nothing could downplay how attractive his chiseled face was. He still looked like a beautiful man, just hidden behind an untamed beard.

He held up two envelopes. "They put these in my box instead. Wanted to pass them along."

"Thanks." I glanced at each one. "Bills...great."

He didn't smile with his mouth, but his eyes lit up slightly. "That's the only thing that's ever in my box, besides junk flyers."

"Well...thanks." I tucked the letters under my arm.

Cypress stayed put, obviously having another motive. "Dino has been pretty down lately. I think he misses you."

"He does?" I asked in surprise.

"When I first moved in to the house next door and he didn't see you anymore, he did the same thing. He gets really bummed out. He's probably afraid the same thing is happening, and he won't see you anymore."

Knowing our dog was in pain broke my heart. "Aww…"

"Do you mind taking him for a walk? Then letting him stay with you? That would get him out of his funk."

"I'd love to."

"Great. I'll be right back." Cypress left my house and walked back to his.

The conversation made me realize that the three of us were a family, despite my need for space. It didn't matter how angry I was or how Vanessa's presence made me feel. Life went on.

Cypress returned with Dino on a leash. "There she is, boy."

Dino took off and charged into my legs. He shook his tail with impressive force and whined with excitement.

"I missed you too." I kneeled on the ground and wrapped my arms around him, feeling him go crazy in my embrace. His fur was so soft, and his slobber got on my knee. "You're so gross, but I love you." I let him kiss me on the mouth before I stood up.

Cypress handed me the leash. "Here's some food too." He held up a plastic bag of hard dog food and set it on the couch. "You two have fun." He gave me a smile that wasn't remotely sincere then walked out.

When I imagined Cypress going home to an empty house without Dino there to keep him company, I felt an ache in my chest. He spent so much time making sure I had what I needed that he never worried about taking care of himself. I'd have to be made of stone not to appreciate everything he did for me. "Cypress?"

He turned back around. "What's up?"

"You wanna come with us?"

Dino spun in circles more, as if he understood what I'd just asked.

Cypress's mouth stretched into a smile, and this time, it wasn't fake. "I'd love to."

———

It was a cool evening. The sky was overcast with thick and heavy clouds, and the sun had no chance of piercing through the haze. But there wasn't any wind, not even a slight breeze that moved over the skin.

There was hardly anyone along the beach, probably because the sky was so murky. The tide was high, so the beach was sloped at a harsh angle and we had to walk on the sand that was elevated above the water.

It was a dog beach, so we didn't need to keep Dino on a leash. He was a well-behaved dog that wasn't hostile to other canines he saw along the way. Sometimes they would smell each other's butts, but they'd be on their way a moment later.

Cypress brought an orange tennis ball, and he would throw it far ahead, making Dino run at full speed to retrieve the ball before it was washed away into the ocean.

"Wow, he's fast," I said. "Look at him go."

"He's a sheep herder for a reason."

"I can't see Dino herding sheep. He would just smell their butts all day."

Cypress chuckled. "You're probably right."

Dino returned with the ball in his mouth. His tongue

hung out the left side of his mouth, getting drops of slobber everywhere.

"Good boy." Cypress took the ball out of his mouth and threw it again.

Dino took off.

There were dolphins swimming near the kelp forest close offshore. Sometimes they jumped out of the water, being playful as they hunted their dinner. Seeing dolphins was a normal sight because I spotted them almost every time I was down here, along with otters and whales. The Monterey Peninsula was a sanctuary for wildlife, so all the creatures flourished in safety.

"So, are you ready to talk to Amelia?" Cypress took the ball from Dino's mouth and threw it again.

I placed my hands in the pockets of my hoodie and walked beside him, my sandals kicking up sand with every step I took. "No." I couldn't ignore my sister forever. She was my family, and we had to stick together through thick and thin. But I didn't want to pretend that everything was okay, to sweep everything under the rug when her actions were completely wrong.

Cypress didn't voice his opinion about my response.

"I'm not ready."

Cypress looked straight as he walked forward, his eyes on Dino.

"She's my sister, and I love her no matter what...but I'm so angry with her."

"I understand."

"That's one thing you don't do, touch each other's boyfriends. The fact that you're my husband just makes it worse."

"Yeah, you're right."

I was surprised he agreed with me so easily.

"But she's in bad shape. She told me she feels worse than she did when Evan left her."

Great tactic to make me feel like shit.

"She's sorry about what she did. Wishes she could take it back. Wishes she hadn't been in such a bad place to begin with so that wouldn't have happened." Cypress turned his gaze on me as he kept walking. "We both know that never would have happened if she hadn't hit rock bottom. She never would have developed romantic feelings for me and just went for me. Even if you and I had never dated, I'm not her type and she's not mine."

"How can she not be your type?" I asked incredulously. "Everyone always said she was the pretty sister when we were growing up. She's gorgeous. Evan is an idiot for leaving her for that dumb girl. She might be younger, but she's definitely not prettier."

"I think Amelia is very pretty. But you look very different."

"Uh, thanks."

He chuckled. "I meant that in a good way. You're also beautiful, but you contain the qualities I prefer. But none of that really matters. All I'm trying to say is, Amelia and I never would have hooked up in a million years. That kiss never would have happened if she wasn't in that dark place and I wasn't the only one helping her. That's the point I'm trying to make."

I understood what he was saying. Amelia wouldn't have done that under a different circumstance. I knew it was true.

"So maybe you could talk to her soon," he said gently. "Bury the hatchet."

"Yeah…I'll think about it."

Cypress faced forward again just when Dino ran up. He grabbed the ball from the dog's mouth and threw it again.

We'd almost reached the opposite end of the beach, and we would have to turn around and head back the other way. "Have you thought more about us?"

I stared at the sand beneath my feet, seeing the soft mounds before I stepped on them with my sandal. "What do you mean?" I turned around and started walking the other way before we hit the rocks. The whole strip of beach was in front of us again as we prepared to head back the way we came.

Cypress mimicked my moves. "You know what I mean, Bree. You were upset when you saw Vanessa, and this kiss with Amelia pushed you over the edge. I want to know where we stand. I have a right to ask."

My heart had softened into mush since Cypress and I started spending time together. I found myself giddy and weak just the way I used to be. I lived for every kiss and every touch. Even though I had my guard up the entire time, he managed to pierce my exterior and get right into my chest. I didn't want to lose him, not the man who constantly looked after me every single day. He'd sacrificed a lot to be with me, more than anyone else ever would. "It was hard seeing Vanessa. It was like a horse kicked me in the chest."

"I can imagine."

"But you didn't do anything wrong. Just the memory got to me. And what happened with Amelia... I can't be mad at you for that either. You didn't kiss her, and when she kissed you, you ended it. I'm still upset about the whole thing, but I can't keep blaming you for my heartache."

Cypress listened, only breaking his concentration when he grabbed Dino's ball and threw it again.

"But I want to be with you. I want to make this work."

He released a quiet sigh, heavy with relief.

"But I think we should try marriage counseling or something. These issues aren't going to go away on their own and—"

"That's fine. Whatever you want."

When I felt his excitement, it reminded me how lucky I was to have him. Ever since I woke up from my haze, he'd been the most committed guy on the planet. Most of our days together were painful and exhausting, but he never gave up on me. He stayed because he loved me.

I stopped walking, and he stopped a second later. He looked at me, knowing I was about to say something.

"Thank you for not giving up on me...on us." Cypress was the foundation of my existence. He was my rock that I relied on. He'd been there for me every single day, the crutch that supported me. When we were old and gray, he would be there taking care of me too. That was real love. "I know I've been difficult—"

"I love you."

I'd heard him say that to me many times, usually in the heat of the moment when we were together. But no matter what context we were in, he said it the exact same way. His eyes hardened slightly, and his posture stiffened.

"I don't care how difficult you are. I don't care how much work this is. You are my wife, and I will do anything and everything to keep you."

My eyes softened as my heart slowed down to a quiet pace. The ocean was loud beside us, and Dino stood there with his ball still clasped in his mouth. I didn't see Cypress as the manwhore who broke my heart all those years ago. Enough time had passed that I didn't see him that way anymore. I saw a new version of him, the committed and caring man who bore no resemblance to his old self at all.

I walked toward him and moved into his body, feeling his strong chest and even stronger heart. My face pressed against the soft fabric of his t-shirt, and I wrapped my arms around him. Fortunately, we were the only people on this side of the beach, just us and our dog. I inhaled his smell and felt the peacefulness wash over me. No matter what came our way, we would get through it together. With Cypress, I never felt like I was alone. I always had someone looking out for me—someone who loved me.

WHEN WE GOT BACK TO MY HOUSE, WE HEADED INTO MY bedroom and dropped our bottoms before we landed on my bed. His t-shirt was still on, and I didn't even take off my sweater. Too rushed to wait an extra two seconds to get everything off, he was between my legs with my knees separated.

He moaned when he felt himself slide into my slit, feeling my flood of arousal meet his thick length.

I grabbed his hips and guided him into me, and we moved hard. Instead of taking our time and making it last, we fucked like it'd been a lifetime since we'd been together. I just wanted to have him—as much as I could get in the shortest amount of time possible.

Cypress took over my bed, making the headboard smack into the wall roughly as he pushed himself deep inside me. He stretched me wide apart with his massive size, skin to skin because we didn't bother having a discussion about the condom.

I knew he hadn't been with anyone else.

I was about to come. I could feel it deep between my legs as he ground his body against my clit. "I want you to come inside me."

He dug his hand into my hair and got a good grip on my

scalp. "You want my come?" His thumb brushed against my cheek and almost came into contact with my mouth.

I licked his thumb then pulled it into my mouth and sucked on it.

Cypress's eyes darkened, and he fucked me harder, his balls smacking against my ass.

I kept sucking, knowing I was about to come.

When I did, it was the best one I'd ever had. It crushed me from the inside out, making me whimper and scream at the same time. I bit down on his finger and gripped his hips, yanking him harder into me.

Cypress came a moment later, filling me with everything he had and not wincing despite the way my teeth dug into his skin. If anything, it made him come harder. He groaned in satisfaction once he gave me all his come, a sleepy look in his eyes.

I kept my hands on his hips so he wouldn't go anywhere. "Give me more."

He pulled his thumb out of my mouth and stuck his hand into my hair again. He adjusted the tilt of my head so I was looking directly into his eyes. "That's my wife."

7

A MELIA

Cypress knocked before he walked inside. "Hey, it's me."

"Hey." I sat at the kitchen table with a beer already waiting for him. He told me he was on his way, so I knew it was him before the door even opened. I made sure Evan stayed away so they wouldn't cross paths. The last thing I needed was Cypress knowing I was screwing my ex.

He'd be pissed.

He sat down, took a long drink of his beer, and then wore a wide smile that made him look like a dork.

"Are you high?"

"No. Why?"

"You don't usually grin like that." I pointed at the corners of his mouth, which were practically underneath his eyes.

"I do when I'm really happy. And I'm super happy right now."

"Really?" I asked. "Something happen with Bree?" If he was making progress with her, then there was a good chance she would make progress with me.

"I feel like I finally have my wife back. She acted the way

she used to last night, aggressive and playful at the same time. We fucked just the way we used to, like two animals that wanted to rip each other apart." He grinned again and took a drink of his beer. "So awesome."

"Oh, that's great. What made her come around?"

Cypress told me they had a long talk at the beach. Something he said must have changed her mind because she was different, a lot more open. She couldn't wait until they got back to the house before clothes starting coming off.

That's what I wanted—for them to work it out.

"She said she still wants to do marriage counseling, which is fine by me. We can do whatever the hell she wants as long as we're together. I said that to her about a hundred times."

"I'm glad you guys are making progress."

"Yeah, I hope this is the final stage. We've been through all the difficult stuff. I can't imagine anything else coming up now."

"Yeah, probably not." I was happy for Cypress, but I would have been happier if I weren't so miserable. He had his wife back, but I still didn't have my sister back.

Cypress read my mind. "I think she'll talk to you soon. We talked about you last night, and she admitted you were in a dark place. I explained to her you never would have kissed me under any other circumstance, and that seemed to give her perspective."

"Thank you."

"So, just hold on a little longer. It'll happen. I promise."

"You promise?"

He nodded. "If she doesn't do it on her own, I'll make her."

"I've never seen anyone make her do anything."

"Well, I'm her husband," he said proudly. "I know how

my woman thinks."

Evan stopped by again, this time with a pint of ice cream.

I opened the door but didn't let him inside. "The girls are already asleep."

"I know. I'm here to see you." He held up the pint. "Thought we could talk and eat right out of the carton—the way we used to."

When the girls were acting out or behaving badly, Evan and I used to sit at the kitchen table and try to figure out what to do. We usually split a tub of ice cream, eating more calories than we should late at night. It affected my waistline more than his, unfortunately.

But I wasn't stupid. I knew this was a ploy to get me into bed. I'd fallen for it enough times, as embarrassing as it was. "No. I'm not sleeping with you anymore, Evan. It was a stupid mistake, and it's not gonna happen again. You can come back tomorrow at five if you want to see the girls. No later than that."

Evan didn't budge. "How can you make the same mistake five times in a row? That's not a mistake, baby."

I rolled my eyes. "This is over...whatever it is."

"Or it's just getting started."

I shut the door in his face.

He stuck his foot out and caught the door before it could close. He pressed the door open with his hand and stepped inside, uninvited.

"You're being awfully rude right now."

"We both know if I made a move, you wouldn't stop me. We'd make love right on that counter, just as we've done hundreds of times in the past. But for tonight, I'm not gonna do that. I come in peace." He set the ice cream on the counter. "I just want to know how you're doing. Promise." He held up his hand like a Boy Scout.

"You broke your last promise to me—to remain faithful to me for the rest of our lives. You can't blame me for not believing you."

He brushed off the comment by grabbing two spoons from the drawer and sitting at the kitchen table. "I got double chocolate. Your favorite and my favorite."

Since I wanted ice cream more than I wanted to argue, I sat across from him and grabbed a spoon.

We ate quietly, each of us sticking to our side of the carton.

Evan watched me with his pretty eyes, examining every move I made. "Why do you want to stop sleeping with me?"

"Because it's gross."

"It didn't seem gross at the time."

"Because I wasn't thinking clearly." I kept scooping the ice cream into my mouth. "I meant what I said. We aren't getting back together, Evan. I've only been sleeping with you because I've hit rock bottom in life. Sleeping with someone familiar is comforting."

"I don't believe that. You still love me, and we both know it. Let's not lie to each other."

"I love you, but not in the way I love Ace." It was a cold thing to say, but I wasn't going to lie about my feelings. I didn't want Evan to make any inaccurate assumptions about what was going on between us.

He stared at the ice cream and left his spoon in the carton, no longer in the mood for the treat. "It really hurts when you say that, but I deserve it. It's karma. I said the same thing to you, and now you're saying it to me."

I didn't say it to hurt him or because I believed in karma. It was just how I felt. "But he and I are never gonna happen. I'm glad we're still friends. I'll settle for that rather than lose him altogether."

"Are you sure the guy doesn't feel the same way?"

"Why?"

"If he's been sleeping with you, he's gotta feel something."

I shrugged. "He said he didn't. Said he just wanted to be friends."

Evan shook his head slightly. "Sounds like an idiot to me."

"It takes one to know one…"

He didn't dodge the insult. He only absorbed it. "How are things with Bree?"

I sighed in response. "She still won't talk to me…"

"I'm sorry, baby." He gave me an apologetic look.

"Don't call me baby."

"I can call you whatever I want."

"You used to call me that all the time, and then you started calling Rebecca that. It reminds me that I was replaced, and I don't want to be called that anymore."

His face fell like I'd slapped him. "I'm sorry…I didn't realize it bothered you."

Everything bothered me.

"I hope things get better with Bree soon. You two are really close. I'm sure she'll forgive you for whatever you did. You're a good person, so your crime can't be that bad."

No, it was pretty bad.

"Can you tell me what you did?"

"It doesn't matter, Evan."

He leaned over the table, getting close to me. "If you think I'm gonna judge you, I'm not. There's nothing you could have done that would make me look at you differently. You're still the most amazing woman in the world to me."

Why did his lines still affect me after what he did? "When you left me, I was in a really dark place. I put on a brave front with you because I didn't want you to understand how much you crippled me. I had too much pride. But behind the scenes, I was a mess. I stopped eating, stopped sleeping. Taking care of the girls was a million times harder because I was doing it by myself, and I didn't care about anything. Then Bree lost her memory, and that was even more devastating. I hit rock bottom, and I could barely take care of myself. But Cypress was there. He did so much for me and the girls. He helped me get back on my feet, picked up the girls from school while I lay in bed and did nothing. He put food on the table when I stopped working. He did everything. One night, I drank too much wine, and it was late. I made an impulse decision to kiss Cypress. It lasted for a few seconds before he pulled away and ended it." I swallowed the lump in my throat, feeling the guilt kill me. "Cypress had to tell her the truth, but he didn't identify me. So I told her...and she hasn't forgiven me."

Evan bowed his head then covered his face with his hands, hiding his reaction from me.

He was probably jealous that I'd kissed my brother-in-law. Probably thought less of me for doing something so morally wrong. But there was nothing he could say or do to make me feel worse than I already did.

Evan lowered his hands and revealed eyes filled with tears. The white parts of his eyes had turned red, and the skin around his eyes was puffy and irritated. The only other time I'd seen Evan wear that look was the day we got married, but he was crying from joy, not sadness.

He sniffed then blinked his eyes quickly, trying to dispel

the moisture that had flooded his eyes. He did everything he could to make sure the tears wouldn't fall, but one broke through his defenses.

I stared at him in shock, unable to believe what I was looking at.

He took a deep breath, steadying himself before he spoke. "I...I can't believe I did that to you. I can't believe what I did to my kids..." He pinched the bridge of his nose with his thumb and forefinger and closed his eyes. "God fucking dammit."

I was still speechless, having never seen Evan break down in my life.

"I'm so sorry, Amelia. I...I wish I could take it back. I hate myself for hurting you...knowing what you went through when I ran off with a woman who didn't compare to you. I can't believe I hurt the woman I promised to love forever because I was thinking with my dick instead of my heart. I just... I'm ashamed of myself."

My heart must have been bigger than I thought, because I reached my hand across the table and rested it on his. I wanted to tell him it was okay, but those were words I could never say. His behavior was unacceptable. I pitied him because he was finally understanding the grave mistake he'd made, but I would never give him vindication for it, only forgiveness.

He pulled his hand away and left the table. "I should go. I don't deserve to be here." He walked to the front door with sagging shoulders and dragging feet. He didn't turn around before he walked out, and he didn't close the door behind him.

I didn't go after him because I didn't have anything to say. Now he knew the truth of what his actions had caused. He knew his decision to leave me had consequences. While he was fucking around with a young woman, living the good life, I was struggling to get by.

It would never be okay.

But I was glad he finally took responsibility for what he did, acknowledged his behavior was wrong. He showed remorse for the mistake and finally stepped up to be a father. He could have easily never figured it out. He could have stayed with her forever and disappeared from our lives.

I thought I would be satisfied when his relationship fell apart. I thought I would be happy when he wanted me back. I thought I would feel ecstatic when he walked out of the house in tears.

But now I wanted to cry too.

Because I would always love him.

I WALKED INTO THE OFFICE IN THE MORNING AND FOUND ACE sitting at this desk. He gave me an apologetic look, knowing I was still going through a hard time. I would love to be greeted by his strong embrace instead, but I needed to let that go.

He'd probably slept with a dozen women by now.

I took a look at the schedule, assuming I was downstairs.

"Blade purposely put Bree downstairs today. Well, we both did it on purpose."

I looked at him with an eyebrow raised.

"She thinks you're at Olives today, but I'll say we switched it up at the last minute. If we can get you two in a room together, maybe something will happen. She can't avoid you any longer. It's gone on long enough."

"I don't want to piss her off, Ace."

"Who cares? Go down there and get to work. She can

leave if she really wants to. You're just testing out the waters."

I'd never been so nervous to be in the same room as my sister before.

"How are you doing otherwise?"

Ace used to be my greatest confidant, but I hardly saw him anymore. "Evan came by last night. I told him I kissed Cypress and everything I was going through at the time to explain why I did it. He broke down in tears and left."

"He did?" Ace asked quietly.

"Said he's ashamed for putting me through so much pain."

Ace straightened in his chair, his gaze stoic. "I'm glad he finally realized it."

"Yeah..."

He looked at me when he asked his next question. "Are you two working things out?"

"Not romantically. I'll never take him back after what he did. I just hope we can be good friends and partners again."

He turned back to me, looking me in the eye inquisitively. "And he accepts that?"

I shrugged. "He wanted to get back together, but when I told him about everything he put me through, he walked out. He said he didn't deserve to be there. I suspect that's the end of him trying...at least I hope so."

He continued to stare at me, his gaze intense like it used to be before we made love.

"Well, I should get to work... Wish me luck."

"Yeah...good luck."

I walked downstairs and stepped into the diner I'd worked at almost every morning since I could remember. Everything was exactly the same, except my sister was there, and she was still angry with me.

She was taking an order at a table when I walked inside. She didn't notice me until she headed toward the kitchen and the cooks. She stopped in her tracks when she saw me, her eyes narrowed in anger, and then she pretended I didn't exist.

It never got easier. I wanted to cry at that reaction. I missed the warm way she used to look at me. I was a role model to her, her older sister she always looked up to. Now she looked at me like I was dirt on the floor.

I hated this so much.

I tried to focus on my job so I wouldn't think about the hostility in the room. The only thing that made me feel better was the fact that Bree didn't leave. She could have walked out and gone to the café instead. She could have even gone home if she wanted to.

But she stayed.

I waited on the tables and hustled through the breakfast and lunch rush. The diner was usually packed from open to close since we shut our doors at three in the afternoon. It was the perfect shift for me since I needed to pick up the kids when they got out of school.

Bree was helping a large party of eight people when a young woman walked inside and waited at the counter to be seated. I finished up taking an order from a customer before I walked toward her. The closer I got, the more familiar she looked.

She stared at me with such a heated expression I was a little scared. Her eyes were narrowed with malcontent, and her lips were pressed so tightly together she might break her jaw.

It took me a second to realize who she was.

Rebecca.

I saw her and Evan together once before. It was at a

restaurant. They were together in a booth in the corner, sharing a bottle of wine. It was the first time I saw them together after he left me. I'd walked back to the parking lot, got in my car, and cried.

It was definitely her.

I slowly walked up to her, knowing she knew exactly who I was. She must have known I owned this restaurant. Evan had to have mentioned it to her. The fact that she wasn't with anyone else told me she had a very specific reason for being there.

I stopped seven feet away from her, leaving much more space than I would with any customer. The gang and I always treated guests like family, making them feel welcome in our relaxed atmosphere.

But something told me she was dangerous.

"Can I help you?" I still held the notepad in my hand because I'd just taken someone's order. She would be stupid to attack me in the middle of a crowded room with witnesses. I assumed she just had something mean to say.

She kept glaring at me.

I waited for her to say something, but nothing was forthcoming. I had work to do, so I couldn't linger and wait for her to put words together to form whatever insult was on her mind. I turned around and headed to the kitchen.

"You fucking whore!" Rebecca grabbed me by the back of the hair and threw me down hard onto the ground. I fell on a table and a chair first, hitting my elbow and thigh before I hit the floor. "Stay away from—"

"Don't touch my sister!" Bree came out of nowhere and yanked Rebecca off me. She punched her right in the face then threw her on the ground. "Touch her again, and see what happens. Look at her again, and see what happens."

Bree grabbed Rebecca by the neck and strangled her as she pulled back her right arm to punch her in the face.

I finally recovered from my fall and grabbed Bree's hand before she could kill the girl. "Bree, don't. Stop."

"No, this bitch is gonna die." Bree pushed me off and grabbed Rebecca by the throat.

"Bree, no!" I yanked her off and dragged her away. "She's not worth it. Let her go. She's obviously got a pathetic life to come down here and assault us like that."

Rebecca finally scooted away, coughing and gripping her throat.

Bree didn't fight me anymore, but she looked maniacal. "Touch my sister again, and I swear I'll kill you. Bury your body so there's nothing but your teeth left." She leaned forward and spat on her.

Damn.

Rebecca finally got up and left the restaurant, walking as fast as she could without running.

Jose helped us both off the ground. "Should we call the cops?"

"Yes," Bree said. "I'm pressing charges on that bitch."

"No," I said. "Bree, you nearly choked her to death. If we file a report, she can file one too. I say we drop it." I grabbed Bree by the elbow and took her out back where the employees had their breaks. We both needed some privacy after that blowout.

"Are you okay?" Bree asked immediately. "How's your arm? Your leg?"

"I'm fine." Maybe it was just the adrenaline, but I didn't feel the pain. "She just caught me by surprise."

"You shouldn't have turned your back on her. Never turn your back on a psycho bitch."

"Lesson learned," I said with a weak chuckle.

"Are you sure you're okay?"

"Bree, I'm fine. Thanks for having my back in there."

"Of course. You're my—" Her eyes fell in sadness when she realized we hadn't spoken in two weeks.

I'd forgotten about it for the last few minutes. Despite being terrorized by Evan's ex-girlfriend, it was nice to feel close to my sister again.

Bree finished what she was saying in a quiet voice. "You're my sister. I always have your back."

"I know."

Bree stared at me in silence, a vulnerable look coming over her face. "I'm sorry for not talking to you for so long. It was stupid. I love you."

Now Rebecca wasn't on my mind at all. Nothing but happiness lived in my body. My chest finally relaxed now that the stress had disappeared. I was finally happy. "I'm sorry too. I love you." I hugged her next to the dumpster, grateful to have my sister back in my life. "I'm sorry about what I did. It was stupid—"

"Forget it," Bree said quickly. "It's in the past, and let's leave it there." She pulled away with a smile on her face. "I've done stupid stuff too. No one is perfect."

I pinched her cheek, just the way I did when we were kids. "You're perfect to me."

I CALLED EVAN WHEN THE GIRLS WERE IN THE OTHER ROOM. We hadn't spoken since he walked out of the house in tears the other night. He answered the phone in a quiet voice, not as confident as he usually sounded. "Hey. What's up?"

I'd never heard him sound so low. "If you aren't doing

anything, can you come by? I need to talk to you about something important."

"Are you okay?"

"I'm fine. But I have something to tell you."

He sighed into the phone. "I know I'm gonna sound like a jackass for saying this, but I hope you're pregnant."

If I were pregnant, then that would strongly increase his chances of getting back together with me. That was the only explanation I could think of. "No...I'm not."

"I'll be right there."

He arrived at the house fifteen minutes later, probably driving straight from the office. He left his BMW at the curb then walked inside. He didn't look the same as he did before. There was a darkness to him, a shadow in his eyes. He leaned against the counter and didn't come anywhere near me. "What's up, Amy?" He hardly ever used my nickname, but he probably did it because baby was no longer available.

He obviously had no idea what happened with Rebecca. He would have said something the second he answered the phone.

"Rebecca came to the diner this morning."

He raised his head and narrowed his eyes. His body suddenly tightened, and his spine straightened. "What did she say?"

"She called me a whore then attacked me."

Evan didn't react because the news was so overwhelming. It would take anyone a few seconds to absorb the words and understand them. "Wait...what?" He took a step toward me and raised his palm, clearly agitated. "She attacked you?"

I nodded. "She pushed me onto a table and chair, and I

fell to the ground. Bree fought her off before Rebecca ran out of the restaurant."

He gripped his skull with both hands and nearly dug his nails into his scalp. "What the fuck? Are you fucking kidding me?"

"Shh." I placed my forefinger over my mouth. "The girls."

"I don't give a shit. Rebecca assaulted you?"

"Yes."

"Jesus fucking Christ." He stepped away from me and walked in a circle, his knuckles white and his forearms tense. "Fucking bitch."

"Enough with the cussing, Evan."

He ignored me before he came back to me and circled his arms around my waist. "Are you okay? You look okay, but tell me you're okay." His hand moved to my neck, and he tilted my chin up to look me in the face and make sure I didn't have any bruises.

"I'm okay. She didn't hurt me or Bree."

"Thank god." He pressed his forehead to mine before he kissed my hairline. "I'm so sorry, Amy." He pulled me into his chest and hugged me, his powerful body hiding me from the rest of the world. "I love you... I would have died if she'd hurt you."

His affection was nice. He had the same effect on me that he always did, just like he had when we were married. I missed the way he used to love me, the way he used to protect me. "But she didn't...so everything is okay."

"No, everything is not okay." He pulled away and looked at me with a furious gaze. "Did you call the cops?"

"No. I didn't want to press charges."

"Why the hell not? She assaulted you."

"I know what it's like when the man you love leaves you. She's probably just not taking it well—"

"I don't give a damn. You don't go around attacking people when you don't get your way."

"Evan, drop it."

"I'm not gonna drop it. I'm gonna talk to her and make sure she never bothers you again. I promise it won't happen again."

"I know." I believed he would do anything to keep me safe. "And the girls—"

"Don't even say it," he whispered. "Rebecca shouldn't have touched you, but she wouldn't do anything to them. She's psycho, but not insane."

As long as he thought the girls were safe, then I didn't care what she did to me.

"I'm gonna take care of this now. I'm not gonna be able to think about anything else until it's resolved." He stepped back, his gaze heavy with sadness. "Again, I'm sorry..."

"It wasn't your fault, Evan. Have the two of you been fighting lately?"

"Not really. But she's been trying to get me back. Calls me late at night. Swings by the apartment. When she comes by my place and I'm not there...she knows I'm here. The fact that we're getting back together just sends her over the deep end."

"Who said we were getting back together?"

"Well...that's how she sees it. She knows we're sleeping together."

I didn't press him on it, knowing it was a fair assumption to make.

"I'll let you know how it goes." He opened the door and took one more look at me. "I'm sorry I let you down."

8

_____

"What do you want to watch?" I flipped through the channels because there was nothing on.

Cypress sat beside me with his arm over the back of the couch. "I don't care. I'm planning on making out with you."

"We just got busy for an hour."

He waggled his eyebrows. "You know I'm always ready for you."

"Well, I need a break because I'm a little sore. It's not like you're gentle."

He winked. "Like you want me to be gentle."

A knock sounded on the door, and Dino sat up with his ears straight.

"I wonder who that is..." It could be Amelia. I told Cypress that we made up, but I didn't mention the attack by Rebecca. Amelia and I decided to keep it to ourselves. If the guys knew, they would flip out.

I opened the door and came face-to-face with my old brother-in-law.

Evan.

The pig.

"What the fuck do you want?" Everything tumbled out of my mouth immediately. It was rude and cold, but I didn't care. I didn't like Evan. It's not like it was a secret. Everyone had had a year to get used to their divorce, but I didn't. It was still new to me. On top of that, his psycho girlfriend attacked my sister.

That shit ain't gonna fly.

Evan didn't seem offended by the cold greeting. He took the hit without reacting. "Can I talk to you for a few minutes? I have something to say."

I crossed my arms over my chest. "What makes you think I give a damn about anything you have to say?"

He took the insult well for a second time. "It's about what happened earlier today." He glanced at the couch where Cypress was sitting, obviously unsure if he knew anything about the episode.

I wanted to keep that a secret. "Hold on." I shut the door and walked to the couch. "Can I speak to Evan in private?"

"Sure." He rose from the couch, and Dino stuck to him like glue. "You want me to go home or what?"

"If you don't mind." I hadn't told anyone she was sleeping with Evan again. As her sister, I had an unspoken vow to keep all of her secrets from everyone.

"I don't mind if I get to come back."

"Yes, you get to come back."

He gave me a quick kiss on the lips before he walked out with Dino. He gave Evan a cold glare as he passed and headed back to his house next door.

"Come in." I couldn't believe I was inviting the devil into my house.

"Thanks." Evan shut the door behind him and stood in

the living room. The fireplace was roaring and the TV was still on, but he didn't take a seat.

"What's up?" I asked, hating the fact that I was looking at this guy.

"I wanted to apologize for what happened today. I had no idea she was so unhinged, and I'm sorry you were ever in danger. I'm not only humiliated but terrified. If something had happened to either one of you, I never would have forgiven myself."

"You shouldn't forgive yourself for being with her to begin with. This is all your fault."

He bowed his head. "I know."

"How could you leave Amelia for a stupid bitch like her?"

He sighed. "I'd do anything to take it back. Trust me, you have no idea how much I hate myself, how much I hate my life. I had a beautiful family, and I threw it away for someone who didn't matter. I miss my wife. Now I have an apartment by myself, and it's so quiet that it haunts me." He slid his hands into his pockets and stared at the floor. "I miss seeing my girls every day. I miss Amelia cooking for me. I miss everything. But I fucked it up."

I tried not to feel sympathetic because he didn't deserve it, but when he sounded so sincere, it was hard not to.

"Anyway...I talked to Rebecca, and I promise it won't happen again. I told Amelia to press charges, but she didn't want to do that. But it's been handled. I don't want you guys to feel scared."

"Scared?" I asked incredulously. "I'm not scared of that cunt. Anytime, anyplace, I'll knock her out."

"I believe you."

Now that everything had been said and done, I wanted him to leave. I tapped my fingers against my arm as I waited.

"I know it's too late to say this, but I'm sorry for what I did to your sister. I know you've both had a rough time in life, and I didn't take care of her when I promised to. I let you down, and I owe you an apology."

"I don't accept your apology, Evan. If you were really upset, you would leave her alone. You had her, but you threw her away. Now it's time for her to be with someone else." Not Ace, specifically, but I wished it were Ace.

What Evan said next surprised me. "I know she's in love with Ace. But he was the one who called things off before I made my move. So I think it's fair that I try to be a family again. It's not like I'm interfering."

Ace called things off? They slept together one time months ago. Why would Amelia even tell Evan about her one-night stand? "Ace ended things?"

"Yeah. They fooled around for a while, but then he lost interest."

Awhile? "How long?"

Evan faltered when he realized his assumption had been wrong. I didn't know anything about this. "I...I'm not sure."

I stepped forward. "Evan, tell me."

"I'm not sure," he said with a sigh. "Maybe a few months. I thought she told you."

She'd been sleeping with Ace for months? They had a private relationship, and she didn't even tell me? Ace was hooking up with her, but he still didn't want to be with her? He just let Evan have her? This was so stupid my brain hurt. I couldn't believe she'd lied to me—again. "I knew they hooked up one time, but I didn't know it was an ongoing thing."

Evan rubbed the back of his neck. "I know you don't like me, and you're never going to like me—"

"Damn right."

"But I love Amelia, and I want to be with her. I want to be a family again. If I have any chance of having that, I have to try. You know Amelia has been sleeping with me—"

"You've been taking advantage of her."

His eyes narrowed in anger. "I've done a lot of stupid things I'm not proud of, but I've never taken advantage of Amy. Everything between us has been consensual. She still loves me, and I'll always love her. We were married for eight years. Love like that doesn't just go away."

"It went away when you left her." I would never forgive him, not ever. I'd forgiven Cypress because that was a different circumstance. We were seeing each other for a few months when it happened. If we'd been married with children, then the act would have been unforgivable.

Evan absorbed the insult with a clenched jaw. "I know I have a chance with her. Ace walked away, and I'm here. Amelia told me we'll never get back together, but I know we could make it work if I'm patient with her. I intend to be as patient with her for as long as she needs."

I didn't want this to happen. I didn't give a damn if Evan was the father of her kids. She deserved better. "Evan, if you really love her, now is your chance to prove it. Just leave her alone and let her find someone else. Let her find a man who gets it right the first time around."

He shook his head. "I can't do that. I made a stupid mistake, and I was living in a fog. But when that fog bank disappeared, I could see clearly. I want to be with Amelia for the rest of my life, and I'll be the best damn husband in the world. I won't even look at another woman. I'll be everything that she deserves."

Why couldn't Ace fight for her like this? I knew Amelia would give in to Evan eventually since she was already sleeping with him. That never would have happened if Ace hadn't walked away so soon. I was certain Evan was being sincere, but he didn't get a second chance when there was someone better out there. "I hope you crash and burn."

I POUNDED ON THE DOOR UNTIL AMELIA FINALLY ANSWERED.

"What?" she blurted. "Everything okay?"

I yanked her outside and shut the door so the girls wouldn't overhear us. "You've been sleeping with Ace for months, and you didn't tell me?"

Her eyes snapped open in disbelief.

"Yeah, I know. How could you keep that from me?"

She still didn't respond, obviously surprised that I knew so much.

"And it went on for months? Were you just hooking up? Was this a relationship?"

"Bree...who told you?"

"Does it matter?" I put both hands on my hips.

Flustered and uncomfortable, Amelia could hardly look me in the eye. "Look, we didn't plan on it happening. It just kept happening...over and over. We tried to stop, but then we'd be alone in a room together and we didn't have the restraint."

"So this was just a hookup?"

"Yeah," she answered. "I hoped it would turn into something more the longer we kept doing it. But Ace was the one who called it off. He didn't give much of a reason, just said it was wrong."

I bet he called it off when Evan was back in the picture—the damn idiot.

"Who told you? I know it wasn't Ace."

"Evan."

Her mouth dropped. "What? Evan? How?"

"He came by the house and apologized about Rebecca. He mentioned Ace in passing, and then I pressed him on the topic until I got everything out of him."

She crossed her arms over her chest and sighed. "Goddammit, Evan."

"You're mad that you couldn't lie to me again?"

She gave me the same attitude Mom used to give. "I don't have to tell you every little detail about my sex life, alright? I knew what I was doing with Ace was stupid, and I wanted that stupidity to remain between Ace and me."

"But I could have helped you. If I'd known, I could have..." I had to keep my promise to Ace, so I shut my mouth.

"Helped me?" she asked. "Helped me how?"

"I don't know," I said with a shrug. "Never mind." I changed the subject before she could press me on it. "Then Evan apologized to me for hurting you when he left. I didn't accept his apology."

"What else did he say?"

"He's gonna try to get you back. He acknowledges that he doesn't deserve you, but he knows you still love him. The fact that you're sleeping with him encourages him."

Amelia watched me, but her eyes showed her thoughts running wild.

"Amy, please don't get back together with Evan."

"I'm not," she said quietly.

"Yes, you are. I see it happening right in front of my eyes. You're sleeping with him, aren't you?"

"I told him that was over."

"But you still love him, right?"

She shrugged in acknowledgment. "No matter how long I live, I'll always love the man I married. I can't control that.

Honestly, I wouldn't want it any other way. He gave me two beautiful girls. I could never hate him."

"But that doesn't mean you should go back to him."

"I never said I was, Bree."

"What about Ace?"

"What about him?" she asked.

"You still love him, right?"

She rolled her eyes. "He doesn't want me. He wanted to fuck me for a while, but that's it. I need to forget about him and just move on."

"He doesn't just want to fuck you."

"Then why did he leave?"

Ugh, this sucked. I just wanted to blurt it out and tell her the truth. But my oath to Ace stopped me from betraying him. I was in the middle of the dumbest soap opera in the world. These two people could be together right now if they just stopped being so stupid. "Maybe he's afraid to get involved with you when Evan is around."

"That doesn't make any sense."

"It does. Maybe he's afraid you'll get back together with Evan and dump him."

She shook her head. "That would never happen."

"Maybe he doesn't realize that. You should tell him..."

"No. Ace is a confident man. He knows he doesn't have to compete with anyone."

I was gonna scream. "Just don't get back together with Evan, okay? Promise me."

She stared at me but didn't move her lips.

"Amy," I pressed. "Promise me."

"You know I can't make a promise like that. I honestly have no intention of getting back together with him right now, but in years to come, who knows? I'm not gonna make a promise I can't keep."

That was both good news and bad news. "Fine. I've gotta go." I turned around and walked away.

"Uh, that was abrupt," Amelia said. "Where are you going?"

"I just have to take care of something. I'll talk to you later." I wasn't going home or back to Cypress.

I was going to Ace.

———

I POUNDED ON HIS DOOR JUST AS I DID TO AMELIA'S. I DIDN'T have the patience to knock once and take a step back. After my arm became fatigued from slamming against the wood, I rang the doorbell over and over.

"What?" Ace yanked the door open in just his sweat-pants, looking pissed off by the annoying way I just got his attention. "Shit, I was taking a piss. Could you wait two seconds?"

"No." I invited myself inside. "I'm tired of waiting. You need to get your ass in gear and tell Amelia how you really feel. This game you're playing is annoying, and I'm sick of it."

"I'm not playing any games."

I stomped my foot. "I know you've been sleeping with her for months now. You only broke it off recently."

The blood drained from his face.

"Don't worry, she didn't rat you out. Evan did."

"Evan?" he asked. "He knew about it?"

"Yeah. And once he found out you stopped seeing her, he's been trying to get her back. He sees her as fair game."

Ace shut the door, his muscles rippling with the move-ment. He was so ripped it seemed like his body might split down the middle because his physique was so strong. "She is fair game. And I told you this would happen."

"Well, she told Evan that she's still in love with you."

Instead of tightening his body further, his entire physique relaxed in astonishment. "She said that? To him?"

I wanted to grip my scalp and scream. "Yes. I've been trying to tell you that. She wants to be with you. But if you keep waiting, Evan is gonna get under her skin. It's only a matter of time."

He moved his hands to his hips and stared across his living room at nothing in particular.

"Ace." I waved my hand in front of his face. "Yo."

"Hmm?" he asked without looking at me.

"You still aren't going to do anything? This is your one and only chance. Do something now or lose her forever. Because if you don't do anything, she's gonna keep sleeping with Evan until she falls for him again."

"Wait...she's sleeping with him?"

I didn't want to share her secrets, but I thought Ace had the right to know. "Yeah."

He ran his hand through his hair, his face tinted red with anger.

"But you can't be mad. You left her, and she was depressed. So it's not a surprise she jumped into bed with him. You rejected her."

"I didn't reject her."

"From her point of view, you did. So what are you going to do?"

He paced in his living room, his fingers resting against his chin. "I don't know."

"You don't know? Are you freaking kidding me?"

"It's complicated, okay? She's sleeping with him now."

"But she would stop if you came into the picture."

"That's what she says. Who knows how she would really feel if I said anything to her."

I narrowed my eyes. "Ace, I used to respect you. I used to see you as a strong man who fought for what he wanted. He wasn't intimidated by anyone. But right now, frankly, you're being a pussy."

He stared me down coldly.

"So put on a shirt. You're coming with me."

"Where are we going?"

I marched to the door. "Just put on a shirt."

9

<small>BLADE</small>

A week went by, and I didn't speak to Celeste.

I didn't stop by her bakery to see her.

I pretended she didn't exist.

Life became boring and mundane. I went to work then went home and played video games. Sometimes I would jog on the beach before the sun set, working out my frustration until my body was exhausted and I could get some sleep.

Sometimes I wondered if I was overreacting.

We never said we were exclusive. If she was seeing another guy in Carmel, would it have bothered me the same way? Was it the fact that the guy was in France? In the back of my mind, I knew the real reason why I was so upset.

I'd already fallen for her.

She was smart, ambitious, and intelligent. She was funny, sexy, and easygoing. There weren't a lot of women like that in the world, and I was lucky enough to find one. She was my dream woman, the kind of lady who didn't need a man to take care of her because she could take care of herself.

Of course she had a boyfriend. Women like her weren't single—ever.

Was I a complete idiot for thinking I could actually have her?

Yes. A big idiot.

I tried to forget about her and return to my life the way it used to be. I considered picking up a woman in a bar so I wouldn't feel so alone, but the idea of talking to a woman and pretending to have a good time was anticlimactic.

There was only one woman I wanted.

I went to Cypress's place after work so we could play the new PS4 game that just came out. Bree wasn't home, so he had free time.

"How are things going with her?" Our beers sat on the table, and we had the controllers in our hands.

"Really good," Cypress said. "We had a long talk, and she warmed up to me again. We've been having a lot of sex too." He waggled his eyebrows. "I think we're finally in a good place. Shouldn't be any more bumps in the road."

"Don't jinx yourself."

"I think we've had all the bad luck we're gonna have. We pulled through." We were working as a team in the game, cooperatively killing all the aliens in space so we could save Earth from extinction. "Anything new with Celeste...?"

"We aren't seeing each other anymore."

"I know, but have you talked to her?"

"No." I kept my eyes on the game.

"Has she tried talking to you?"

"No." I didn't expect her to either.

"That's too bad. I know you liked her."

"Yeah..." Should have known it was too good to be true.

"You don't want to keep hooking up with her for the summer?"

Ace told me to do that, but I couldn't go through with it. Too difficult. "No. I'll get over it and find someone else."

Cypress dropped the subject and focused on the game. Dino lay right beside him on the couch, leaning against him with his chin resting on his thigh.

My phone vibrated on the table, and I glanced down to check it.

It was from Celeste. *Hey, can we meet somewhere? I'd like to say something to you.*

I stared at the phone for another second and stopped paying attention to the game. An alien came by and blew me to pieces, and I barely noticed.

"Dude, what the hell are you doing?" Cypress said. "How are we gonna save Earth at this rate?"

I set the controller down and grabbed the phone. "Celeste texted me."

"She did?" He paused the game. "That's ironic. What did she say?"

"Says she wants to meet up." I kept staring at the phone like she might text me again.

"For a booty call?" Cypress asked.

"No. She wants to talk."

Cypress grabbed the phone and read the message before he handed it back. "What are you going to do?"

"I don't know..."

"I wonder what she wants to say. Maybe she dumped her boyfriend for you."

"I doubt it."

"How will you know until you talk to her?"

"So you think I should meet her?" I asked.

"Obviously. If you don't, you're always going to wonder what she wanted to say."

True. It would haunt me. "You're right."

"Text her."

I texted her back. *Sure. Where?*

How about that place where we had drinks with your friends?

Sure. I can be there in an hour.

I'll see you there.

"We're meeting in an hour." I tossed the phone on the coffee table.

"Nervous?"

"Yeah." I wouldn't admit that to someone else, but I could say it to him. "I don't know what it is about this girl..."

"I don't think anyone knows why they're into someone else. You just know."

"I guess." Now I didn't want to play anymore. I couldn't concentrate. "I'm gonna go home and change."

"Let me know how it goes."

My stomach was tied up in knots, and a burst of adrenaline had spiked in my blood. No woman made me feel this way, made me feel high and low at the exact same time. "I will."

I WALKED INTO THE BAR AND SAW HER SITTING ALONE AT A table. She already had a gin and tonic sitting in front of her, and she wore a beautiful blue dress that showed off her entire back. Only a few straps covered her gorgeous skin.

I got hard at the sight of her.

I wished she didn't have that effect on me. I wished I weren't so impressed, so floored by this woman. She made me weak. She made me feel sensations I didn't want to feel. I didn't like it.

When I reached her table, she looked up at me. With thick eyelashes, painted lips, and beautiful hair, she looked like she was about to compete in the Miss Universe pageant —and rock it. That gold necklace she always wore was around her throat, and she wore another silver ring on her right hand. She sat perfectly straight, holding the same posture as a queen.

I sat down, immediately feeling resentful and angry again. Celeste never betrayed me, but it felt like she ripped my heart out anyway. I needed to stop being so harsh and judgmental. It wasn't who I was. If she were a different woman, I'd probably even admire the open relationship idea.

But not when it was a woman I wanted so much.

I stared at her, and my mind went blank. I should have said hi or something, but I didn't. All I could think about was kissing her, fucking her, and chaining her up to my bed so she could never go back to France ever again.

I wanted to kidnap her.

Shit, I had it bad.

Celeste was the first one to speak. "Thanks for meeting me."

I nodded, my mouth still out of service.

Her fingers wrapped around her glass, her nails painted a bright red color. Last time I saw them, they were blue. I noticed subtle aspects of her appearance that I never noticed with anyone else. I knew when she wore the same outfit I'd already seen, and I knew when she did her hair differently.

I paid attention.

"How are you?" she asked.

I didn't want to make idle chitchat or beat around the

bush. I was wound too tightly for pleasantries. "What did you want to say to me?" If I answered her question truthfully, I'd have to tell her I was just as upset as I was when I walked out of her house. I wouldn't allow her to understand how much she hurt me, how much she affected me.

Celeste didn't flinch at my coldness. "I've been thinking about you all week. I didn't like the way we left things. I didn't like the way I hurt you. That's what I wanted to say to you." She turned blunt, making this into a business conversation.

"That's it?" I asked. "You didn't like the way we left things?" I was hoping for something more from her, more substantial. "That's what happens when people break up. They stop talking and move on."

"I know," she said. "But I don't want to move on."

I stared at her lips, watching the way they remained partially opened. I missed the way her lipstick would leave a stain around the base of my cock after she sucked me off. Anytime I looked at that sexy mouth, it was all I could think about.

"Blade, I miss you." She looked me in the eye as she said it. "I've thought about you every day. I've thought about texting you a lot, but I never did it. I just...I don't know. Do you miss me?"

Like she needed to ask that. "Then what do you want to do about it? You still have a boyfriend."

"I thought maybe you just needed some time to cool off. You were surprised and needed to digest it."

"I don't want to be with a woman who's committed to another man." Even if he knew about me, I didn't like it. I didn't like knowing she talked to him regularly, told him about her life in Carmel. I was a fuck buddy on the side, not a person who actually mattered.

"So...you still feel the same way?"

I nodded.

She looked down at her glass before she took a drink.

I knew she wanted to go back to being fuck buddies. She wanted to screw for the summer before she went back to her boyfriend in France. Then she would come back next summer and probably want to do the same thing. It was every guy's dream but my nightmare. The anger made the truth roll off my tongue. "Celeste, you mean something to me. I don't just want to fuck you. I want to make love to you. I want you to be mine. I know we haven't known each other very long, but...I've never felt this way for a woman before. Something tells me you're special to me, that this could actually turn into something. But if you're gonna keep seeing someone else, then this isn't going to work. I don't want to be a summer fling. I want more. If you can't give that to me...then this is over." I put the ultimatum on the table, and now she had to decide. I was naïve to think she would actually pick me, but my heart told me there was a chance. She wouldn't be sitting across from me right now if I didn't mean anything to her.

She stared at me in silence, her lips pressed tightly together as she considered what I said.

It was the longest minute of my life.

"You're asking me to be with you instead of him."

"Yes."

"When you live in America and I live in France?"

"Yes," I repeated.

She tucked her hair behind her ear, flustered. "Honestly, I've had a lot of summer flings in Carmel, but never one like this."

The simple sentence made me jealous of all the men who'd fucked her before me. It was stupid and immature, but it bothered me. I was just another name on a list of men she'd already forgotten.

"You're different," she said. "I knew it the first time I saw you. I knew it when we kissed. I knew it the first time we were together. I know what you're talking about...because I feel it too. I've never doubted my relationship with Henry until our paths crossed."

I didn't want to know his name.

"Now, I'm torn. You're forcing me to make a decision, and the fact that I can't make it concerns me."

So she was seriously considering me?

"I understand how you feel, Blade. I understand you don't want to settle for some of me when you want all of me. But you're asking me to walk away from a man I've been with for five years."

"If you've ever slept with another man besides him, then you don't love him."

"Don't presume you know how I feel," she said coldly.

"But I do know how you feel. When you're truly in love, you don't want a summer fling. Frankly, you wouldn't be running this bakery across the world if it meant you had to be away from him. You could hire someone to run the damn thing. That isn't love, Celeste."

"And how would you know?" she said defensively.

Now it was obvious to me. "Because I want you to stay here with me. I want you to dump him for me. I want to be with you every single day. That's how I know, Celeste."

Her eyes immediately softened when she absorbed exactly what I said.

I confessed to something I didn't even know I felt. It just came tumbling out in the heat of the moment. I didn't keep my cards close to my chest like I should have. "If you were mine, you would never want to be with another guy. I would never want to be with another woman. I would give you every reason to stay. I don't know this guy, but he doesn't deserve you. He shouldn't want to be with other women. And he definitely shouldn't want you to be with other men. Would you keep doing this when you're married? Would anything ever change? What about when a friend of yours sees him with someone else? You just act like you're fine with it?" The relationship didn't make any sense to me. Even if she explained it to me, I still wouldn't grasp it.

She stared at her drink before she answered. "The open relationship idea was his. He said it's difficult to remain faithful when he travels all the time. So we started doing it that way. We talk about the other people we've been with, but we don't go into details. I agreed to the idea because I appreciated his honesty. There's nothing I hate more than a liar. He's never been a liar. I know he would be a good father and provider. He's ambitious and compassionate, two things I like in a man. That's how we got here."

"So, this is a business relationship."

"Not necessarily."

"It sounds like it," I said coldly. "You're sacrificing love for convenience."

She drank from her glass.

"I can offer all of that and more. I'm a very successful man, and I've got a heart of gold. And I can promise you I'll never want another woman besides you. Every time you go back to France to visit your friends and family, I'm coming with you. I want passion and a partnership. Don't settle for this guy."

She stared at me with a defeated look. "Blade, we haven't known each other very long—"

"Trust your heart." I placed my hand over my heart. "I trust mine. It's telling me something right now. Yours must be too. You wouldn't have asked to see me tonight if I didn't mean anything to you."

She didn't disagree.

"Be with me, Celeste."

She looked into her glass, losing her confidence. "I can't make that kind of decision right on the spot. I need more time."

"How much time?"

"I don't know...until the end of the summer."

She wanted me to keep seeing her, to put my heart on the line until she made her final decision. If she picked him in the end, I would be crushed.

"I understand if I'm asking too much. I just need to spend more time with you before I leave my life behind. You aren't just asking me to leave Henry. You're asking me to live here full time. You can't expect me to make a decision like that after seeing you for less than a month."

She was right. It was unreasonable. "You're seriously considering me?"

She looked me in the eye.

I leaned forward. "If I have a real chance, then I'll meet you halfway. I'll give you until the end of the summer."

"Thank you..."

"But I have one condition."

"Okay."

"You can't see him. I don't want him to visit you or you visit him." I wasn't going to keep sleeping with her if he was around to interfere. Then I would really be sharing her, and that wouldn't be fair to me.

"That's fair."

"Then we have a deal." A very strange deal.

We stared at each other across the table and ignored everyone else in the room. She didn't touch her drink, and I didn't bother ordering a beer. Neither one of us wanted to be there.

We wanted to be alone.

10

AMELIA

I'd just put the girls to bed when there was a knock on my door.

Must be Evan.

I hadn't seen him all day, so it didn't surprise me that he dropped by. He probably wanted to get laid—even though that wasn't going to happen. I opened the door and came face-to-face with my sister—and Ace.

Seeing them outside my door was normal. But at nine in the evening, it was pretty strange. "What's going on, guys?"

"Ace wants to talk to you." Bree walked inside with Ace trailing behind her. "The two of you are gonna sit down and talk." She pulled Ace's sleeve and guided him to a chair at the table. He fell with a thud, his body heavy for the wooden chair. "You." She pointed at me. "Get over here."

"Bree...what's going on?" I did as she said, unsure what my sister was up to. If my sister was trying to force Ace to be with me, she wasn't doing me any favors. That wasn't romantic at all. "Please tell me you aren't about to embarrass me right now."

"Nope." Bree stood beside Ace and looked down into his face. "Ace has something to tell you. I'll leave you two at it." She patted him on the shoulder and walked out, leaving us alone in the silent kitchen. The only sound we heard was the dishwasher cleaning the plates we used for dinner.

I watched Ace as I waited for him to talk to me. I didn't know what this was about, but my imagination ran wild. I missed having him in my bed with me. I missed doing it against the garage door because we couldn't make it to the bedroom. It was impossible for me to be alone with him without thinking dirty things.

Ace stared at the table before he finally met my gaze. He shrugged before he spoke, the confidence rising in his expression. "I'm not sure where to start."

"The beginning usually works."

"Alright, the beginning..." He smiled slightly before he spoke. "You told me you wanted to be with me, that you've had feelings for me for a while. When I told you I didn't feel the same, I was lying."

My eyes narrowed. "You were...?"

"Yeah. The truth is, I didn't want to get involved with you because of Evan. I knew you were going to get back together with him eventually. But that didn't stop me from sleeping with you...all those times. But I broke it off with you when you told me he was trying to get you back. I just assumed I couldn't compete with him, that I should bow out so you guys could be a family again."

I couldn't believe this. I could have been with Ace months ago, but he hid this from me. I wouldn't have slept with Evan in the first place if Ace hadn't broken my heart.

"Bree sticks her nose where it doesn't belong, so she confronted me about it. I told her the truth but made her promise not tell you. This whole charade is her way of getting out of it." He rested his hand on the table, three feet away from me. "She told me you still want to be with me. She also said if I didn't do something now...you might get back together with him. So I'm throwing my cards on the table. I'm showing you my true colors. I'm finally being honest. I know I shouldn't have waited so long, but I thought I was doing the right thing."

I still couldn't believe this. This entire time he'd felt the way I did. "I don't understand, Ace. You want me to get back together with Evan, or you don't?"

"Both," he said. "I don't want to stand in the way of you guys being a family. If you want to be with him, I'll understand. But I want to know your answer right now. Because if I start to love you, and I get used to being with the girls all the time, and then you change your mind and want to be with Evan...it would kill me. Literally." He leaned forward as he looked at me. "So I need to know. You can take some time to think about it. But really think about it."

"Ace, I've been in love with you for months..."

"I know." He gave me the same look he did when we were making love. It was intense and beautiful. "So I hope you pick me. But if there's any doubt, you should think it over. Right now, we could still go back to being friends. But if we do this and you want to be with him, it's gonna be difficult for us to find a new way to work with each other. It won't be the same, Amelia. And more than anything, I don't want to have you then lose you. It would suck."

My eyes softened.

"So, that's the truth. All of it. Ball is in your court, sweetheart."

"I wish you told me this sooner."

"I thought I was doing the right thing...at the time."

If Ace and I were still seeing each other, I wouldn't have

gotten into bed with Evan. Now that I'd spent so much time with him, I didn't hate him as much as I did before. I actually liked him. I'd be lying if I said I wasn't torn.

Ace seemed to understand that. "You know where to find me." He rose from the chair and dismissed himself from the conversation.

I wasn't ready for him to leave yet, not when he'd just walked into my life and told me all the things I wanted to hear. "Ace."

He stopped.

I got up and walked toward him, feeling my fingertips go numb the second I was close to him. My heart worked ten times harder because the proximity was the biggest rush of adrenaline I'd ever received. I'd dreamt of nights when he was mine. I'd fantasized about the four of us being a family, of Ace being the husband who would always be faithful to me. We would grow old together and be buried beside one another.

I hated myself for being unsure if I should pick Ace or not. But I couldn't just let him walk out the door without feeling him, without kissing him. I rose on my tiptoes and kissed his mouth, feeling the coarse hair from his jaw as soon as we touched. Our mouths melted together like warm chocolate, and I felt that tightness between my legs. I immediately fell into him, moving into the counter as his tongue dove into my mouth.

The chemistry was just as strong as ever, more powerful than it used to be. It made me shiver and cling to him more, desperate for the warmth I was addicted to. His hand moved into my hair the way I liked, and his rough fingertips caressed my soft skin.

I loved it when he touched me like that.

My hands explored his powerful body, and I moved my

tongue into his mouth, feeling his own dance with mine. I breathed into him as he breathed into me, and before I knew it, my hands were at the top of his jeans and getting them loose.

I got the button and fly undone then lifted his shirt over his head.

Ace went with it, getting my top and bra off. He kissed my neck as he undid my jeans before he groped my left tit. When our clothes were gone, he lifted me onto the counter and sucked both of my tits until my nipples were nearly raw. His length was hard and long against the counter, and I couldn't wait to feel that thick length inside me. My fingers dug into his hair, and I stopped myself from moaning by sheer force of will.

His mouth returned to mine as he positioned me on the counter, tilting my hips and placing my legs over his shoulders. He cradled me against him even though my body was folded tightly, and he inserted his big cock inside me.

"Oh..."

Ace pressed his mouth harder against mine to silence my moans. If the girls woke up and they found us like this, they would be scarred for life. He gripped my ass and rocked into me on the counter, fucking me just the way I liked. He treated me like I was the most desirable woman on the planet. I didn't have stretch marks or a tummy from being pregnant twice. I was just a beautiful woman being enjoyed.

When my moans were under control, Ace pressed his lips against my ear, exhaling hot breaths into my canal. "Baby...I missed you."

My nails dug into his back as I hung on. "God, I missed you more."

We moved back and forth on the counter where I had

just prepared dinner an hour ago. My back was stretched in an odd way since my legs were so high, but I didn't care because it felt so good. We gripped each other like animals, wanting more of one another but never getting enough.

Ace made me come in record time, pushing me into an orgasm so strong it actually hurt. I breathed into his mouth and did the best I could to stay silent, knowing we were already making too much noise as it was.

My pussy tightened around his dick, and I gushed my come all over him, sheathing him in more lubrication.

He must have felt it because he moaned. "Baby…"

I loved it when he called me that. I loved it when he made me feel like his. "Ace…"

He continued to thrust inside me, his enormous body working hard. "Can I come inside you?"

All the times Evan and I had slept together, he wore a condom. After what he did, I would never trust him to be clean unless he provided a test. "Please…"

Ace pressed his forehead to mine and gave his final pumps before he released with a quiet moan. He gave me his mounds of come, which felt heavy and warm inside me. He breathed hard against me, doing his best to remain quiet even though our bodies felt amazing together. "Fuck…"

My fingers moved through his damp hair, and I kissed him, out of breath and sweaty. I already missed him, but after that, I missed him even more. "Sleep with me…" I missed feeling him next to me, his quiet breathing that reminded me I was safe throughout the night.

He kissed me. "We need to have another round anyway."

BREE AND CYPRESS WERE IN THE OFFICE WHEN I WALKED

inside. Bree immediately grinned at me, probably assuming Ace and I got busy last night.

Not that she was wrong.

I sat at my desk and ignored her obvious look. "Morning."

"Morning," Cypress said, ignorant to what was really going on.

Bree didn't say anything. She just stared. "Cypress, could you get started with the register downstairs? Amelia and I need to have girl talk."

"I feel like you're always kicking me out." He smiled before he walked out, obviously teasing her about it. "You better make it up to me later." He shut the door and headed down the stairs.

Before he was gone from sight, Bree launched into action. "So, what happened?"

"Ace told me how he felt."

"And...?"

"We kissed."

She leaned over my desk. "And...?"

"We did it."

"Yes!" She threw her arm in the air. "I can't believe this took so long. I'm glad you guys finally got your shit together."

I gave her a glare. "Maybe if you told me how he felt, it wouldn't have taken so long."

A guilty look stretched across her face. "So, the sex was good, huh?"

I let her change the subject. "It's always good."

"And now you guys are officially dating, and everything is right with the world. I'll catch Cypress up on everything. Now that he knows you guys are together, he should be mad that you were humping behind everyone's backs."

"Well, hold on." I knew my sister wouldn't like this part of the story. "Ace told me to take some time to figure out who I want to be with. He said he doesn't want me to pick him unless I'm absolutely sure I don't want to be with Evan again."

My sister looked like she might stab me with a pencil. "How can you possibly be unsure, Amelia?"

"I want to be with Ace, but Evan is kinda in the back of my mind."

"Then push him out," Bree snapped. "You aren't going back to him. He's a cheater."

"I know, I know," I said calmly. "But he's the father of my children and—"

"Who gives a shit? Do I need to remind you that he left you for a tramp who tried to jump you?"

Like I'd ever forget how terrible that year was. "Bree, I know what he did was wrong, but I can tell he's sorry. I can tell he's different now. I'm not making excuses for him, but I really don't think he would do something like that again."

Bree wasn't having it. "Amelia, he divorced you a week after he left. He moved in with that girl. He didn't even glance behind when he left."

"I'm aware."

"Then how can you possibly think you could be with him again?"

"Because we're a family, Bree. I have two girls who love their father. I would be lying if I said I didn't miss having the four of us together. And if we could work it out, I know the girls would be really happy."

"I get you want to do the best thing for the kids, but this is your life." She pointed at me. "You should be happy. Ace will definitely make you happy. You never have to worry about his loyalty. He's a straight shooter. He's the best guy."

"Trust me, I know Ace is the better guy."

"Then what are we arguing for? Pick him."

"I just need a little time to think about it."

She rolled her eyes. "Goddammit, Ace. If he'd just said something sooner..."

"We have to play with the hand we're dealt," I said. "I just want to be sure. Ace is right. He deserves to know that I'm not gonna leave him and go back to Evan. I'd rather figure this out now than hurt either one of them later."

Bree sighed and crossed her arms over her chest. "Ugh..."

11

Bree

I couldn't believe Amelia was even considering Evan.

God, I hated him.

Yes, he seemed sincere when he apologized to me. He'd been a great father. He came all the way to my house to apologize to me even though he knew I hated him. But that didn't change anything.

He hurt my sister.

He broke her, actually.

She shouldn't give him another chance just so they could be a family again. Ace was a great guy, the better guy.

She'd better pick him.

Cypress and I walked side by side on the way home from work. We spent the afternoon in different restaurants but met up once our shifts were over. His hand snaked into mine, and he interlocked our fingers as we headed down 7th.

Once I felt his touch, I smiled.

"Everything okay with you and Amelia?"

"Yeah, we're fine."

"You seemed to be talking pretty intently earlier..."

I felt bad keeping the truth from him, but now wasn't the time to come clean about it. After Amelia made her decision, I would tell him what happened. Once he knew Ace kept sleeping with Amelia behind everyone's backs, he'd flip. He was as protective of Amelia as if she really were his sister. "You know how sisters are..."

He chuckled under his breath. "Alright. Keep your secrets."

"They aren't my secrets to share. Otherwise, I would."

We walked up to our two houses that stood side by side. It seemed like a waste to own two properties when we were so close together. It was a waste of money and resources. Plus, Dino had to be shared between the two of us.

"So, sex now or later?" Cypress asked when we stood outside.

"Right to the point, huh?" I asked with a laugh.

"I have a beautiful wife." His hands circled my waist, and he pulled me into his chest. "And I want to have sex with her —all the time." He rubbed his nose against mine before he kissed me.

I kept my eyes open as I kissed him back, seeing the undying affection in his eyes. "How about we shower first?"

"I guess that's okay. I smell like pancakes."

"There are worse things to smell like."

He chuckled then kissed me on the mouth. "See you in a bit." He walked into his house, and Dino's barks met my ears before the door shut.

I walked into my house and got ready, thinking about my husband and dog next door. I smelled like melted cheese and sourdough bread, so I rinsed off in the shower and changed my clothes. I put on a cute thong since I had worn my comfortable underwear while I was at work. I didn't want Cypress to catch me in that.

My mind kept drifting away from what I was doing and focusing on the man next door. I married him, but I couldn't recall my wedding day. When I first got my memory back, I despised him. But now, everything was different.

I missed him.

I was just with him, and I still missed him.

How was that possible?

I redid my makeup and walked next door. I let myself inside since Cypress wouldn't care. Dino ran up to me and gave me plenty of love, dragging his paws down my leg and getting his tongue all over me. I smothered with him with kisses and scratched him behind the ears before I walked into Cypress's bedroom.

He just finished pulling his shirt over his head when I walked in. "You aren't wearing lingerie."

"Was I supposed to be wearing lingerie?"

"A wife's duty is to wear lingerie anytime she can."

"Did I say that in my vows?" I asked with a smile.

"No...but it was implied." He wrapped his arms around my waist and kissed me like he hadn't just seen me thirty minutes ago.

I kissed him back, my hands exploring his tight arms. I'd touched his skin so many times that I memorized how it felt. His smell was second nature to me, and the moment the scent was in the air, I recognized it. My mouth had memorized the feel of his lips long ago.

Cypress continued to kiss me until my mouth stopped responding. I just stood there and breathed, unable to move or do anything else.

Cypress pulled away and gave me a look of concern. "Sweetheart, what's wrong?"

"There's nothing wrong…"

"It sure seems that way."

The feeling snuck up on me sooner than I expected it to. When I finally let my guard down, truly let the walls open, the passion flooded in. Cypress found his way into my heart and claimed it at once. "I love you…"

His eyes softened in a way they never had before. His fingers immediately dug into my hips, and he tilted his head as the intensity grew in his eyes.

"I guess I'm still a little uneasy about trusting you, but I don't think you would ever hurt me again. I know that you love me. I see it when you look at me. And…as much as I don't want to love you, I do."

His hands moved to my cheeks, and he pressed a kiss to my forehead. "It feels so good to hear you say that. I remember the last time you told me you loved me. You left the house to go to work, and you kissed me on the mouth before you said it. I still remember it as vividly as the day it happened." His hands slid down my body to my hips.

"I was thinking…maybe we could move back in together."

The concern left his face, and a subtle look of joy remained behind. "Yeah?"

"Yeah. If we're gonna be husband and wife…we should act like it."

"Is that really what you want?" he asked. "Because I would love to. But I can also be patient if that's what you need."

"No…I want to live with you. We can start marriage counseling and work our way through it. I know I want to make this work. I know I want to be with you. I think it's time that we take another step."

He smiled before he wrapped his arms around me and

pulled me to his chest. He buried his face in my hair and released a deep sigh of happiness. He held me that way for a long time, and soon his chest started to rise and fall at deeper intervals.

I pulled away to see his face, wondering if my suspicion was right.

His eyes were wet, but there were no tears. Subtle hints of redness and blotchiness were on his face. He met my gaze without any shame. "It's been rough...these past eighteen months. There were a lot of times when I lost hope. But knowing it's finally over...that we're really in this together... means the world to me." His big hands ran up my arms, his fingertips caressing my skin.

"I'm so sorry..."

His eyes melted. "Sorry for what, sweetheart?"

"For putting you through so much—"

"Don't apologize to me. I understand why you felt the way you did. No one can hold that against you."

"But it took me so long, and you've done so much for me—"

"Doesn't matter. I'm your husband, and I will always take care of you. I'm never gonna go away, because you're my world. You're my life." He pressed his forehead to mine. "Till death parts us, it's you and me."

Cypress had drifted off as he lay beside me in bed. Dino was at the foot of the mattress, sighing every few minutes because he was restless. Cypress and I had done nothing but make love since I said I wanted to move in together. We didn't even have dinner.

Comfortable beside him in bed, I watched him sleep.

His jaw was more relaxed when he was dreaming, and he had a boyish charm he didn't carry when he was awake. I loved the scruff along his jaw. It was coarse against my fingertips, but I liked feeling it every time he kissed me.

My life had taken so many unexpected turns, and I couldn't believe where I was at that moment. Cypress Heston was my husband, and we'd been married for over two years. We were happy together, and he loved me more than I could understand. I wouldn't have believed it if he hadn't spent the last six months proving it to me every day.

Like he knew I was watching him, he opened his eyes. He released a quiet sigh as he stretched his body, twisting his back and moving his legs. "I would have slept all through the night, but I'm hungry."

"I'm hungry too."

Dino whined.

"And our dog needs a walk," I said. "Or he needs to poop."

Cypress ran his hand through his hair. "He wants a walk. I can tell."

"I'll go into the kitchen and see if there's anything I can make."

"I love having a wife," he said with a smile.

I rolled my eyes and pulled on his shirt before I walked into the kitchen. Dino came with me, hoping we were about to do something fun. I found a few ingredients in the fridge, so I chopped up slices of raw chicken and broccoli and decided to make a stir-fry. Just when the pans got hot, someone came to the door.

I walked to the entryway and peeked through the peephole, assuming it was Blade or Ace.

But it was Vanessa.

What the fuck?

I was only in Cypress's t-shirt, but I didn't care. I wanted this bitch to see me like this, with messy hair and chapped lips. I yanked the door open and smiled. "Yes? Can I help you?"

She obviously didn't expect me to be there because her eyes widened. "Uh...hi."

I waved. "Nice to see you again. So, what can I do for you?" She was in skintight jeans and a top that stuck to her like a second layer of skin. Every time I was having a good day, this bitch ruined it. It was like she did it on purpose.

"I...I was wondering if I could speak to Cypress. Is he here?"

It was his house, wasn't it? "Yeah, hold on. He needs to put on some clothes." I shut the door and walked down the hall.

"Who's at the door?" Cypress asked as he pulled on his jeans and t-shirt.

"Vanessa." I could barely contain the rage in my voice.

Cypress did a double take. "What? Right now?"

"Yep." And she knew where he lived. That was interesting. I crossed my arms over my chest and stared him down.

Cypress looked more irritated than I'd ever seen him. "She's never been here before. I don't know how she knows where I live. I swear."

I walked off and headed back to the kitchen, my anger getting to me. I got back to work over the stove.

Cypress opened the door. "Vanessa, what are you doing here?"

"Sorry, I didn't realize you would have company..."

"I'm married," he snapped. "She's not company. She's my wife."

Take that, bitch.

"Can we talk outside?" she asked quietly so I couldn't hear.

"Fine, whatever." His footsteps sounded as he walked into the kitchen. "I'll be right back. Is that okay?"

"You don't have to ask my permission, Cypress." I didn't turn away from the stove to look at him.

"I'll be right back. I'll make sure she doesn't bother us again." He walked out and shut the door behind him.

I was so angry right now. I wanted to throw the pan at that woman's face. What did she want to talk to him about? Nothing good, I could only assume. After a few seconds of standing there, I realized one of the windows in the front of the house was open.

Should I eavesdrop?

That would be wrong.

But I couldn't contain my jealousy and curiosity. The woman who tried to steal my boyfriend and now my husband was right outside.

I was going for it.

I crawled under the windows so they wouldn't see me, and I took a seat on the hardwood floor with my back against the wall. They both spoke quietly, but I could understand their hushed words.

"Vanessa, are you out of your mind right now?" Cypress asked with suppressed rage. "Are you trying to piss me off?"

"I just wanted to talk—"

"What is there to talk about? You could just call me if you had to."

"I thought it was better to do it face-to-face..."

Cypress sighed loudly. "Why are you doing this to me? I'm married. *Married*. What part of that don't you understand?"

"I thought she didn't have her memory back."

"Wouldn't matter even if she didn't. I'm still married to her. I'm still off the market. I still don't want to be with you."

Ha. Take that, skank.

"Come on, Cypress. What kind of relationship is this? This isn't gonna last."

"She has her memory back, and we're doing great. We're gonna be together forever. You need to let it go, Vanessa."

Bet she didn't like that.

When she didn't say anything, I assumed she wore a pissed look. "You know it's always been you and me..."

Now I was pissed.

"It was us years ago. When I said I loved you, I meant it. But I've moved on. You need to move on too."

"You didn't seem moved on when you slept with me when you were with her," she snapped.

Bitch.

"I made a mistake, and I still regret that to this day. But I changed. I realized Bree was the woman I wanted to spend my life with, and I'm gonna spend my life with her. I don't want to hurt you, but I don't want you, Vanessa. You can keep swooping around like a damn vulture, but you aren't going to get any scraps. I'm committed to my wife. You can do whatever you want to try to persuade me otherwise, but it won't make a difference. But for your sake, I hope you don't waste your time."

She didn't have a comeback to that.

"You need to leave me alone, Vanessa. You can't just show up on my doorstep like this. How did you know where I lived anyway?"

"The post office," she answered.

So Cypress was telling the truth.

"If she's had this memory problem once, she might have

it again," Vanessa said. "And you'll be back to where you were. And you're just gonna stay?"

"You need to look up the word marriage in a dictionary because you don't obviously don't understand what it means."

Boom.

"Vanessa," Cypress said. "Even if Bree and I broke up, I still wouldn't want to be with you. Does that sink into your head?"

"I don't believe that."

"Well, you should. I'm not attracted to women who don't respect marriage. I don't want a woman who's fine with stealing someone's husband. You seduced me once, but you won't do it again." His feet sounded against the stone as he headed back to the house.

Shit. I crawled across the ground and hopped back into the kitchen just before he opened the door. I turned the burners back on and tried to steady my breathing so I wouldn't seem winded. The food was cold, so I pushed it around to make it seem like it was sizzling.

The door shut, and Cypress walked farther into the house.

I didn't turn around and ask him about his conversation. I was too scared that he knew I'd been listening. I worked the spatula in the pan and watched the food start to simmer again. Hopefully, he didn't know it was cold just a minute ago. "Dinner is almost ready..."

He opened the fridge and grabbed a beer before he opened it at the counter. "Please don't tell me we're back to where we were. Please don't tell me you're gonna let that woman get under your skin like last time." He set the bottle on the counter and made a loud clank. "Don't let her have so much power over us." He leaned against the counter as he looked at me, his desperation obvious by the way he gripped the counter.

I set the spatula on the counter and let the food simmer. Cypress was right. When I saw her in that restaurant, she got me all worked up. Now that I'd heard Cypress talk to her outside, I knew I really had no reason to be threatened. Maybe he picked her once in the past, but he wouldn't pick her again. "What did she say to you?"

"Just a bunch of bullshit. It doesn't matter."

Bullshit was a great way to describe it.

"Tell me you're still with me. Tell me we're still moving in together." He grabbed the dials on the stove and turned them off.

"I need to cook—"

"I don't give a shit about dinner." He grabbed my elbow and turned me so I was forced to look at him.

He crowded me, pushing me back until we were on the other side of the kitchen. The kitchen was heavy with the smell of food, but it didn't seem like we would be eating anytime soon.

I looked up at my husband, who was nearly a foot taller than me. "I'm not going anywhere, Cypress. You can relax."

"I can?" His large hands gripped my hips, and he positioned me against the counter. He always pressed me against things, like prey that couldn't run away. He held his face close to mine, his breathing heavy.

"Yes." My hands snaked up his arms, and I felt the hardness of his wedding ring against my hip. "I know you're mine."

He pressed his forehead to mine and released a quiet sigh. "Sweetheart...I'm all yours until the day I die."

12

BLADE

She rode me nice and slow, taking in every inch of my hard cock until she pulled it down again. Up and down she moved, her beautiful tits in my face. Her nipples were subtly pink, and their hardness felt perfect against my tongue.

Never seen anything sexier.

My hands appreciated her luscious ass, gripping it and squeezing it as she moved up and down. I liked her slow pace because I was already struggling not to come. The second we walked inside my house, we landed on the couch and started going at it.

She moved her hands up my chest to my shoulders, and she rolled her head back, her tits hardening as her breathing increased. *"Oui..."*

I loved those French words. "Baby..." I gripped her ass harder, guiding her up and down my length.

"Oui..."

"Come on my dick, baby." I pressed my thumb against her clit and rubbed her hard, moving my digit in a circular motion just the way she did to herself.

She dug her nails into my skin, and the sexiest expression formed on her face. She closed her eyes, her long lashes moving down toward her cheek. She released a cry that echoed in my house, the kind that probably reached the neighbors.

I felt her moisture ooze all over me, sheathing me all the way to my balls. I loved her come. It felt incredible.

"Your turn." She grabbed my hands and placed them over her big tits, making me squeeze them hard as she worked her hips on top of me, taking me over and over again. "Give it to me, Blade."

I was on the verge of coming, but I wanted a little more. "Talk to me in French."

"*Je te veux.*"

I gripped her tits harder and felt my cock thicken.

"*Fais-moi l'amour.*"

I didn't know what she was saying, but my dirty mind could do the imagining for me. I pulled her down my length until I was completely inside her before I released. I had a great orgasm, filling her pussy with all my seed. Every time I fucked her, I was more obsessed with this woman.

Too obsessed.

When my come was sitting inside her, I kept her on my lap. I was surrounded by her arousal, and she was soaked with mine. Her tits were still in my face, and my mind was focused on sex even though I was satisfied.

She didn't get off of me, just as content as I was.

We hadn't mentioned our previous conversation after we had it because there was nothing more to say. My priority was making her choose me instead of him, making her realize she could be loved by me in a way she'd never been loved by anyone before.

She ran her fingers through her hair, dissipating the

sweat that formed at her hairline. When she was on top of me, she rode me at a smooth pace, but her toned body had to work hard to move up and down my long length.

She was a pro.

It was the first time she'd been at my house, but I hadn't given her a tour because we were too occupied by fucking. While I liked to be in charge, my favorite position was having her on top. I loved watching a woman take my cock the way she liked, using me to please herself. I loved having beautiful tits in my face as my hands helped her move up and down. Celeste was a natural at it, so she must like the position too.

"Can I make you dinner?" I'd take her out if that's what she preferred, but when we were in public, we couldn't hook up. When we were behind closed doors, there was a lot more opportunity for sex. We had sex before dinner, during dinner, and always after dinner.

"You cook?"

"I own restaurants. Of course I know how to cook."

"Wasn't sure if you were just a businessman."

"No. We work together to find new entrees for our customers. We take culinary classes together, and sometimes we have working dinners where we come up with new stuff to try. So, I know a thing or two."

"Wow." She ran her hands up my chest. "A handsome man who also knows how to cook. Very impressive."

"I'll impress you even more very soon."

"Ooh...you have my attention." She slowly pulled my cock out of her, some of my come stuck to the head of my dick.

"You're welcome to shower while I start cooking."

"I think I'll take you up on that offer." She picked up her panties and her dress from the floor, standing completely naked in my living room. The blinds were shut so my neigh-bors couldn't see us, and I liked seeing a beautiful woman walk around in just her bare skin. She took the stairs and helped herself to the master bedroom.

I got to work in the kitchen and started preparing the chicken and pasta.

A knock sounded on the door.

I could hear the shower running, so I knew Celeste wasn't going to walk down the stairs naked anytime soon. "It's open," I called from the counter next to the sink.

Cypress walked inside in running shorts and a t-shirt. Judging from the sweat stain around his neck, he'd just finished with a run. "Hey. I walked in at the right time." He came to my side and looked down at the cutting board just as I finished preparing the asparagus.

"You aren't getting any of this. Celeste is upstairs."

Cypress tilted his head toward the ceiling, listening for the sound of the running water. "A shower this early in the evening could only mean one thing..." He nudged me in the side before he winked.

I winked back. "I'm a gentleman, so I'll never tell."

"You just did," he said with a laugh.

I carried the prepared food to the pan on the stove and got to cooking.

"Wow, you're making her dinner too. You really do like her."

"I don't think *like* is a strong enough word."

Cypress grabbed a bottle of water out of the fridge and took a drink. "Since she's here, I'm assuming the two of you worked things out?"

"Yeah. I told her I didn't want to settle for being her fling and she should leave her loser boyfriend for me."

"Why is he a loser?" Cypress twisted the cap back on and

left the bottle on the counter. He leaned against the fridge with his arms across his chest.

"He doesn't care if she sleeps with other guys. Of course he's a loser."

Cypress nodded in agreement. "Very true. So where does that leave you?"

"I have until the end of the summer to convince her to be with me."

"And live here permanently?"

"Yeah."

Cypress whistled under his breath. "Good luck, man."

"I can do it."

"You sound confident."

"She and I have a connection. I can feel it every time I'm with her. Call me crazy, but I can tell she feels it too. There's no other reason why she would agree to give me a chance if she didn't feel that way. She's seriously considering moving here for me."

"Wow. You must be good in bed."

"Duh."

Cypress chuckled. "Anything we can do to help? Talk you up?"

"Nah. I have to do this one solo. But make her feel like family."

He rolled his eyes. "Like we wouldn't have done that anyway."

The shower turned off upstairs.

I glanced at the ceiling even though I couldn't see through solid walls. "Looks like she's done. You should probably get out of here."

"You aren't going to invite me to dinner?" he teased.

"Not unless you wanna watch us have sex."

He cringed in disgust. "I'm good."

Before Cypress could walk away, I asked about Bree. They seemed to be doing well and things were back on track, but anything could change with them. "How's the wife?"

"Good," he said with a quiet sigh. "We were doing really good until Vanessa showed up on my doorstep."

I looked away from the pan and dropped the spatula on the counter since dinner didn't seem important anymore. The chicken sizzled and popped in the oil, but I needed to wait a few minutes before I turned it over anyway. "What? Why did Vanessa show up on your doorstep?"

He rolled his eyes. "Wants to get back together or hook up. I don't even think she wants me that bad. She just doesn't like the fact that I chose Bree over her."

"She's been trying to get you for years now. Doesn't she have a life?"

He shrugged. "I don't get it either. She's a pretty woman, so it's not like she can't find someone else."

"And she just showed up at your house?"

"And, of course, Bree was there."

"Yikes." Having an ex stop by your house never made you look good. "Bree was pissed?"

"No, she took it pretty well, actually. Said she trusted me."

"Whoa...that's a big deal."

"I know." He drank from his water again. "When she saw Vanessa the first time, she wanted to get divorced again."

"What changed?"

"I'm not sure. She's just warmed up to me lately, even said we should move in together."

"That's awesome. You're still doing that, right?"

"Yeah. Thankfully."

After all the back-and-forth nonsense they went

through, it seemed like things were finally getting better. "It sounds like everything is on the right track, then. Hopefully, Vanessa leaves you alone."

"Might have to ask Ace to put the moves on her so she'll forget about me."

"He is a sex machine. May as well use him for his talents."

"Exactly." Cypress glanced to the ceiling when he heard footsteps. "Looks like your woman is almost finished. I should get going. Enjoy your dinner." He walked by me and patted me on the shoulder. "By the way, I've got my money on you."

"Thanks, man." I held up my hand in the form of a wave and watched him walk out and shut the door behind him. I turned my efforts back to the food and started boiling the pasta. Celeste came down just a few minutes later in one of my long t-shirts instead of the dress she'd been wearing when she came over.

I preferred this outfit over the last one.

She sauntered over to me at the stove then gave me a warm kiss. "Sounded like you were talking to yourself."

"No," I said with a chuckle. "Cypress stopped by."

"Oh, that's good." She rubbed her hand up my arm. "I'm relieved."

"I'm not a freak, don't worry."

"How is he? He's a nice guy."

"He just stopped by to say hi. Told me about his marriage problems."

"It didn't seem like they were having problems last time I saw them." She grabbed the salt from the counter and poured some into the water with the pasta, adding her own preferences to my cooking.

"It comes and goes..." I'd never told Celeste about Bree's condition, so I mentioned it to her now.

"Wow. That's unbelievable."

"It's been a crazy ride. It's nice having her back again, but she and Cypress have struggled a lot."

"Doesn't surprise me," she said with her accent. "That would be hard to come back from."

"But they're making it work. Sounds like things are finally going well. They just had a few bumps."

"I'm glad things are better. They're cute together." She looked into the pan and watched me sauté the chicken and veggies. "Mmm...that looks good. You really are quite the chef."

"I hope it tastes as good as it looks. I want you to come back for more."

She grabbed my ass and gave it a squeeze. "I already do come back for more."

At this rate, we would never get through dinner. Actually, we wouldn't have anything to eat because I was probably going to burn it since I wasn't paying attention. I set the spatula down and crowded her against the counter, the pan still sizzling with the food. "Be careful, baby. I'll give you more if you want more."

She grabbed my hips and pulled me farther into her, meeting my challenge with her own. "Always assume I want more, Blade."

WHEN I WOKE UP THE NEXT MORNING, MY LADY WAS STILL right next to me.

I was already calling her my lady when she wasn't even mine yet. I was being too confident in my assumption that she would pick me, but I'd rather be certain than uneasy. I was a confident man, and I knew Celeste would appreciate that since she was so strong herself. If I wanted to keep a powerful woman like her, I had to be just as powerful.

I could take her to expensive and fancy places for dinner, but that wasn't what Celeste was looking for. I didn't want to impress her with my wealth or my charm. I wanted to impress her with something much more personal than that.

I wanted to show her that being with me every day could be much more exciting than anything Henry had to offer. Because when it was just the two of us, we didn't need anything else.

I opened my eyes and stared at her, seeing the top of her tits since the sheet was low. Every inch of her beautiful skin was flawless and soft. I loved kissing her everywhere, tasting the invisible rose petals off her body. I loved everything about her, from her slender neck to the way her petite feet felt against my chest. Every inch of her was divine.

I wanted every inch to be mine.

She opened her eyes a few minutes later, her face naturally pretty without makeup. She usually wore a lot of it every time I saw her, heavy foundation and even heavier eye shadow, but she looked beautiful either way. With virgin skin, her eyes looked smaller and her lips less plump, but something about her appearance made me adore her more. She didn't need makeup to hide her flaws. She only accented all of her already lovely qualities.

"Morning," I whispered, feeling my cock grow underneath the sheets.

She gently stretched beside me, arching her back and pushing her arms above her head. "Morning." She stuck out her chest in the process, her nipples firming now that she was awake and more exposed to the cool air.

My eyes immediately went to her breasts, my cock hardening further in response. Sometimes I wondered if my obsession with her was mostly physical rather than emotional, but everything about her turned me on. The fact that she owned her own businesses and was so independent turned me on. Basically, all of her features intensified my attraction to her.

"You look beautiful first thing in the morning."

All the features of her face softened in response, from the closure of her eyes to the fall of her lips. "Thank you."

I pulled her leg over my waist and slid my hand to her ass, feeling nothing but skin between us. We made love last night then went straight to sleep. I hadn't had a passionate relationship like this in a long time. Just a bunch of one-night stands that were good but not great.

"You look sexy in the morning too," she whispered. "I like your messy hair and sleepy eyes."

"You think sleepy eyes are sexy?"

"I think they're sexy since you spent all night sleeping next to me."

My fingertips dug into her skin, feeling the tight muscles of her ass. She knew exactly what to say to make me feel like a desirable man.

"I know I should go home soon, but I don't want to."

"Then don't." She could stay here for a week straight, and I wouldn't be burdened. "I've got a shower, food, and clothes. You don't need anything else."

"You make a powerful argument."

My hand slid up her soft back until I reached the back of her neck where her hair was. I felt the strands with my fingertips and observed her gentle pulse underneath the touch. I noticed her phone hardly ever went off when we were together. She slept beside me all night, and her boyfriend never wondered what she was doing.

Disgusted me.

Because of his stupidity, I was going to take her away from him.

Idiot.

"Can I ask you something?" Her hand moved up my stomach to my chest, her favorite feature she loved to touch. Her hands were attracted to my muscles, and she loved to grip on to them whenever we were intimate together.

Feeling her touch me made me lose my train of thought for a second. "Anything."

"So...what's your love life like? Have you had any girlfriends recently? Any serious relationships?"

Not really. "No."

"No?" she asked. "No elaboration?" She smiled, telling me she wasn't trying to pry. She was just curious.

"I haven't found anyone I like enough to have a relationship with. My life is usually a combination of hookups and one-night stands. I've always wanted to get married and have a family someday, but the right woman never walked into my life." Until now. The second I laid eyes on her, I knew she was different. Something about her made me think of a future with wedding bells and kids, which were things that never had been on my mind.

She continued to give me that adoring look, with her eyes partially lidded and her lips parted. "So, I'm the only woman you've been with for more than a few days?"

"Pretty much."

"I feel special..."

"You are special." I kissed the corner of her mouth and pressed my hard-on against her, telling her I wanted her before we got the day started. I wasn't getting out of that bed and into the shower until I'd pleased her and myself.

AT THE END OF THE NIGHT, I WALKED HER HOME AND SAID goodnight on the doorstep. I wanted her to sleep over again, but I didn't want to apply too much pressure. Things were going well, and I didn't want to ruin it by being too possessive. "Good night." I wrapped my arms around her and kissed her in front of the door, giving her something to think about before she went to bed.

Her arms rested on top of mine, and she gave me a fierce kiss with those plump lips. She kissed me like a woman who loved a man. I knew her embrace wasn't purely physical, but so much more than that.

When it heated up in less than two seconds, I knew where it would go unless I behaved like a gentleman. I pulled away because I'd fucked her so much for the past few days that there was no way she wasn't sore. She was just too classy to say anything.

"Good night," I whispered against her mouth.

"Good night," she said in return, her hands still resting on my arms.

I placed a kiss on her forehead before I stepped back and let her walk into the house.

With a look full of reluctance, she stared at me like she didn't want to go inside without me. She never locked her front door, so she turned the knob and walked inside. The last goodbye I got was a blown kiss.

I smiled then walked up the street back to my place. It was on the opposite side of Ocean and on 4th Street. There weren't many sidewalks in the city, so I walked in the middle of the road, knowing there wouldn't be any cars after the sun went down. People drove here to enjoy the beach, but once daylight was gone, everyone cleared out.

My phone rang in my pocket, and I fished it out to answer it. I hoped it was Celeste, asking me to come back and spend the night with her.

But it was my mom.

Oh no. I'd been dreading this conversation for a long time, and now it was finally here. I'd planned on calling her on my own, but she beat me to the punch. I took a deep breath before I answered. "Hey, Mom."

My mom's tone was full of the usual happiness she possessed. She was on edge, obviously still uncomfortable by the last memory she had of calling me. "Hey, Blade. I hope I'm not calling too late…"

Humiliation flooded through me, knowing my mom assumed I was with Celeste at the moment. "No. I don't usually go to bed until eleven. I'm still a night owl."

"Yes, I remember." She fell silent, either because she didn't know how to commandeer the conversation or because she wanted me to deal with the burden of the topic.

Since it was my fault, I stepped forward. "I'm sorry about that phone call last month. When she answered, she assumed you were one of my friends…" Did that make it better? Or was this conversation even more awkward now?

"That's okay, Blade. I was just…taken aback."

"Yeah, I can imagine."

"So…who is this girl?"

"Her name is Celeste." My mom asked about my love life sometimes, but she didn't pry. I knew she wanted me to get married and have kids. My brother didn't seem any closer to settling down, so she probably thought I was her only hope of having grandkids. Talk about pressure.

"Will I be meeting Celeste, or is she...just a friend?"

My mom wasn't stupid. She knew I slept around. I used to sneak out in high school all the time. Not a lot had changed since then. My hormone levels never dropped off, and I was just as horny now as I was then. "I hope so, but I'm not sure yet."

My mom's tone changed over the phone even though she didn't say anything. Her pregnant silence was enough. "Does that mean you like this girl, sweetheart?"

The second she used that term of endearment, I knew she was in a better mood. She was hopeful that I'd finally be in a serious relationship. She didn't care if Celeste answered the phone that way if she was someone I truly liked. "I do, actually. She's really cool. She owns a coffee shop here in Carmel. I met her a few months ago, and we've been hanging out ever since."

"A few months?" she asked in surprise. "Oh, that's wonderful."

"Yeah, she's pretty great."

"Are your father and I going to meet this woman?"

I didn't have a clue how she would feel about that. She might not want to meet my parents until she knew she wanted to be with me. "Uh, I'm not sure yet. We're still in the beginning phase of the relationship."

"A few months is a long intro, and you two seem pretty comfortable with each other..."

I rolled my eyes when my mom made a jab at me. "We'll see."

"Well, your father and I would love to meet her whenever you're ready."

Like she needed to remind me. "I know. So, were you calling for a particular reason?" Maybe she just wanted to address the elephant in the room and didn't have anything else to say, but knowing her, she had a few points of discussion.

"We're having a BBQ on Saturday. Wanted to know if you'd like to come."

"Yeah, sure. I'll be there."

"And Celeste is more than welcome to come as well..."

I wasn't sure if I'd even bother asking her. "I'll pass that along."

"Great. Just let me know."

"I will, Mom." During the conversation, I crossed Ocean and approached my house. Now I was standing in front of it and digging my hand into my pocket to find the key. "I'll talk to you later. I just got home, and I've got to pee."

"Alright, sweetheart. Love you."

My mom said that to me every time we got off the phone. It used to annoy me, but now that I knew Celeste lost her mother, I felt ungrateful not appreciating my mother's love. "Love you too, Mom."

13

AMELIA

I spent the rest of the day weighing Ace against Evan.

They were two completely different men, both with great qualities. Ace was the obvious choice because he'd been nothing but wonderful to me since the day we met. When things heated up between us, he was even more kind and gentle. He helped me with the girls without my even having to ask. He was honest, loyal, and trustworthy.

Evan didn't have a lot going for him other than the fact that he was the father of my children and my ex-husband. But being married to him for eight years left a permanent mark on my heart that could never be erased. The eight years I spent with him were nothing but joyful. I was happy every single day until he walked out.

But I also knew he'd changed. When he apologized, he meant it. When he cried in front of me, those tears were real. He understood the severity of his actions and truly regretted the poor decision he made. If he could go back in time and erase his choice, he would.

I knew that was the truth.

So I could forgive him and be happy again, probably have a better marriage than I did before, or I could be with the man who wasn't stupid enough to fuck up in the first place.

To any objective person, the answer was clear.

But it was blurry for me.

I helped the girls with their homework when we came home from school, made dinner, and then got them ready for bed. It was only a matter of time before Evan showed up. He hadn't told me how his conversation with Rebecca had gone, and even if he didn't have anything to report, he would still stop by.

I was sitting on the couch drinking wine in front of the fire when my phone lit up with a text message from Evan.

I'm outside. Are you awake?

I wasn't sure why we had these clandestine meetings sometimes. It was as if he didn't want the girls to know he had a private relationship with me. Maybe he just didn't want to get their hopes up if it didn't work out. They would love nothing more than to have him back in the house every single day.

I didn't bother to text him back before I opened the door.

He was in a black hoodie with jeans, his fair face handsome in comparison to his dark clothing. "Hey."

"Hey."

After sharing a look with me, he let himself inside and stepped into the kitchen.

I shut the door and locked it before I looked at him. I wasn't sleeping with him again, not when I was stuck in this love triangle. I'd slept with Ace, and I probably shouldn't have done that, but I couldn't help myself.

Evan stood too close to me, close enough for a kiss if I wanted to make it happen.

I stepped back, needing the space. "What's up?"

Evan glanced down at my arms and torso, obviously put off by the way I stepped away from him. "I'm sure Bree told you I stopped by her house by now."

"Yeah…she mentioned it." And he told her about my relationship with Ace. I would be mad at him under different circumstances, but since it led to something great with Ace, I couldn't complain.

"I didn't know she didn't know about Ace…never would have told her otherwise."

"I know, Evan." When I sighed, I released all the pent-up annoyance I had for him. I let it disappear before I looked at him again. "Don't worry about it. She and I talked it out… and we're fine."

"I'm glad to hear that. Then you must know I took care of Rebecca."

I nodded.

"She won't bother you again. I promise."

I nodded again. "Thanks. I hope she feels better soon."

"She's just having a hard time adjusting to it. She knows we're trying to make our relationship work. She was intolerant to it, but I explained to her that we were married and we have two kids…we're a family. I think she's just too young to get it."

I bit my tongue because I wanted to make a jab at her age, but that would paint me in an ugly light, so I didn't say anything at all. I didn't get any satisfaction out of seeing her in pain even though she didn't care about stealing my husband from me. Since I knew how shitty it felt to watch a man leave you, I only felt sympathy for her.

"But she won't be a problem anymore," he whispered.

"I never said we were working on our relationship, Evan." I had to make that clear so he didn't make any assumptions. I shouldn't have slept with him, but I was making poor decisions at the time because I was miserable.

"It doesn't matter. I told her I'm trying to get you back, and that's definitely true, regardless of how you feel. She knows I want to be your husband again, to live here with the kids again."

I stepped back and leaned against the counter in the kitchen, my heart working fast in my chest. I had to tell him about Ace, but now I was dreading it. He was determined to make it work between us, but now he had even more obstacles to overcome.

"Baby..." He cringed when he realized he said the nickname that I didn't want to hear. "Amelia...what's wrong?"

Ace just called me by that name the other night, and I'd loved hearing it. I loved feeling him inside me, just his skin against mine. I dug my nails into his shoulders as I listened to his hot breaths of pleasure. "There's something I need to tell you...and you aren't going to want to hear it."

He moved to the counter across from me and crossed his arms over his chest. He stared me down with a stoic expression, refusing to let his thoughts be obvious on his face. "What is it?"

"Ace came over the other night and told me he had feelings for me..."

Evan didn't react.

"He said he'd had feelings for me for a while. He backed out of our relationship because he thought it was the right thing to do. He assumed I would take you back, and he didn't want to stand in the way of us being a family." I couldn't look him in the eye right away. I had to muster up the courage even though I had nothing to be ashamed of.

"But now he says he wants to be with me."

Evan's expression was as cold and hard as ever.

"So he wants me to choose..."

The only reaction Evan gave was sliding his hand through his hair. His movements were slow because he was spending most of his focus on thinking. He sighed quietly under his breath, his voice so low I could barely hear it.

I wasn't sure what kind of reaction I expected from him. He wouldn't be happy, obviously. I just told him I was in love with Ace a few weeks ago. The whole reason why we were screwing was because I was depressed that Ace left.

"And this is your way of telling me you're going to be with him now?" He crossed his arms over his chest and wore an ice-cold look. His eyes were narrowed the way they were when he really angry about something. His jaw was clenched tighter than ever before, but the rest of his body was sluggish with defeat.

"No...I told him I needed to think about it. Ace says he wants a final decision, no going back and forth. He doesn't want me to be with him, only to change my mind later and come back to you. So, if I want to make this work again, I need to figure it out now. He said he wouldn't be angry with me if I chose you. We could still be the good friends we've always been. But he wants me to really think about it." I stared at the floor for a moment, no longer wanting to look at the hardness of Evan's face.

"So I have a chance?" he whispered.

I looked up again. "Yeah...you do."

He sighed again, but this time it was in relief. "I'm touched that you're willing to consider me again...after what I did."

Most people in the world would think less of me for being so soft, but I couldn't stop my feelings. I'd loved Evan the moment I saw him, and every day after that. Love like that couldn't be erased in a year. "I know you're sorry for what you did. There are plenty of days when I miss being a family, miss being a wife. As much as I try to stay angry at you, I can't. You're the father of my girls..."

He nodded. "I'm a very lucky man. I wish I'd understood that a year ago."

Me too.

"So...how much time do you need to make your decision?"

"I don't know..." How would I choose between two amazing men? Everyone would tell me to pick Ace, and they were probably right. But my wedding dress was still in the closet, and my ring was still sitting in the nightstand. Memories like that couldn't be easily erased. They lingered on forever...in both my mind and my heart.

Evan rubbed his hand across his jaw as he looked at the floor. "When Ace was here the other night...did you...never mind." He dropped his hand and looked out the window. "Forget I said anything."

I knew exactly what he was asking, and since we were in this situation, I thought he had the right to know. "Yes."

He closed his eyes, cringing at the response.

"I'm still in love with Ace. I think he's one of the most amazing guys I've ever met. Despite what you've put me through, I know I can trust again. I know I can trust him to always be faithful to me. He's great with the girls, and he's such a good friend to me. If he'd said something to me months ago...I would have jumped into his arms. But now I'm confused. I hate you for what you did to me. You hurt me so much that I couldn't get out of bed. But the second you were back in my life, I felt that electrical touch whenever we were close to each other. Every time you kissed me, I melted. I didn't think about Rebecca because it just felt like us again. And when you finally understood how much you hurt me...I knew you were truly sorry for what you did. When you said you wished you could take it back, I knew you meant it. My trust has been broken, but I don't think you would ever betray me again."

He looked at me with a focused expression, his gaze hard and intense at the same time. "Then pick me."

"Not so simple..."

He stepped toward me, approaching me on my side of the kitchen. "I love you with all my heart." His hands moved to my hips, and he gave me a gentle squeeze. "We can be a family again. I could move back in and be here every day. We could have dinner together every night and help the girls with their homework. Sleep in late every Sunday and make pancakes in the morning..."

"I know..."

He cupped my face with one hand and brushed my cheek with his thumb. "I know I made the stupidest mistake of my life, but please forgive me. Amy, please. I'll do anything to make it up to you. I'll spend the rest of our lives showing you how sorry I am."

"I know, Evan. I've already forgiven you."

He pressed his forehead to mine. "Then be with me. Please don't pick him."

I closed my eyes and tried not to cry. I didn't like seeing Evan beg me like this, let himself be so vulnerable like this. He was always strong and affectionate at the same time, never so desperate.

"Ace is a great guy," he admitted. "Honestly, if you aren't going to be with me, he's my first pick. He'd treat you right, and he'd be good to the girls. The idea of having some other guy watch my daughters makes me sick to my stomach...but not Ace. I can't lie to you and say he doesn't deserve you more than I do...because he does. He didn't fuck up. I did. But...I love you. I really love you. I love you in the strongest and fiercest kind of way. I know what it's like to lose you, to live without you, and now I never want to go through that ever again. I'm gonna be everything you deserve in a husband. I'll be the most committed, loyal, and affectionate husband in the goddamn world. Yes, I made a stupid mistake, but I learned from it. I learned that I was an idiot for ever letting you go." He wrapped his arms around me and pulled me into his chest. His face moved into the crook of my neck, and he breathed quietly. "It's selfish of me to ask you to pick me...but I'm gonna be selfish."

BREE TEXTED ME AFTER WORK. *EVERYONE IS COMING OVER TO whip up new specials. You in?*

It was a working dinner. We hadn't had one of those in a while. I hadn't done anything other than think about Evan and Ace, so I might as well do something more productive. Evan had stayed late last night talking about our relationship. He didn't spend the night because he knew that wouldn't be appropriate anymore. *Yeah, I'll be there.* I texted Evan next, knowing I didn't need to ask Sara to babysit all the time. *Would you mind watching the girls for a few hours? I have to work tonight.*

The three dots popped up immediately. *You're working the night shift?* I could hear the tone of surprise in the message.

The gang is getting together to prepare new specials for the next two weeks. We used to do it all the time, so Evan knew what I was talking about. We hadn't done it lately because we'd all had too much on our plates.

Gotcha. I'll be there in a few.

He arrived thirty minutes later, wearing a shirt that fit his arms nicely. "Hey."

"Hey." I was wearing jeans and a t-shirt, knowing my clothes were probably going to get stained in Bree's kitchen. He looked at me as if I were wearing a ball gown and pearls. I missed the way he used to look at me like that. It was nice. "Thanks for helping me out."

"You don't need to thank me. We're a team."

I grabbed my purse and pulled it over my shoulder, keeping my distance from him. I didn't want to get too close to him for fear of where it would be lead. "I'll see you in a few hours."

"Bring me some leftovers, okay?" he asked with a smile.

"There probably won't be anything left. Blade is a pig." I smiled back before I walked out and headed to Bree's house a few blocks away. Ace was going to be there, but Evan didn't mention him. There was no way for me to avoid Ace, just as there was no way for me to avoid Evan.

I arrived fifteen minutes later and walked inside.

"I say we try the chicken piccata," Bree said at the counter.

"No," Blade snapped. "That's such a blah dish. You can get that anywhere."

"It's not blah," Bree countered. "Right, Cypress?"

Cypress shrugged. "No, it's not blah..."

Blade rolled his eyes. "Of course, he's gonna agree with whatever you say. Not fair. What do you think, Ace?"

Ace didn't answer their questions because he'd been staring at me since I walked in the door. It was a look that should only occur behind closed doors, but he didn't seem to care. "Hey." He walked toward me and hugged me.

Blade and Cypress both watched us, their eyebrows raised.

They clearly had no idea what was going on.

Ace held me with his solid arms, and immediately, I forgot about Evan. I just thought about this strong man who had always been there for me no matter what. Last time we were along together, we made love on my kitchen counter, our bodies moving together perfectly.

"You look nice," he whispered against my ear.

"Thanks...you do too."

He finally pulled away, but his eyes were still on me, announcing to everyone in the room that we weren't just friends. Even someone as dense as Blade would notice.

Cypress eyed us back and forth before he cocked his head to the side. "Uh...something going on?"

I looked at Bree.

She shook her head, telling me she hadn't told them about Ace.

I wasn't planning on telling them, not to be deceitful, but to protect Ace from Cypress's wrath. He was the overprotective brother I never had.

Ace didn't look afraid before he answered. "I told Amelia that I wanted to be with her. She's thinking it over, but that's not gonna stop me from hugging her."

Cypress looked even more confused than before. "Wait...what?"

I took over so Ace wouldn't have to say anymore. "Ace and I have been hooking up for the past few months. I told him how I felt about him, but he ended things. Turns out, he walked away because he thought I was going to get back together with Evan, and he didn't want to interfere.

But I've fallen in love with him in the process...so here we are."

Cypress stared at me blankly, like he couldn't digest all that information in such a limited amount of time. Blade looked just as lost. "So...then you guys are together?" Cypress asked. "That's what you're telling us?"

"Not quite," I said. "I've been spending a lot more time with Evan, and now I'm kinda confused about what to do..." It was an awkward thing to say in front of Ace, but since we were all together 24/7, there was no point in holding back. He would just hear it from someone else anyway.

"Whoa, back up," Cypress said. "You're thinking about taking Evan back?"

"The biggest scumbag on the planet?" Blade asked incredulously. "That guy could—"

"Guys." Ace silenced them with just a single word. "Look, we all don't like Evan for what he did, me included. But they were married for eight years, and they're still a family. Evan seems sorry for what he did. I don't think he's ever going to mess around again. But none of that even matters because it's not our decision, and it's none of our business. Amelia is family, and we have to respect how she feels because this is the father of her kids. Alright?"

That shut them up.

"I'm not gonna lie and say I don't want her to pick me," Ace continued. "She should be with me. I'm the most loyal and honest guy on the planet. I'd protect her...and love her. But if she wants to be with Evan, it won't affect our friendship or affection for one another. We just wanted to say that so everything is out in the open."

How could I not pick Ace after that? He was so confident and smooth. I didn't know too many guys like that. He defended me just when the pack was about to rip me apart.

Cypress finally relaxed, taking Ace's words to heart.

Blade backed off too.

"I'm sorry I kept fooling around with her behind everyone's backs," Ace continued. "But for my part, it meant something to me. I wasn't using her. I wanted to be with her. I was just hesitant because I knew Evan would come back into the picture...and I was right. It was only a matter of time before he realized what he threw away."

Heavy silence filled the air as everyone held their breath, waiting for Cypress to have some kind of reaction. Bree kept eyeing him hesitantly, wondering if he would explode or simmer.

Cypress realized everyone was staring at him, so he finally said something. "I'm not mad, everyone. Calm down. Under the circumstances, there's nothing to be upset about."

That went over well.

"So you're basically stuck in a love triangle now?" Blade asked.

"I wouldn't call it a love triangle," I said. "Just...a triangle."

Bree came to my aid when she knew I was uncomfortable. "Anyway, we need to get cookin'. Otherwise, we'll be here all night. Blade, flatten the chicken. Cypress, get the pans going."

I loved my sister. "I'll take care of the pasta."

"MAN, I'LL NEVER EAT AGAIN." BLADE SAT BACK AGAINST THE dining chair and rubbed his nonexistent stomach.

"Yeah, right." Bree rolled her eyes. "You'll be hungry again in thirty minutes."

"If Celeste is cooking," Blade said. "That woman always makes me hungry...for a lot of things."

Now I rolled my eyes. "TMI."

"You wanna talk about TMI?" Blade asked. "What about that little speech Ace gave about your hookups? That was a lot of info to get in ten seconds." He rubbed his stomach again.

Ace changed the subject. "Everything was good, if you ask me. I think we should incorporate everything."

"Not the quesadilla," Cypress said. "Way too cheesy."

"I agree," I said. "Most people around here are health conscious. They won't eat that."

"Cheese is amazing," Blade said. "Everyone should eat it. The French love cheese. That's all I see Celeste eat —and wine."

"Did you like the quesadilla?" Cypress asked.

After a long pause, Blade shrugged. "Eh."

"Then the quesadilla is out," Ace said. "But we'll keep everything else. I think the piccata will be a nice addition to Olives. We haven't updated the specials in a while."

"True," Cypress said. "Now who's gonna clean this up?" He looked at Bree.

She narrowed her eyes. "Because I'm a woman, I'm expected to clean?"

"No," Cypress said. "You just like things done in a particular way. Whenever I help, you get mad and redo it."

Ace laughed. "That's very true."

Bree rolled her eyes, but a smile was on her lips.

"I was kidding anyway," Cypress said. "We can knock this out in ten minutes if we do it together."

We all worked in the kitchen, and within fifteen minutes, it was done. It was getting late and we all had work in the morning, so we said our goodbyes and walked home.

Though Ace's house was in the opposite direction, he walked me back to my place.

We walked together in silence, but the emptiness was heavy with the things we didn't say. My hands were in the pockets of my jeans, and he glanced at me every thirty seconds.

I finally said something. "I don't mind you walking me home, but Evan is with the girls."

"Does he have a problem with me now?"

"Actually, no. He said you were a good guy, and he would understand if I picked you."

Ace nodded in approval. "Didn't expect him to say that. Sounds like he's matured."

"Yeah...I think he has."

We walked up my street, but when we were a few houses down, Ace stopped.

I knew a conversation was coming.

"Have you thought any more about who you're going to pick?"

"Yeah...a lot."

"And?"

"I don't have an answer, Ace. I'm not sure how to decide."

Ace didn't show even a hint of frustration. "I can understand the dilemma. I wish I'd done something sooner instead of waiting so long. Your sister was right..."

She was dead right. If Ace had told me how he felt sooner, I wouldn't have let Evan into my heart again. But that was in the past, and it didn't matter now. "I think I should choose you. You're the better guy, Ace. When you broke things off...I was so upset. You make me feel good about myself..."

His eyes softened.

"But with Evan...there's a lot of history there. When we

were married, we were happy. And we have our girls…"

"I know," he whispered. "I'm not going to give you my two cents on the matter because I'm obviously biased. But you'll make the right decision on your own."

He was right; he would be completely biased. But my curiosity got the best of me. "I want to know what you think, Ace. As a friend…"

He cocked his head to the side. "You're sure about that?"

I nodded.

"I think if you go back to him, you'll be happy. I don't think Evan will do anything that stupid again. But you'll always be haunted by what he did. It'll be a shadow over your lives forever. Everyone will know what happened and think less of you for going back to him. I also think you're one of the most selfless people in the world who always does the right thing for everyone else, so you want to be with Evan to make him happy. You know he's sorry for what he did, and you love him so much that you want to give him what he wants. You want to make the girls happy by having their father around all the time. But what about what you want, Amelia?"

I stared into his face, which was barely visible since the sun was gone and there was only one streetlight on the road. His words pierced right through me, hitting in every vulnerable place I had. His words carried so much truth, there was no way I could ignore their power.

Ace knew his words struck me in the right spot when his expression softened. "Maybe you should go on one date with each of us. One dinner, one time. After you go out with both of us, you make your decision. Seems fair."

"That sounds like an episode of *The Bachelor*."

He shrugged. "We both want the girl, so we'll go through the charade."

Ace was good-looking and sweet. He could have any woman he wanted without having to subject himself to such an indignity. "What do you say?"

"I'll run it by him."

"Let me know how it goes." He didn't kiss me goodnight. Instead, he gave me a hard hug before he walked the opposite way down the street, sparing me the difficult interaction I would have with Evan if he walked me to the front door.

I went inside my house and found Evan in the living room with the girls. They were playing with their dolls, and Evan had a boy doll of his own. They seemed to be having tea together, something the girls usually did with their stuffed animals.

Watching them together ignited a pain in my chest. Before Evan had left me, I'd counted my family as my biggest blessing. No matter how difficult things got, we always had each other. I would always come home to this— even if we were living in a shack.

It was all I ever wanted.

When Evan noticed I was there, he put the doll down and met me in the entryway. "How was work?"

"Fattening."

He smiled at me, looking handsome without even trying. "Sounds like fun."

"I'm just glad we didn't go over the dessert menu."

"I definitely would have crashed if you had." He glanced at the girls before he turned back to me. "They had their baths and brushed their teeth. They just wanted to see you before bed."

"Aww..." Times like that made me love being a mom. Sometimes they could be brats from hell, and sometimes they could be the sweetest angels in the world.

Evan continued to stand there like he had more to say,

but words didn't form on his lips.

"I talked to Ace about our situation."

He stared at me.

"He said I should go on one date with each of you before I make my decision."

Evan crossed his arms over his chest. "Sounds fair. I'm in."

I'd thought Evan would reject the idea. "You're sure?"

"Yeah. But I want to go last."

"Why?"

"Whoever goes last is the last person you'll be thinking about. Did he lay out any rules?"

"No..."

"I don't mind not having rules."

I knew that meant sex was on the table. Both men wanted to show me what they could do to persuade me I should pick them. I felt like a slut because I'd never done anything like that, but if neither of them cared, I wouldn't object. "I'll talk to him."

"Alright." He wrapped his arm around me and kissed me on the forehead. "Good night."

I closed my eyes when he kissed me, the same reaction I always had. "Good night..."

"Let me know." He walked out and shut the door behind him.

I watched the girls continue to play with their dolls in front of the TV, laughing and living in their own little world. It was easy to enjoy the sight and not think about anything else. Soon, I would have to make a decision about who I wanted to be with. It was a difficult choice because I knew how permanent it was.

Whomever I picked would be the man I spent the rest of my life with.

14

We walked into the house after work and let Dino into the backyard so he could do his business. After being cooped up in the house all day, he was eager to be outside under the sun with the breeze in his fur.

Cypress left the back doors wide open then grabbed a beer from the fridge. "Want one?"

"No thanks."

"You used to drink beer all the time."

"I did?" I found it unlikely I'd acquired a taste for it. I usually preferred wine or a cocktail.

"Yep. It was the only thing I would pick up at the store, so you got used to it." He twisted off the cap then took a drink.

"You know, you could easily lie to me about stuff just to get me to do it."

"True..." He waggled his eyebrows. "Maybe now isn't the best time to tell you how you always gave me a blow job every day when we came home from work..."

I rolled my eyes and walked away. "Nice try."

He chuckled then came up behind me. "So, what do you want to do?"

"Well, maybe we can get started on moving things over."

"Yeah?" He grabbed my arm and gently turned me around so we were face-to-face. "I would love to. But where should we live? Here or there?"

"I assumed at my place. That's where we lived before, right?"

"Yeah. Sounds good to me. I bought this place for a great price, so I should be able to get a good price on it in return."

"Cool. So...where do we start? Are all my things packed away in boxes somewhere?'"

"No." His hands moved around my waist, and he gave me that affectionate look I was used to. "Most of your clothes are still in my closet. Our pictures are in a few photo albums here in the living room. Most of this furniture is new stuff I bought once I moved out, so we could donate it. Honestly, there's not much. It should take a day."

"That's nice."

"I'll leave the furniture inside when I put up the for sale sign. Maybe someone will want everything."

"Everything is in good condition."

"Yeah. I have our wedding china, so we'll need to keep that. I have some other things too..."

We were really doing this. Cypress was really going to move in with me and start over...or pick up where we left off. I wasn't entirely sure. But either way, we were moving forward.

Cypress watched me with his blue eyes. "Are you sure you wanna do this? Because there's no rush. I'll wait forever —you know that."

"I'm sure, Cypress."

"Because you're gonna have to see my face all the time.

You're gonna have to share your toothpaste with me, and sometimes your toothbrush. I'm gonna make moves every morning and every night, so there's gonna be lots of sex. And not to mention, you're gonna find my dirty socks all over the place."

I smiled because none of that sounded bad. "I'll manage."

"And you're gonna wake up to dog breath too."

I cocked an eyebrow.

"From Dino, not me."

I chuckled when I understood what he said. "Oh, okay. I feel better now."

"So that's a firm yes? Because I'm gonna put this house on the market immediately."

"I'm sure." Cypress had proved himself to me a million times over. He was committed to this marriage, even when I wasn't even aware we were together. He kept his vow and loved me every single day, never giving up on me even when I threw in the towel. I knew he was a different person than he was when we were together the first time. He was so different I hardly believed he was the same person.

But he was my husband.

And I loved him.

A smile melted across his face, and he pressed his forehead against mine. "Then let's get started."

"I'M GLAD YOU AREN'T MAD AT ACE."

Cypress pulled all the boxes down from the top shelf and placed them on the floor of the walk-in closet. "Why would I be?"

"Because he was fooling around with her for so long. You were pissed when he slept with her one time."

"That was different." Cypress glanced at all the labels on the boxes before he stood up. "I thought he just used her. But now I know they had a relationship...and I hope that relationship continues."

"I don't want her to pick Evan either. I hate that guy."

"You don't hate him more than I do." He pushed his clothes to the side in the closet, revealing all of my stuff on hangers. On the shelf next to it was a jewelry box.

"She would be stupid not to pick Ace."

"I know...but she might not."

"I don't know how I'm going to accept it."

"Me neither," he said. "I know I should give him another chance because your family gave me another chance...but it'll still be hard."

"It's not the same thing at all, Cypress." Evan was married with two kids, and he took off, leaving Amelia high and dry. Cypress and I had only been dating for a few months. We weren't married for eight years. "Don't compare yourself to that asshole. You're nothing like him."

Cypress turned away. "Here's all the stuff you've kept over the years. Souvenirs from our trips, extra pictures, just a bunch of things I knew you wouldn't want to part with... even though you don't remember it."

"Thanks." I opened the first book and found a blue blanket. It didn't seem important enough to keep, but it must have some significance.

"That's the blanket we used to take to the beach all the time. My mom knitted it for us."

"Ooh..." I felt it in my fingertips. "It's nice."

Cypress opened some old boxes and started placing his

clothes inside. Old jeans and sweaters went into the pile. "I'm glad I only have to carry this next door."

"Yeah..." I spotted the garment bag at the end of the clothing line. Something was inside, and it reached all the way to the floor. Only one thing came to mind, and I wondered if my suspicion was correct. "Cypress?"

He loaded the box to the top then closed the lid. "Hmm?"

"Is this my wedding dress?" I pushed the other clothes aside so I could get a better look at it. I could see some of the white color of the fabric, but most of it was covered by the plastic.

Cypress turned to me, his eyes unreadable. "Yeah."

I grabbed the zipper and slowly pulled it down. Inside the bag was a beautiful white gown with a rhinestone pattern in the center where the two straps met. It was in perfect condition except for the bottom of the dress, which was stained with dirt because it dragged on the floor when I wore it.

I couldn't believe I'd worn this.

I had a wedding day.

I'd been a bride.

The happiest day of my life came and went, and I couldn't remember it at all.

Looking at it brought tears to my eyes. I was heartbroken that I couldn't remember such an important day. I couldn't remember what it was like to walk down the aisle to my husband. I couldn't remember what it was like when he got down on one knee and asked me to marry him. I didn't remember the food at our wedding or our honeymoon.

I didn't remember any of it.

"Sweetheart..." Cypress circled his arms around me and pressed his lips against my hairline. "What's wrong?"

I released the bottom of the dress and stared at it as it hung on the hanger. "I'm just sad I don't remember it... I don't remember anything. This dress is so beautiful, and I don't remember picking it out."

He kissed my forehead. "It must be hard..."

"I missed the happiest day of my life. That gown had been on me, but I can't remember the way it felt. I can't remember how the fabric felt against my fingertips. I can't remember when you took it off of me..."

"Well, I remember. I remember for the both of us."

I moved my face into his chest so he couldn't see my tears. "What was it like?"

Cypress pulled me to his chest and rested his chin on my head. "We decided we wanted to see each other before the ceremony. It was just us and the photographers. Down the street was this beautiful door covered with ivy. I stood there, looking the other way. When you were ready, you tapped me on the shoulder and I turned around.

"You were already in tears because you couldn't stop crying. And then I couldn't stop crying."

I sniffed into his chest.

"Your hair was long and in curls. You did your own makeup because you didn't like the way the artist did it, and I was happy you redid it that way. You looked just like you, the woman I fell in love with. We stood together, and the photographers took our pictures as we cried and said we loved each other. It's a moment I'll never forget... I think it's my favorite memory from that day."

I closed my eyes and tried to feel a memory I'd never experienced. I tried to absorb his words and understand exactly how it felt.

"We had grilled cheese sandwiches and tomato soup for one of the appetizers. People loved it."

I chuckled.

"Dinner was great. We had different food stations that people enjoyed. We even had a macaroni bar."

"That sounds good..."

"For our first dance, we danced to 'Magnet and Steel.'"

"What kind of cake did we have?"

"Carrot and chocolate."

"Carrot is my favorite..."

"It's mine too. We spent most of the night dancing with our friends. We had a photo booth. When the wedding was over, we went downtown to a bar with everyone, and since it was Halloween, everyone thought we were dressed up for the holiday."

I chuckled again.

"Then we went back to the room at two in the morning, made love, took a short nap, and then left for the airport."

"It sounded nice..."

"It was the best day of my life." He pulled away so he could look me in the eye. "And I'll never forget it."

I'd do anything to get back the years I'd lost. They were in my brain somewhere, I just couldn't access them. I loved Cypress, but I wished I knew how I loved him before. I wished I remembered everything about our relationship, even the difficult times.

"I know you're sad you don't remember everything. But we're gonna make a lot of incredible memories together. We still have our whole lives together. There's so much more for us to experience."

"I know..."

He kissed my forehead and squeezed both of my hands. "Today, we're making a memory together. It's the first day of the rest of our lives."

ALL OF HIS CLOTHES WERE NOW AT MY HOUSE, ALONG WITH everything else he needed on a daily basis. He'd already talked to his Realtor about putting the house back on the market, and Dino made himself at home like he'd never left.

Now my closet wasn't just full of my things. Cypress's t-shirts took up half of the room. His boxers and socks had now taken up some of my drawers, kicking my stuff out. His electric toothbrush sat on the counter with the cord plugged into the wall. His razor was there as well.

Now I lived with a man.

I lived with my husband.

We woke up in the morning at the same time, had sex, and then went to work. We stopped a coffee shop and got coffee before we entered the office on Mission Street. It already felt like a routine even though only a few days had gone by.

Amelia was in the office when we walked inside, but the guys had already left for their positions.

"So, how's the love life?" I asked.

Amelia closed her laptop because she was finished doing whatever she needed to do. "I'm going to go on a date with each one of them. After that, I'll make my decision."

Did she really need to go on a date to figure it out? "When is that happening?"

"Not sure yet. But soon."

"Two guys fighting for you...that must be fun."

"They aren't fighting," she said. "It's more of the oppo-site." She eyed Cypress at his desk before she turned back to me. "You guys seem to be doing well..."

Cypress flipped through some paperwork before he stood up again. "I'll let you two have girl talk. I'll see you later, sweetheart." He gave me a smile before he walked out, his coffee still in his hand.

"How's the new roommate?" Amelia asked.

"Good. It's been weird, but it also feels right, you know?'"

"I know it feels right because you guys used to be so happy. I know things will get even better."

"We moved all of his stuff over to my place except the furniture. But I haven't seen my ring...I thought we would come across it by now, but we haven't. I found my wedding dress though."

"Oh, that gown is so beautiful. Did you love it?"

"I fell in love. It made me sad that I can't remember wearing it..."

"Well, I remember how beautiful you looked. Take my word for it."

"Thanks, sis."

She drank her coffee as she kept her eyes on me. "So, sounds like you and Cypress are really making it work this time."

"Yeah. I didn't think I could forgive him, but I trust him. It's crazy that I trust him after what he did. Do you think it's stupid?" Cypress did a terrible thing, and it only took a few months for me to love him with all my heart. Sometimes I wondered if that was too fast, if his rugged handsomeness was affecting my ability to think clearly.

"Not at all," she said. "Cypress is nothing like he used to be. It took him an entire year to get on my good side, even though he more than proved it a long time ago. When I look at Cypress, I don't think about what he did. I think about how incredible he is now. I think about how loyal, loving, and passionate he is. You're his whole world, Bree. You never need to worry about his eyes wandering where they shouldn't. He only has eyes for you."

"Thanks...I needed to hear that."

"His house won't be on the market for long. Someone is going to snatch it up."

"You're right. He's not even asking much for it. He just wants to get rid of it."

She smiled before she drank her coffee.

"What?" I'd known that look since we were little.

"He probably wants to get rid of it so you won't change your mind," she said with a chuckle.

"I'm not going to change my mind. I think we have a lot of work to do, but I think it'll work out. I just wish we weren't going straight into marriage..."

Amelia gave me a peculiar look. "I don't understand your meaning."

"I just wish we could experience all the steps all over again, like dating and then moving in together...and then getting married. We're skipping right to the end, but I wish I could experience all of those parts."

"Bree...if you aren't ready to move in—"

"It's not that I'm not ready. I just wish I'd gotten to experience everything before this. It's hard to explain..."

Amelia placed her hand on my thigh and gave me a gentle pat. "No, I get it. I wish I could say something to make it better, to tell you enough stories that you can feel like you remember...but I can't. You'll have to believe me when I say you and Cypress were in love and happy for a long time before you got married. And when you became husband and wife, you loved each other even more."

15

BLADE

"Why are we here?" I sat at the table with Ace and Amelia in the middle of the lunch hour. Bree was at the café because she was purposely not invited to this meeting. Seeing the rush of customers while I sat on my ass and did nothing made me twitch in discomfort. I wasn't used to doing nothing.

Cypress finally fell into the chair and joined us after he finished up in the kitchen at Olives. We had iced teas in front of us along with a big plate of hummus and pita bread. "Thanks for meeting me."

"What's this about?" I asked. "And why can't Bree know about it?"

"Having secrets from your wife isn't a good way to start a marriage," Ace warned.

"It's not a bad secret," Cypress said. "I just need your help with something."

"What is it?" Amelia asked.

Cypress looked out the window, like Bree might walk by any minute. "Things have been going well with her, but she's upset she can't remember anything. She can't remember my proposal, she can't remember the wedding, and it breaks my heart. I know it kills her."

"She said the same thing to me," Amelia said. "It makes me sad."

"Unless you've made a scientific discovery, I don't see how you can change any of that." I didn't want to sound like an asshole, but that was just the truth.

"I can't change of that," Cypress said. "But what if I recreated it?"

Everyone took a moment to understand what he meant. Ace was the first one to smile, getting it quicker than the rest of us. Amelia's eyes softened as she looked at Cypress, the emotion written all over her face. It took me a moment longer to grasp his intentions. "How can you redo everything?"

"I'm not going to redo everything," Cypress said. "But I'm going to propose again. And we're going to have another wedding."

"Aww...that's the sweetest thing I've ever heard." Amelia fanned away the tears in her eyes. "Cypress, she would love that."

"That's awesome, man," Ace said. "But October is a month away. Are you going to propose to her now and then have the wedding next year?"

"Actually, I called the Perry House and told them what happened. They asked the couple that currently has Halloween booked if they'd be willing to give it up for me, and they said yes. They wanted to get married in Hawaii anyway. So it's all mine." He smiled, the kind of grin that reached every feature of his face.

"Seriously?" I asked. "That's the coolest thing I've ever heard."

"We're gonna put together a wedding in a month," Amelia said. "We can help you, Cypress."

"Thank you," Cypress said. "Now that we live together, I can't hide all this from her. I need you guys to help me out."

"Totally," Ace said. "We're there."

"Yeah, I'm in," I said. "Whatever I can do to help."

"When are you going to propose, then?" Amelia asked.

"I was thinking the night before," Cypress said. "We would go down to the beach and have a picnic. I'd ask her to marry me, and she would say yes. We'd have a great night with sex and booze, and the next morning I would tell her we're getting married."

"And only give her that day to prepare?" I asked incredulously.

"She already has her dress," Amelia said. "I remember what all of her flowers looked like and her jewelry. I still have my bridesmaid dress. I can put it all together for her. I can invite everyone on the guest list too. We could totally pull this off."

"I think this is the best idea you've ever had," Ace said. "Bree won't have to miss anything. We can recreate those memories for her so she can have them forever."

"It's perfect," Amelia said. "You're so sweet, Cypress."

Cypress shrugged. "I promised to make her happy every single day for the rest of my life. And that's what I'm going to do."

I looked at Cypress in a new way, and I knew everyone else did too. He'd never given up on Bree, even when the doctors said her condition would never improve. He'd been faithful to her when most men wouldn't have. But this was the biggest gesture of all, repeating everything he'd experienced just so she could have it too.

CELESTE SAT ACROSS FROM ME AT THE TABLE WITH HER CONE held in her fingers. She opened her mouth and dragged her tongue across the cold cream, licking it up before she pulled her tongue back into her mouth.

I couldn't eat my ice cream because I was so distracted.

Jesus.

She licked the sides before she took a smile bite from the top of the ice cream. She ate much slower than I did, so her ice cream melted and dripped down the sides of the sugar cone. No matter how quickly she ate, she couldn't keep up.

I didn't care about my ice cream anymore. I was more interested in watching her.

"What?" she asked when she noticed my stare.

"Nothing."

Her eyes narrowed in an angry way, but since she wasn't actually angry, it was cute. "Liar."

"I've never seen a woman look so sexy eating ice cream."

"Remind you of anything...?" She dragged her tongue from the base to the top, taking it slow.

Now my ice cream had started to melt because I stopped eating it. All I could think about were those fantastic blow jobs she gave me. She worked her tongue like a pro, and she swallowed my come like she was starving.

I had a boner right in the middle of the ice cream parlor.

I started eating my ice cream again, knowing it would melt everywhere if I didn't swallow it down.

She finished hers, her eyes locked on mine. When she got to the cone, she bit off entire pieces and swallowed them down.

Thank god she was almost finished. I took her to ice cream because I wanted to have a nice date, dinner, and dessert. All we seemed to do was get busy, and I wanted to show her we could have more than just good sex. We could have a great conversation too...even though she just proved me wrong. Everything led back to sex. "My mom called me the other day."

"She did?" She finally finished her cone and set the waxed paper on the table. "Oh no...how did that go?"

"It was awkward. Not gonna sugarcoat it."

She cringed. "Yikes..."

"I told her we didn't know it was her on the other line. We thought it was Ace."

"I doubt that made a difference."

"Not really. But she asked if she might see you around, and I said yes. She immediately perked up then."

Celeste couldn't wipe the surprised expression off her face. "What? Why would that make her happy? She must think I'm a slut."

"I've never brought a woman around before. If I bring someone, she knows they're special. And she also knows that could mean marriage and kids...so she isn't going to care about your first interaction."

She wore a doubtful expression. "She's not gonna care that I told her you were getting laid before I hung up on her?"

"No. Not if you're important to me."

Celeste's expression softened slightly. "That's actually pretty sweet. She just wants you to be happy."

"Yeah. My mom is pretty great. A little clingy sometimes, but great. I think she wouldn't be so concerned about me if I were married. I'm perfectly capable of taking care of myself, but I think she feels better knowing I have a partner in life. She won't always be around, and she wants to know I'll be okay when she's gone."

"Aww...that's what parents do."

That opened up the way to my next question. "They're having a BBQ tomorrow. Would you like to come?"

"Me?" she asked incredulously.

"Yes." I moved my hand across the table and rested my hand on hers. "You."

"With your parents?"

"And my brother."

"Sounds pretty intimate."

I rubbed my thumb over his hand, fearing she would she say no. It was a soon to meet my family, especially if we couldn't work things out. I'd always thought if I introduced a woman to my parents, she would be the one. If Celeste went back to Henry, then I would be putting myself out there for no reason. When I brought my future wife to meet my parents later, she would know she wasn't the first one I wanted to be with.

I was taking a risk.

Celeste looked me in the eye with an unsteady gaze. It wasn't clear what she was thinking, but she didn't look confident like she usually did. "Do you think that's a good idea...?"

I had no clue. "I want you to meet my family. I want you to know that if you decide to stay here, not only are you adopting my friends as your own, but my family as well. You belong somewhere."

She turned her hand over and felt my hand with her fingertips. Her skin was smoother than mine, always smelling like rose petals. "Okay. I think that could be fun."

I smiled, but I also felt a jolt in my chest. I'd never been so excited and scared at the same time. The end of the summer was approaching, and if she got on that plane and left me, I wouldn't recover. I would be torn into a million pieces, facing my first heartbreak. "Great."

"WOW. SHE'S MEETING YOUR PARENTS?" ACE ASKED.

"Yeah." I sat in the bar with Ace and Cypress, the girls both working at Olives for the evening. Every once in a while, we had to work the late shifts. Employees needed time off from time to time. I drank my cold beer right out of the bottle. "My mom is having a BBQ, so I thought I would go for it."

"You don't think that will be awkward?" Ace asked.

"Like, superawkward?" Cypress asked.

"As soon as I told my mom that she might stick around, she was happy. She wants me to get married so bad I don't think she cares about that phone call." My mom used to ask me about my love life in my early twenties. She hinted at grandchildren and other things all the time. But now she didn't ask anymore because I was almost thirty. Her greatest fear was me spending the rest of my life alone, so ignoring an inappropriate phone call was nothing in comparison to accepting that fate.

"Celeste agreed?" Cypress asked.

"She was hesitant at first," I said. "But she got on board pretty quickly. I'm thinking if I integrate her with my life, she might be more likely to choose me. She's leaving a lot behind by staying here, so I need to give her a community to stick around for."

"You want us to hang out with her?" Ace asked.

I didn't want either of them alone with my woman. "Absolutely not."

"What?" Cypress asked. "I'm married, and Ace is...unavailable."

"You guys are hot," I said. "I don't want her alone with you so she can stare at your muscles all day."

Cypress grinned so hard his face looked different. "We're hot, huh?"

Ace flexed both of his arms. "She wants to stare at our muscles all day?"

I rolled my eyes. "You know what I mean."

"Yeah," Cypress said. "You think we're hot. It's pretty clear."

"I'm totally straight," I said. "There's not a doubt in my mind when I'm with Celeste. I never get tired of her. I just don't want her to spend too much time with you and wish I were buff."

"You aren't buff, but you're ripped," Ace said. "Chicks dig that."

Cypress placed his hand against his chest. "I know my wife does."

"When is the BBQ?" Ace asked.

"Tomorrow. I know my brother is gonna flirt with her, so I'm gonna have to kick his ass." My brother and I weren't close, but we got along well. He would tease me when he realized there was a serious woman in the picture. That was just how he was. "When does *The Bachelor* start?" I asked Ace.

"Tomorrow," Ace answered. "We're meeting over there to flip a coin."

"Flip a coin for what?" Cypress asked.

"Who gets to go last." Ace drank his beer and watched the TV in the corner. "There's no rules for the date, so... whoever goes last has the advantage. He'll be the last one she thinks about. You know what I mean?"

"So, it's okay for each of you to sleep with her?" I asked incredulously.

"Yep," Ace answered.

"You're okay with that?" Cypress asked.

Ace shrugged. "I guess it's kinda weird, but she was sleeping with him for the past month anyway."

"She was sleeping with him?" Cypress asked incredulously. "And you at the same time?"

"No," Ace corrected. "We had our fling. I left her. And then she hooked up with him. There wasn't any overlap."

"But still," Cypress said. "I hate that guy...wish she'd never slept with him."

"It's my fault," Ace said. "If I hadn't left, none of this would have happened."

I didn't say anything to try to make him feel better because there was nothing to say. Ace was right. He should have spoken up. "So, ta the end of the two dates, she's going to make her decision?"

Ace nodded. "Yep. The whole thing was my idea, actually."

"You suggested that?" Cypress asked.

"I just want it to be over," Ace said. "I gave her a timeline, and we each get a full night to persuade her. It'll be over in a few days, and then we can move on."

"She'd better pick you," Cypress said.

"Yeah," I said in agreement. "She would be an idiot to go back to him."

Ace only shrugged, too nice to say anything else. "How's the wife, Cypress?"

"Good," Cypress said. "It's just like it was before. She takes up most of the bathroom with her makeup and hair stuff, and she rolls my socks in this strange way before she shoves them in my drawer. We switch off making dinner. It's really nice. I finally feel like I'm home. Dino is really happy too. He's always loved Bree more than me."

I liked knowing my friend was happy. Cypress had been through a lot, more than most of us. He finally had what he wanted after waiting so long. It wasn't perfect, but it was good enough. "I'm glad you guys are working it out. She'll be so happy with the wedding."

"Yeah, I know she's been looking for her ring," Cypress said. "When we moved stuff out of the house, she went through the jewelry box and looked in my nightstands. She asked about it once before, but I never gave her an answer."

"At least she wants to wear it again," Ace said. "Better than her wanting a new one or something."

"I just hope she doesn't ask me about it again," Cypress said. "I wear my ring all the time, so she probably wants to wear hers. If she can be patient a little longer, it'll make my life easier. I don't want to just hand it to her, you know? Like it's not a big deal and move on. I want it to be special."

"I never knew you were such a romantic until Bree lost her memory," Ace said. "You're the most romantic dude on the planet."

Cypress eyed his beer. "What can I say? I guess I kinda like my wife." He grinned.

"Kinda like her?" I teased. "I think you really like her, if you ask me."

"Nah," Ace said. "He just thinks she's alright." He chuckled and drank his beer.

"What about you?" Cypress asked me. "Do you really like Celeste? Think she's just alright?"

I knew the truth a while ago, but I was too uncomfortable to admit it out loud—even to myself. The only reason why I would be going through a charade like this was if this woman really meant something to me. I'd been with lots of beautiful and daring women, but none of them ever captured my attention.

Not like Celeste.

"I think it's obvious," I finally answered.

"We're a bit dense," Ace said. "So you should just tell us."

I looked away, unable to meet their gazes. I'd never said the words out loud before, especially not to my friends. "I'm in love with her."

CELESTE ARRIVED AT MY DOOR WITH A GLASS DISH IN HER hands. "I wasn't sure if I should bring something, so I made some muffins."

"Awesome." I took it from her hands and set it on the table by the door. "My family will get a kick out of that." My arms slid around her body, and I kissed her in the doorway, my hand moving into her hair and my mouth caressing hers. Her soft mouth nibbled my bottom lip gently in the sexiest embrace.

Whenever I kissed her, I didn't care about doing anything else. My brain shut off, and all I felt was a carnal instinct to make love to this woman with my mouth, to worship her body with my hands and make her feel more beautiful than she ever felt in her life. I got off on pleasing her, something that I never really experienced before. I had fantasies with other women, kinky stuff that turned me on. But making Celeste come was my ultimate fantasy now.

When things heated up and I started to lift up her dress, someone knocked on the door.

I growled against her mouth.

She sucked on my bottom lip before she pulled away. "We're gonna be late anyway..."

"You think I give a damn about being late?" I pulled away from her and opened the door, not caring about whoever the hell it was on the other side.

"Yo." Cypress held up a six-pack of beer. "Can we crash the BBQ?"

"We've got hamburgers and buns in the car," Ace said. "And lots of chips."

"I made potato salad," Amelia said.

I stared at all my friends, surprised they were standing there. "Uh...sure. I didn't realize you were interested in coming."

"Of course, man." Cypress clapped me on the shoulder. "We wouldn't miss it." He turned to Celeste and gave her a bear hug. "Hey, you. You look nice."

"Thanks." She hugged him back, caught off guard by his affection.

Ace high-fived her next before he hugged her. "Did you make any muffins today?"

"Actually, I did," Celeste said.

"Awesome," Ace said. "My day just got better."

Bree and Amelia hugged her next, greeting her like they'd been friends for years.

There was something suspicious about the whole thing. "So, what's all of this about?"

"Nothing," Cypress said. "We just thought it might be kinda awkward after that phone call with your mom, so we thought being there could help break the ice a bit."

Still sounded fishy to me. "Well, we should get going. You wanna meet us there?"

"Let's do it," Ace said as he walked out the door. "We'll see you there."

I followed them outside with Celeste.

"I didn't know they were coming."

I locked the door behind me and took her hand. "That makes two of us."

———

WE PULLED UP TO THE HOUSE AND WALKED THROUGH THE SIDE gate to the backyard. Celeste didn't seem nervous, even though any other woman would be. The first words she'd said to my mom weren't exactly classy. But she held her head high, her shoulders back, and she wore a brilliant smile.

My mom hopped up from the kitchen table the second she saw us. "My son." She wrapped her arms around me and hugged me like she hadn't seen me in years.

"Hey, Mom." I hugged her back, letting her squeeze me like a child.

She pulled away and turned to Celeste next. "Oh my god..." She looked into her eyes like she saw something. Then her hands moved over her chest. "You're beautiful." She hugged her just the way she hugged me, squeezing her like a daughter.

Wow. This went over a lot smoother than I expected.

Celeste flinched before she could find something to say in response. "Thank you. It's nice to meet you, Mrs. Thomas."

"Call me Denise." Mom pulled away and gave her a genuine smile. "We're so happy to have you here."

"She made muffins." I nodded to the dish sitting on the table next to the BBQ. "Celeste is an excellent baker, so I can guarantee they're great. I eat her muffins all the time." I realized what I said after it was too late, and I tried to hide my humiliation.

If Mom picked up on it, she didn't notice. "Let me introduce you to Mark, Blade's father."

My dad hugged her, gave her a nice smile, and welcomed her like he did with everyone else. My dad was really easygoing and laid-back. That was where I got my personality from, thankfully. I could have brought home anyone, and my dad wouldn't have cared—even a dude.

My friends came around the back a second later.

"You brought everyone?" Mom asked happily.

"Yeah, they wanted to tag along," I said. "They brought more burgers so there'll be plenty to go around."

My mom and dad hugged all of them and caught up on lost time.

Derek came out of the house with a beer in his hand. Celeste's back was to him, so she didn't notice him right away. He looked her up and down then gave me a thumbs-up with a wink.

Asshole.

Derek walked up to us and ignored me, choosing to address her instead. "Derek. Nice to meet you." He shook her hand. "You must be Celeste."

"Yeah," she answered. "And you must be the brother."

"Whoa." Derek smiled. "Love the accent. You're from France?"

"Yeah," she answered. "Paris."

Derek gave me an incredulous look, like he couldn't believe I actually found a woman so perfect.

Well, I did. Take that, bitch. My arm circled her waist, and I brought her into my side, not wanting my brother to get too close to her. Derek teased me most of the time, but I didn't want him to make Celeste uncomfortable. She was used to guys gawking at her, but I didn't want her to feel like prey with my family.

My friends gathered around the table with their beers and soda, making conversation with Derek. The second my mom was free, she moved in on Celeste again. "I can't help but notice your accent. Are you French?"

"Yeah," Celeste answered. "Born and raised in Paris."

"Ooh...that's wonderful." My mom continued to smile, but it quickly turned into a forced expression. "I've always wanted to go. Maybe one day Mark will retire, and we can finally travel."

"It's a beautiful place," Celeste said. "I'm sure you'll love it."

"I would love to hear more about it," Mom said. "I just have to get the produce and condiments out of the fridge. I'll be right back."

"I can help you," Celeste volunteered.

"Oh, that will be nice," Mom said. "Thank you." They walked off together.

Dad started manning the grill with Derek, so I took a seat with the gang. Since we were finally alone together, I cut straight to the chase. "You guys could be doing anything on a Saturday. What gives?"

"We just wanted to hang," Ace said.

"Cut the shit," I said. "We see each other more than we should, and you know it. We're sickly codependent on each other."

Cypress glanced at everyone else before he came clean. "When you said you were in love with this woman, we knew we needed to step it up. We want her to be part of the group, to feel welcomed by us. We have to give her another reason to stay, to be her family away from family."

I shouldn't have been surprised by the gesture. I knew my friends would do anything for me, just as I would do anything for them. Now that they knew this woman was special to me, someone I wanted to love for the indefinite future, they banded together to help. They wanted Celeste to stay as much as I did—because they wanted me to be happy.

CELESTE WAS TALKING TO MY DAD ABOUT SOCCER, AND MY friends were hanging out with Derek on the patio. I went inside to help my mom clean up and to gauge her impression of Celeste. Thankfully, it didn't seem like that phone conversation ever happened. My mom didn't mention it, and after the first hour of spending time together, it didn't seem to be on anyone's mind.

"Need help, Mom?" I came next to her at the kitchen sink and started scraping old food into the garbage.

"That's nice of you, sweetheart. But I'm okay."

"Mom, you always do everything around here. Let me help you."

She smiled and stopped fighting me. "Okay."

I scraped the food into the garbage and stacked the dishes so she could rinse them off. "The burgers were good. I ate two."

"I know," she said with a smile. "Ace ate three."

"Well, he's a beast. That guy eats, like, ten thousand calories a day."

"I feel bad for his mother, having to cook so much for him all the time."

"I feel bad for her because he probably ate her," I teased.

Mom laughed.

Now that the mood was set, I went for the answer I was looking for. "What do you think of her?"

"You care about my opinion?" she challenged.

"You're my mom. Of course, I care. You know I've always been a mama's boy."

She smiled. "She's lovely, Blade. Truly." A painful sigh accompanied her words, making her look as depressed as she was at her grandmother's funeral.

That didn't sound good. "If that's true, why do you sound so disappointed?"

"I'm not disappointed, sweetheart. She's very kind and smart. She's a successful and strong woman, the kind of woman I'd always hoped you would be with. She'll give you beautiful children and raise them to be wonderful people."

"If you like her so much, why do you sound so sad?"

"Because...never mind."

"Mom, tell me."

"I can't," she whispered. "It's selfish."

"Mom." I turned off the water. "Come on. Talk to me."

She wiped her hands with the dish towel and set it on the counter. "Well, if she's from France...I can only assume that's where she wants to be. So, she'll take you away from me." Her voice caught with the sadness that was drowning her. "My son will be on the other side of the world, and I'll never see you..." She was about to break down in tears.

"Mom..." I rolled my eyes. "I'm never moving there. She and I have already talked about it, and if she wants to be with me, we would live here. I can't leave my restaurants or my friends and family. I'm sure we'll visit for good chunks of time, but no, we wouldn't live there."

"Oh, thank god." She gripped her chest before she hugged me hard. "You have no idea how relieved I am."

I patted her on the back. "Like I could do that to you, Mom."

She pulled away, her tears gone and her smile beaming.

"Then I love her. She's absolutely wonderful. Your father really likes her too. We hope we'll be seeing more of her."

"I hope so too."

"How long have you been seeing her?"

"A few months. I've kinda fallen hard for her..."

Mom smiled. "Does she know that?"

"It's pretty obvious."

"Does she feel the same way?"

"I'm not certain. She's debating whether to go back to France or not at the end of the summer."

"Blade, that's just a few weeks away."

"Yeah, I know." I wasn't going to tell my mom about Henry. That was Celeste's business, and I wouldn't share it with anyone. Might make her look bad. After that phone call, she didn't need anything else to tarnish her image. "So, I'll know soon enough."

"Well, she'd have to be an idiot not to love you. You're a perfect man, Blade. Your father and I couldn't be happier with the way you turned out. You're handsome, successful, smart, and so sweet."

My mom flattered me every single time I saw her. She thought Derek and I were the most amazing people on the planet—even though we weren't. "Thanks, Mom. But you're a little biased."

"Am not."

I raised an eyebrow.

"Okay...I am a little biased."

I chuckled. "I'm glad you can admit it."

"Since you only have a few weeks left, you shouldn't be in here with me." She patted my side. "Join Celeste."

I looked out the window and saw her sitting with my friends. Ace just said something that must have been funny, because Celeste laughed. Her eyes lit up with joy, and she wore the cutest smile.

I hoped I could witness that smile once the summer was over.

And for the rest of my life.

16

AMELIA

Bree and Cypress came over to watch the girls for the rest of the evening. They were going to drop them off at school the next morning so I wouldn't have to worry about being home at a certain time.

It was kinda awkward.

Everyone knew I was going to sleep with both Evan and Ace on separate nights. I'd never had my personal life on display like that. Even I thought it was a little slutty...but I was going to do it anyway.

Evan got there first, looking good in tight jeans and a t-shirt. If he was going to take me out, it was somewhere low-key. "Hey." He wore a confident smile and greeted me with a hug.

"Hey."

Ace walked in a moment later, looking just as handsome with his rock-hard body. He looked Evan in the eye and greeted him with a handshake.

Only an extremely confident man could do that.

"I've got the quarter." I held it up so they both could see

it. I couldn't believe I was about to do this. I was going to flip it, they were going to call it in the air, and whoever won got to take me out last.

It was barbaric.

"3...2...1." I flipped the quarter into the air.

Evan called it first. "Heads."

I caught the quarter in my hand and looked into my palm. "It's heads."

Evan didn't gloat, but a small smile crept onto his lips. "I'll go last, then." He didn't make small talk or say hello to Bree and Cypress in the living room before he left. He walked out and didn't look at me twice.

Now it was just Ace and me.

It took a moment for the awkwardness to wear off. Anytime both men were in the same room together, it was so saturated with unspoken tension. Both of them were calm and mature about the situation, but that didn't mean they didn't despise one another.

"Are you ready to go?" Ace asked.

"Yeah. Where are we going?"

"I thought we would pick up some sandwiches and go down to the beach to watch the sunset."

Sounded romantic to me. "That sounds nice."

"Great." He walked into the living room. "It's gonna be cold tonight so grab some sweaters, girls."

"Okay!" Rose jumped in the air, excited she got to come with us.

Lily immediately packed her toys into her backpack.

Uh...what was I missing here? I lowered my voice and came to Ace's side. "I asked Bree and Cypress to watch them because I thought it was just going to be the two of us..."

"Well, I want it to be the four of us." At six foot three, he looked down at me like mountain looking at a river. His blue eyes were the softest feature he possessed, and they softened even more when he looked at me. Whenever we kissed, I felt the hardness of his features melt away.

For the first time in my life, I was speechless.

Ace stared at me for another moment before he grabbed Rose's backpack and helped her with her things. He pulled her sweater over her head, helped her with her shoes, and did the same with Lily.

Bree grinned from her seat on the sofa, watching Ace take care of my girls better than I did. Then she turned to me, a knowing look in her eyes. She didn't need to state what was on her mind. It was as clear as a neon sign.

I had to pick him.

WE GRABBED SANDWICHES FROM THE BAKERY THEN WALKED down together to the beach. Ace kept an eye on the girls as he continued his conversation with me, effectively juggling two things at once.

"How was the diner?" he asked, his eyes on the girls as they walked in front of us.

"Pretty good. I got coconut syrup all over my shirt, and I smelled like Hawaii from the rest of the day."

He chuckled. "There are worse things to smell like."

"Very true. I'm just glad it didn't get in my hair. Would have taken weeks to get it out."

We walked past the other people going up the hill toward the restaurants. When we reached the sand, the girls pulled off their shoes and started to run down the hill.

"No running." Ace didn't even raise his voice, and the girls listened to him.

They didn't obey me like that. They usually had a bit of

an attitude but didn't directly defy me...one of the perks of motherhood. We walked down the sand and moved to the left where the tourists never went. It was also a great place to see dolphins because they hunted fish in the kelp beds.

Ace pulled out a blanket from his backpack and laid it on the ground. The girls' backpacks were placed at the edges so it wouldn't fly up in the breeze, and we gathered around and ate our sandwiches together.

"Uncle Ace?" Lily asked.

"What's up?" he asked after he finished chewing his sandwich.

"How do you eat so much?" She pointed at his sandwich. "You ate half of it in one bite." She giggled at her own question.

"I'm part bear," Ace said with a straight face.

"Part bear?" Rose asked. "But...you aren't a bear."

"I know," Ace said. "That's why I'm part bear."

"You don't have any hair," Lily said.

"Yeah," Rose added. "Bears have hair."

"I transform when the sun goes down," Ace said. "That's why you never see me late at night."

Both of their eyes opened wide.

I tried not to laugh.

Lily looked down at her sandwich before she took the biggest bite she could. "Look, I did it too. I'm a bear."

Rose tried to do the same thing, but she could only take a tiny bite. "Me too."

"Looks like we're all bears," Ace said.

"What about Mommy?" Rose pointed at my sandwich. "Be a bear too."

"Okay." I shoved most of the sandwich into my mouth even though it wasn't my best moment. I was on a date, and I smeared mayo over my mouth. I tried to chew, but so much was stuffed inside it was difficult. I wiped my face with a napkin and finally got it down. "I did it."

"We're all bears." Lily raised her arms in the air like a creature. "Roar."

Rose howled.

Ace chuckled. "Bears don't howl. Wolves do."

"Ohh..." Rose interlocked her fingers together. "Whoops."

The girls finished their dinner then carried their buckets closer to the water. They started to dig, making sand castles that were quickly swept away by the water.

Ace and I were finally alone together, and all I could think about was how good he was with my kids. "You're great with them."

"They're easy. Very sweet." He scooted closer to me on the blanket, his arm touching mine. "They get it from you."

I smiled and felt my cheeks blush. "I don't know that... they call me Momzilla sometimes."

"That's just how kids are. They complain about their mom until they become adults. Then they finally appreciate you."

"Well, they aren't going to be adults for a long time, so I have a ways to go."

"It'll be worth it." He leaned into me and pressed a kiss to the corner of my mouth. "And then we'll have some more kids, and we'll do it all over again."

"More kids?" I asked. He was pretty confident to make such an assumption.

"It's not that I don't love the girls, but I'd like to have the full experience too. I'd love to see you pregnant, waddling around the house. I'd love to get you ice cream in the middle of the night. I'd love to be in the delivery room when our kid is born. I'd love to wake up in the middle of the night when they start to cry...the whole thing."

I never expected Ace to say anything like that to me. He always seemed like a manwhore who didn't care about marriage and kids. He didn't seem like the kind of guy who ever wanted a family. "I didn't know you wanted to have kids."

"I do—with the right person." He leaned closer to me and looked me in the eye.

His gaze was so intense that I looked away. "You think about that kind of stuff?"

"Definitely. I think we'll have a great life together. We'll work together, balancing our time being parents and just being us. It'll be wonderful."

"You say it like it's gonna happen."

"Because it is going to happen," he said quietly.

"I thought you said you weren't going to interfere in my decision?" He was directly contradicting himself.

"I'm not trying to interfere with your decision. But I know you're going to pick me."

"How?"

He looked out at the water where the girls were playing. "I just do. I wish I'd known it sooner, but now I do."

Lily and Rose came back after all their sand castles had been destroyed. Sand stuck to their plastic buckets, and their shovels were still wet. "We suck at making sand castles. Can you help us, Uncle Ace?" Lily asked.

"You make the best sand castles," Rose said.

"Sure," Ace said with a smile. "But Mom makes better ones. You wanna help us?"

I knew his idea of a date wasn't a fancy dinner with candles and a white tablecloth. He didn't want to have a gourmet meal that was overpriced. He wanted to show me what our lives would be like every single day—the four of us. "I'd love to."

––––––––––

WHEN WE CAME HOME, WE GOT THE GIRLS IN THE BATH, DRIED their hair, brushed their teeth, and put them to bed. Having Ace there made the nighttime ritual a lot easier. Two parents were always better than one.

There was an extra bedroom in the house so the girls could each have their own room, but they'd wanted to stay together. I knew when they became teenagers that would quickly change. They'd want their own rooms and scream whenever the other borrowed their clothes. But for now, they were still two little girls.

I kissed them each on the heads then turned off the light before I shut the door.

Ace was in the hallway with a hard expression on his face. He watched me like I was a TV screen, analyzing every single move I made. He practically counted my breaths and the number of times I blinked.

I recognized the tension between us. It wasn't awkward or difficult. It was a different kind of tension, the kind that led us into the bedroom. He took me by the hand and pulled me into the master bedroom on the opposite side of the house. The lights were off, and he didn't bother turning them on. He pulled his shirt over his head then immediately yanked off mine. My arms moved above my head, and his fingers caressed mine even when the fabric was free. With a strong grip, he placed my hands against his chest before he pressed his face to mine. He didn't kiss me, purposely restraining himself from letting his soft lips touch mine.

He undid my jeans as he kept his eyes locked to mine. It

was more intimate than sex, having a connection like this. I could feel all of his emotions, all of his desires. Undressing was my least favorite part of sex, but he somehow turned it into foreplay.

He pulled my jeans down to my ankles then pulled my panties down too. He was on his knees when I was naked, and he pressed his lips against the skin of my legs, particularly my inner thighs. He worshiped me with his mouth, moving across my skin but never moving to the place where I wanted to feel him most.

"Ace..." My fingers dug into his hair, and I used his strong frame for balance. He was going to make me come without even touching the area that was throbbing.

He stood up almost immediately after I said his name and dropped his jeans and boxers. I helped him get them down and ended up on my knees. But instead of kissing him the way he did to me, my mouth immediately went to his length, and I took him all the way to the back of my throat.

Ace moaned quietly, telling me how much he enjoyed it. His hand moved into my hair, and he caressed the back of my neck. He gently thrust into me, matching my pace and not changing it. His big dick moved into my mouth and made my saliva drip from the corner of my mouth.

Even though it hurt to sit on my knees, having his length inside my mouth felt incredible. I wanted to make him feel as good as he did for me. My tongue worked his length, cushioning him from my teeth.

He pulled my mouth away, and a string of saliva stretched between my mouth and the head of his cock. When he pulled me to my feet, it broke apart. Ace guided me onto the bed, positioning me at the edge so my ass hung over. My legs were cradled in his arms, and he scooted me until I was perfectly positioned underneath him. As strong as a Roman soldier, his physique was lined with powerful muscles that had the strength to pick up a car. His ass was firm and tight, and his narrow waist led up to rock-hard abs. He pressed his cock into my entrance then slid inside, parting me until his entire dick was deep within me.

I couldn't think.

My hands latched on to his forearms, and I tossed my head back. My eyes closed, and I treasured this exquisite feeling, this sensation of being a wanted woman.

His powerful hands kept me in place as he thrust into me, giving me his thick cock over and over. He took his time and didn't pound into me the way he did when we usually hooked up. He took it slow, enjoying every inch of our bodies as they moved over each other.

It was incredible. All I did was lie there and enjoy him, but that was the sexy part of it. He wanted me so much that he pinned me down so he could enjoy it, do exactly what he wanted to my body. He conquered it and took his pleasure.

I opened my eyes and looked into his gaze, seeing a man who was both my friend and my lover. If I spent the rest of my life this, I would be happy. I would feel treasured, protected, and loved. Our appearances would change as time passed, but we would still love each other just as much. The fire and passion between us couldn't be extinguished, not even by time.

We moved like that for a long time, and I stopped myself from coming even though my body was desperate for a release. I wanted to wait until he was ready, wanting to come at the exact same moment.

But he was making it impossible for me to wait. "I want to come with you..." My hands slid up his forearms, and I gripped the crook between his forearm and bicep.

He moved his hands to the bed and leaned farther over me, his body rubbing right against my clit.

Oh god.

He thrust into me deeper and harder, giving me every inch of his length that could fit inside me. His face was just inches from mine, and his beautiful body worked to please me. I loved watching his muscles ripple and shift with every movement he made. "Baby, I love you."

I inhaled a deep breath when I heard him say those words. They were words I already felt in my heart. They were words that scarred me when I saw him with Lady. After months of fooling around in dark corners where no one would catch us, I'd thought I didn't mean anything to him.

But I was wrong.

"I love you too."

He pressed his face to mine and finally gave me the kiss I'd been waiting for. I was full of his cock, treasured by his big hands, and out of breath from his kiss. I'd never felt more desirable in my entire life.

"Come for me," he said into my mouth. He shoved his cock farther inside me, moving into my tight channel and stretching me apart.

My arms locked around his neck, and I breathed into his mouth. I couldn't kiss him when I was this close to exploding. I could barely think straight. My thighs parted farther apart so I could take more of his length, ready to be the recipient of all that come. "Ace..." My pussy gripped his dick violently as I came, my moans surprised by his mouth against mine.

He paused with his length fully inside me and released, giving me his come at the same time.

"God, yes..." I grabbed his ass and kept him inside me, feeling the warmth and weight of his seed. My mouth was open, and I couldn't close it because I wasn't getting enough air. My body was in overdrive, and there wasn't enough gasoline to keep me going.

He released a quiet moan as he finished, his entire body flexed with the exertion.

My hands glided to his hair, and I finally kissed him, the heat slowly passing.

He stayed buried inside me, his cock softening. "I'm not gonna stop until you tell me to."

"Good." I sucked his bottom lip into my mouth. "I never want you to stop."

When we woke up the next morning, I didn't ask Ace to leave early. We both woke up to the sound of my alarm and got ready. Ace took a shower, put on the clothes he wore the night before, and made the girls breakfast while I got ready.

We walked out together, and before Ace walked to the office, he gave me a kiss goodbye.

"Bye, Uncle Ace." Rose waved before she hopped into the car.

Lily waved too. "Bye."

Ace raised his hand and smiled, looking more handsome than I'd ever seen him. "See you later." He gave me a final look before he started walking to work.

We didn't talk about last night. We didn't talk about my date with Evan. Nothing was said at all.

The ball was entirely in my court.

I dropped off the girls at school then went to work. Ace wasn't there because he must have already headed to Olives or the café, but Bree was there.

And her eyes were stuck on me like pointed daggers.

"Here we go..." I grabbed the schedule and concentrated on my name before she started her speech.

"If you don't pick Ace, I'm gonna slap you."

There it was. "Thanks for letting me know."

"I'm not watching the girls tonight."

"That's fine. I'll ask Sara."

"You can't be serious." Bree got to her feet, her hands on her hips. "You can't sleep with Evan after your date with Ace. You just can't. The guy took your kids on the date. You'd be an idiot not to pick him."

She spoke to me like I wasn't already aware of all of this. "Bree, you're telling me everything I already know. This is something I need to figure out on my own. I already asked Sara, so she's coming by. You don't need to worry about betraying your loyalty to Ace."

"It's not about loyalty," she said. "Remember when you told me I was being stupid about Cypress?"

Absolutely.

"Well, now we're in reverse. You're being stupid about Ace, and I need to tell you that."

"Bree, drop it."

She rolled her eyes. "You're as stubborn as a mule."

"Evan is the father of my—"

"Yeah, yeah. I've already heard this." She walked out of the office and left me there alone.

Instead of going to work right away, I sat at my desk and considered what she'd said. I knew how my family felt about the situation. I knew how Ace felt. And I even knew how I felt. But the answer still wasn't that simple.

———

MY HEART WAS BEATING A MILLION MILES A MINUTE. THE

second I heard the knock on the door, the adrenaline spiked in my blood. Like a thousand horses were racing in my temples, I could feel the pulse in my head.

Sara was in the living room with the girls, so I answered the door.

Evan walked inside in jeans and a collared shirt. His hair had just been cut. It didn't make much of a difference, but I noticed any little change he made. His jaw had just been shaved too, and I liked the clean look around his mouth. "Hey."

"Hey."

He walked farther inside and said hello to the girls. Just like when they were excited to see Ace, they were excited to see him. They both hugged him at the same time and sprinkled his face with kisses.

Ugh, this was hard.

Evan said goodbye then returned to me in the doorway. "You look nice."

I was wearing a dark blue dress with sandals that I stole from Bree. "Thanks." I did my hair differently, curling it instead of the usual straight look. I wore a silver bracelet, but my fingers were still absent of any rings.

My wedding ring was inside my nightstand where I hadn't touched it.

"Ready?" he asked.

"Yeah."

He took my hand and walked me out. Our fingers were interlocked together, and it almost felt like years in the past when we would get a sitter so we could enjoy some alone time. Evan asked me about work on the way, but he didn't ask about Ace.

Not that he wanted to know anything about the date.

He took me to Casanova, and the significance wasn't lost on me.

It was where we had our first date.

Evan had reservations, and we were taken to the exact same table where we ate for the first time. It was underneath a peculiar painting that I hadn't forgotten about. It was more private than the other sections of the room. Van Gogh's table was right beside us, only for looks and not for sitting.

Evan ordered a bottle of my favorite wine then looked at his menu.

When he wasn't looking, I stared at his features. He had a lean jawline and hollow cheeks. With naturally rugged features, he looked like a man who would be at home on a movie poster. He had beautiful eyes, a soft feature in comparison to the rest of his pure masculinity. He only had one freckle, and it was nearly underneath his jaw. It was hard to see unless you already knew it was there.

There were so many things I loved about Evan. He was a great father, he was hardworking, and he had a big heart. I fell in love with him before the end of our first date. I slept with him that night, and it felt right. Not a day went by when I'd wondered if I'd married too young or rushed into having kids.

Because Evan was the one.

But it didn't matter how much I loved him or the kind of history we had. It didn't matter that we would wake up at midnight together just to put the girls' presents under the tree. It didn't matter that we had something beautiful.

Because everything was different now.

Evan looked up at me, detecting the change in atmosphere. He looked at me with those soft eyes, but they quickly hardened in pain. He didn't need to hear me say anything to know what I was thinking.

He knew.

"I'm sorry, Evan…" I was about to break down into tears before we even ordered. The bottle of wine sat there, but we didn't pour a single glass. My heart ached for the pain I was about to cause him, but I knew I had to do it.

His eyes shifted down to the table, and his shoulders slumped. "We haven't even—"

"It's not going to change anything." I knew Ace was the one I wanted to be with. The idea of sleeping with Evan made me feel so guilty that I couldn't go through with it. And the only reason I felt that way was because I was obviously in love with someone else.

Evan still wouldn't look at me. His fingers locked together on the table, and he released a quiet sigh before he looked up. He finally met my gaze, but there was heartbreak in the look. "Amelia, just think about it. We've been married for eight years—"

"I will always love you, Evan." My hands moved on top of his on the rustic wood. My fingers gripped his as if the affection would cushion the heartbreak. "I want to be a family again. I want to go back to what we were…but we can't."

"If Ace weren't in the picture, I know you would take me back."

"But he is in the picture, Evan."

"But if you're willing to work on this marriage with me without him, then don't you think you should do it even if you have feelings for him? You know I'll be understanding of that as we move forward. We have two kids, Amelia. It should be us. We're a family. We already built a life together."

"I know all of that, Evan. But…you left me."

He closed his eyes and clenched his jaw.

"You broke my heart. You left me for another woman. You betrayed my trust. You...you are the one who threw us away. Not me. So don't put the blame on me. I won't allow that."

"I wasn't putting the blame on you, Amelia. I just—"

"You're making me feel guilty for not taking you back, that I'm the one breaking up our family. Evan, you left me for a woman ten years younger than me. My tits aren't as perky as they used to be, and I'm not as thin as I was when we first met. You wanted a younger, fitter woman. Let's not forget that part of the story."

"Like I ever could," he whispered.

"I've forgiven you for it. I know you're sorry. I still wish it never happened. I still wish we were happy together... because we were really happy."

He nodded, his eyes filling with moisture.

"But I deserve someone who wouldn't make that mistake. I know Ace would never betray me. I know he would never hurt me. With him...it feels right. I never looked at him this way before you left me. But now, I can't picture myself with anyone but him."

He closed his eyes, and that's when a tear escaped.

I felt like shit.

He took a deep breath and quickly wiped it away.

"Evan, I'm sorry. I hate hurting you... I love you."

He leaned back in his chair and looked down, doing his best to hide his emotions from me and the rest of the room.

I didn't know what else to say. I'd made my decision, and I'd brought down the blade that executed him. I wished there were a way I could have both, but there wasn't. Neither one of us could erase the past. Evan made his decision to leave me for someone else, to walk away from his family without saying more than two words to me.

I couldn't take him back.

I deserved better.

I deserved more.

WE LEFT THE RESTAURANT WITHOUT ORDERING DINNER. I LEFT a large bill to cover the inconvenience we'd caused. Evan and I walked back to my place together, but we didn't say a single word to each other. He had his hands in his pockets, and he didn't try to grab my hand.

It was a long walk.

We turned onto my street and kept walking, our feet dragging against the road. This night was just as painful for me as it was for him. It was a night we both wanted to end even though the pain would never really go away.

Evan stopped in front of the house, not taking the stone steps to the front door. He kept his distance, probably not wanting to see the kids.

I stared at him, unsure what happened now. I didn't want to repeat myself when it would probably only make him feel worse.

He kept his hands in his pockets and stared at the house.

"I'm sorry, Evan."

He finally looked at me, his eyes lidded with pain. "Don't apologize to me...I fucked this up."

I crossed my arms over my chest.

"I wish Ace weren't in the picture. I wish I could have my wife back...my family back. But you're right. I'm the reason this nightmare is happening. You've already forgiven me... and that's more than I could ask for."

My heart was breaking again.

"You deserve better," he whispered. "Better than me. I'm just so selfish that I don't want to give it to you."

"Evan…"

"You have no idea how much I wish I could go back in time and change everything. I'd give anything…anything at all. It was so fucking stupid." He dragged his hands down his face as the tears started again. "I lost everything that ever mattered to me. I lost the only woman who's ever really loved me. I lost my kids…and another man is replacing me."

"That's not true." I grabbed his hands and pressed my face close to his. "No one could ever replace you, Evan."

"Ace is going to move in and see my girls every day. He's going to be the one to take them to school…pick them up. Make dinner for them and be the man they turn to when they grow up."

"So are you, Evan. We aren't getting back together, but we're still a family. We'll always be a family."

He squeezed my hands back and sniffed.

"I love you, and you love me. Our girls need both of us— and that's something they'll never lose. I don't want you to think that."

"But everything will be different now."

"It's been different for over a year," I said. "But we'll find a new way to be a family. You can still take them to school every morning. You can still take them to dinner. I'll never keep you away from them, and Ace never would either."

"Okay…but I still don't get you."

I looked down at our joined hands because I couldn't meet his gaze. Nothing would cushion the blow that hurt him the most. I didn't want to give him false hope, not when I knew Ace and I would last forever. "But you have every-thing else. And you'll always have a part of me. No matter how much I love Ace, you'll always have a piece of my heart."

Evan moved his lips to my forehead and kissed me, his lips warm and soft against my skin.

I closed my eyes, and now I tried not to cry. When I looked up to meet his gaze, I saw his wet eyes. My tears didn't need to fall for me to know that the same tears were in my eyes. I rose on my tiptoes and pressed my lips to his, giving him the last kiss we would ever have.

He kissed me back, a soft kiss that was full love as well as pain. It wasn't like the other kisses we'd shared throughout our time together. It wasn't full of passion or lust. It was just love...a different kind of love.

I pulled away and stepped back, the tears getting heavier in my eyes. They were about to streak down my cheeks, and I didn't want Evan to witness them. If I broke down, he would do the same. "I'll see you later..."

"I love you," he whispered. "Forever."

Now I couldn't control my emotions. The tears fell and streaked like raindrops on a windshield. "I know...and I love you forever."

I DIDN'T WANT TO CALL ACE RIGHT AWAY AND TELL HIM TO come over. While I didn't regret the decision I made, I was still heartbroken over what I'd lost. In the back of my mind, I'd always hoped Evan and I would find our way back to each other.

But now that would never happen.

I was too emotional, too upset to talk to Ace. Out of respect for Evan, I thought it would be wrong to run off to Ace when our relationship came to such a heartbreaking end. But I didn't want Ace to think I was sleeping with Evan that night. I didn't want him to toss and turn, feeling sick to his stomach at the thought of Evan touching me.

When I was in my empty bed, I texted him. *I want you to know that I told Evan it wasn't going to work out. We didn't even get through dinner. He walked me home, said goodbye, and then left. I don't want to talk to anyone right now, but I wanted you to know I'm alone for the night.*

The three dots from his phone immediately popped up. He'd obviously kept his phone on hand the entire time, hoping I would text him. *Thanks for letting me know. Good night, baby.*

My eyes crinkled at the affectionate name, knowing he'd just claimed me as his forever. *Good night.*

I lay on my side of the bed and stared at the empty spot beside me. This mattress was the one Evan and I had shared since the day we got married. It was where we made love for the first time as a married couple. It had a lot of memories.

If I made the right decision, why did I feel so terrible? Was Ace right about me? That I cared more about other people than I cared about myself? That his heartbreak is what broke me?

I shouldn't second-guess myself. When I sat across from Evan at dinner, I knew exactly how I felt. It was unmistakable. The pit of my stomach was heavy with stress, and my body was answering a question my heart couldn't.

That Ace was my choice.

I didn't sleep that night even though I was exhausted. I just lay there, drifting in and out of consciousness. Even though the time drifted by slowly, it seemed to pass in the blink of an eye. Before I knew it, my alarm went off and I was out of bed.

I took the girls to school before I headed to work. Ace

probably told everyone my decision, so I wouldn't have to explain anything once I walked inside. When I entered the office, everyone was there.

Blade gave me a sympathetic look, telling me he knew exactly what happened.

Bree wore a slight smile, obviously pleased by my decision.

Cypress looked at me like he always did, like I was his little sister.

Instead of smiling in joy, Ace's face mirrored the sadness on mine. He got out of his chair and walked over to me, carrying a gentleness that was reserved for me. He wrapped his arms around me and pulled me into his chest. "You doing okay, baby?"

All I did was nod.

Bree came up behind me and hugged me, her face resting against my back. "We're here, Amelia."

"Yeah." Cypress walked to our huddle and rubbed my shoulder.

"We're always here." Blade couldn't get to me because I was sandwiched in the middle of everyone, but his proximity was enough affection.

"I know." I closed my eyes and cherished the love everyone gave me. I knew I picked the right man when Ace was so understanding. He didn't gloat at his victory or turn jealous at my sadness. He accepted everything, knowing my feelings were more important than his. "I love you guys."

Ace brushed a kiss across my forehead. "We love you too."

17

BREE

I left my shift early and walked to the diner. The doors were locked, and Cypress was taking care of the register while Amelia was taking care of the tables. I let myself inside and stopped at the counter. "Hi."

Cypress looked at me with an expression he never showed to anyone else. It was a smile, but it was more than just any smile. His eyes crinkled in the corners as the affection came over his face. His shoulders straightened, and his body exuded excitement. "Hey." He said a single word, but it was pregnant with so many things he didn't say.

I leaned over the counter and kissed him, just as every wife kissed her husband after a long day of work.

He kissed me back, his kiss soft and seductive. It was short, but the small embrace was enough to give me chills.

When I pulled away, I licked my lips and headed to Amelia, feeling the heat rise around my neck.

Amelia didn't look at me, but she'd obviously witnessed that kiss. "Don't worry, I'm not looking." She wiped down the table with a damp cloth then stacked the chairs.

I helped her. "How are you?"

"I'm okay," she said with a sigh. "I'm feeling a million things at once right now..."

"You wanna talk about it? Get some coffee?"

"I should finish up here—"

"Amelia, go," Cypress said from the counter. "I got it. I'll pick up the girls from school too."

I smiled, loving my husband even more.

"Thanks, Cypress." She removed her black apron and set it on the table.

She and I walked to the bakery and got two coffees and a snack. We sat at one of the tables in the courtyard while everyone enjoyed their afternoon with their friends and their dogs. Amelia was hesitant to say anything, but her expression said everything she couldn't.

"It'll get better," I finally said. "I'm sure it's hard right now, but it'll pass. You made the right decision."

"I know I did." She held her mug without taking a drink. "I'm happy, but I'm miserable at the same time. I hated hurting Evan like that. I should feel good about it, getting my revenge after what he did...but I take no pleasure in it."

"I know, Amelia. You aren't like that."

"I guess it hurts the most because I know how sorry he is. I know he truly regrets it. I know he really loves me..."

I could tell Evan was sorry. When he came to my house, I could see a look of apology I'd never witnessed before. He wasn't the same man who'd walked out on her. The experienced changed him, made him realize how stupid he was. He knew exactly how much he lost, and that was punishment enough. I actually felt bad for the guy. "Yeah, I agree."

"And if Ace hadn't come into my life...I'd probably have taken him back."

"But you love Ace."

She nodded. "I do love him. I love him because he makes me feel good about myself. I love him because he's a wonderful man. I love him because he's the only person who really understands me..."

Not true. I understood her. But I didn't correct her because it wasn't important.

"I'm very lucky to have him," she said. "He's great with the girls, and they love him so much."

"Yeah..."

"Ace said something to me that really affected my final decision. He said I'm always doing stuff for other people, always caring about what they want more than what I want...so he asked what I wanted."

Ace was a clever man.

"I wanted to take Evan back because I thought it was the right thing to do for all of us...but Ace is the man I really want. I know he'd never hurt me. I know he'd never betray me. I'm not paranoid about what he's doing when I'm not with him. I trust him...and I didn't think I could trust someone after what Evan did."

"Ace is the most trustworthy guy on the planet. He's great."

"I know." She drank from her coffee and stared at the poodle at the nearby table, her eyes full of sadness.

"You should be happy, Amelia. Don't let Evan drag you down."

"He's not dragging me down. I still love him. I hate knowing he's in pain."

"I get that." Amelia was the sweetest person in the world. She didn't like anyone suffering. She would take the entire burden off everyone's shoulders and deal with it in silence if she could. "I wish this had never happened. I wish Evan had never left in the first place. We had a great marriage. Even though it ended, I loved being married to him."

I wished I remembered being married to Cypress. "But it did end. Let's not forget why. Let's not forget the cold way he packed his things and left without looking back. He didn't comfort you when you cried. He didn't try to work it out with you. The whole thing happened in the span of three days. You didn't even have a chance to process it before he was gone."

She gave a slight nod.

"So don't beat yourself up too hard."

"Yeah...you're right."

"You're just too sweet, Amelia."

She smiled. "I used to steal your clothes all the time. I'm not sweet."

"You looked better in them anyway," I said. "Let's not pretend otherwise."

"Oh, shut up," Amelia said with a laugh. "People always told me you were the hotter sister."

"Psh. Yeah, right." That's not what I heard.

Celeste approached our table in a black dress with brown sandals, and until then, I hadn't noticed that this was her bakery. Her dark hair was pulled over one shoulder, and it trailed down in wavy curls. "Hey, ladies."

"Hey." I stood up and hugged her, and Amelia did the same.

"Glad you could swing by," Celeste said. "How's the coffee?"

"It's fantastic," Amelia said. "I already ate my muffin. That was good too."

Celeste pulled up a chair and sat down. "What are you guys up to?"

"We're just getting a snack after work." I figured Amelia

didn't want to talk about her ex-husband and her new boyfriend in front of Celeste.

"Ace and I are together now," Amelia said unexpectedly. "I had to end things with my ex-husband, and I'm just a little bummed about it."

I was surprised Amelia told her that, but since we were all trying to get Celeste to stay for Blade, Amelia was probably doing everything she could to make her feel included. "I don't think she needs to feel bad about anything, and I'm trying to convince her of that."

"Ace is wonderful," Celeste said. "He's been very sweet since the beginning—you guys too."

"Yeah, he's great," Amelia said with a happy sigh.

"Have you been with him since you and Evan talked?" I asked.

"No," Amelia answered. "I felt too guilty running to Ace right away. I feel like I should wait a day or something. I don't want to think about Evan when I'm with Ace, you know? And Ace is patient. He'll understand."

When it came to Amelia, he was the most patient man on the planet. "So, how did you like Blade's parents?"

Celeste's face lit up with a beautiful smile once Blade was mentioned. "They were great. Very warm and sweet. It didn't seem like they remembered that phone conversation. It could have been really awkward, but they went out of their way to make sure that didn't happen."

"His parents are nice," Amelia said. "Derek is nice too—when he's in the right mood."

"He was sweet to me," Celeste said. "But I think that's what made Blade mad."

I wanted to press the more serious questions, like if she was planning on staying or not. Summer was almost over, and she needed to make a decision soon. If she didn't pick

Blade, we would all be hurt. Blade had never felt this strongly for a woman before, and we didn't want her to slip through his fingertips.

Blade was one of the greatest guys I knew. She would be stupid not to pick him. He was honest, sweet, and thoughtful. He would worship the ground she walked on every single day. But I couldn't say any of that, not if I didn't want to make her uncomfortable.

"How are you and Cypress?" Amelia asked.

I felt like we were always talking about my unusual marriage. "We're good. Still happy. I miss him." I found myself missing him when he wasn't around, even if it was only for a few hours. When I walked into the diner and kissed him, I realized I missed him all day while we were apart.

"Aww..." Celeste smiled. "That's sweet."

"It is sweet," Amelia said. "And you know what? I bet he feels the exact same way about you."

I GOT HOME FIRST SINCE HE WAS AT AMELIA'S WITH THE GIRLS. I did a load of laundry, threw dinner in the slow cooker, and tidied up the house before he came home. I showered and did my hair and makeup so I wouldn't smell like food from the café.

Just before dinner was ready, he walked through the front door. In jeans and his favorite hoodie, he had a jaw that was covered with a light shadow. He wore a beautiful grin the second he came inside and spotted me on the couch. "There's something cooking in the kitchen...I've got a pretty wife waiting for me...and there's a fire. It's a nice way to come home."

"I like how dinner came before me on that list," I said with a smile.

"Sweetheart, you are dinner." He sat beside me on the couch, his arm draped over the back and his hand immediately moving to my thigh. He leaned in and kissed me, the kind of kiss that would lead to things we couldn't do in the living room with all the windows open. He sucked my bottom lip then gently nibbled on it, his warm breath seductive in my mouth.

My palm cupped his cheek, and I felt his pulse against my pinkie. It was strong and masculine, beating like a drum.

His hand gripped my leg before he slid it closer to the apex of my thighs.

No one touched me the way he did. He made me feel like the most beautiful woman in any room. He made me feel important, while everyone else was just shadows.

He started to lower me back onto the couch, my back against the cushion and my legs moving around his waist.

Then the slow cooker started beeping.

He chuckled against my mouth before he released growl. "We'll pick this up where we left off..."

We both went into the kitchen, and I prepared the pot roast and spooned it into two bowls. It had been overcast and dreary for the last few days, and a hot stew sounded delicious. We sat at the table together while Dino lay at our feet.

Cypress had his eyes glued to mine as he ate without watching what he was doing.

I wasn't that coordinated.

"I got an offer on the house today."

My hand rested against the bowl with my fingers around the spoon. The way he spoke suggested this would be important, so he had my full attention.

"And they offered more than the asking price." He set his spoon on the saucer then leaned farther over the table, his sweater stretching over his muscles with his movements. His eyes shifted back and forth between my eyes and my lips, gauging my entire reaction.

"That's good, right?" He seemed tense for giving such great news.

"It is. I was going to accept their offer...unless you don't want me to."

"Why wouldn't I want you to?" I asked, dumbfounded.

His eyes narrowed. "So, you're sure this is what you want? You want me to live here with you? Because when I sell that house...I'm not moving out. I'm staying here until I die—and so are you."

When I understood the foundation of his hesitancy, I slid my hand across the table until my fingertips touched the corded veins over his knuckles. I touched him gently, my eyes soft. "Sell it."

18

BLADE

Celeste and I dined in my backyard. I had a back patio made of stone, along with a fire pit. A few years ago, I'd had a brick pizza oven installed, so I made Celeste homemade vegetarian pizza since she didn't eat a lot of meat. She usually drank wine and ate cheese and bread.

"This is good." She sat across from me, her rounded shoulders held back gracefully as she kept up a straight posture. I'd never seen her slouch, even relax for a second unless she was asleep. She always carried herself with confidence and elegance. She stuck out in any room she stepped into, just the way the sun disrupted the night every morning. "I like it."

"Thanks. I made the dough myself."

"No wonder why you're a successful restaurant owner."

"Because I like food." Ever since she'd met my parents, we'd been spending more time together. It was mostly sex, talking, and eating—the three things I loved most.

She glanced up at the white lights that hung up above the patio. I'd just installed them because I thought they would make the backyard look romantic since I had so many rose bushes. They were all in bloom right now, brilliant colors of white and red. "I love the lights...very nice."

"Thanks."

"You could have a dance party out here."

"Do you like to dance?"

"All women love to dance. What about you?" she finished her slice then wiped her fingers on her napkin.

"I like to get down," I said with a smile.

She smiled back. "You look like someone who has good moves on the dance floor."

I shrugged, trying to be humble. "I've dominated a few raves."

She laughed when she knew I was joking. "I didn't know there were a lot of raves here."

"You have to know where to look." I pulled out my phone and pulled a song from my music streaming service. I picked something slow and romantic, something classic and from a different time. The song played through my speakers, and I turned up the volume on my phone.

She eyed me, unsure what I was doing.

"Dance with me?" I stood up and extended my hand.

Her smile dropped instantly, the playful mood between us evaporating like drops of water on a rose petal in the summer sun. She eyed my hand, not with hesitancy, but something else. She eventually placed her hand in mine and rose to her feet.

I took her into the center of the patio, right under the white lights, and I held her directly against me. I took her hand in mine and guided her back and forth, my face just inches from hers. I wanted to bury my face in her neck because I loved the smell of her hair. I wanted to brush my lips against her smooth skin and taste her.

But I wanted to look at her more.

Her red painted lips and bright eyes were the images I saw in my dreams. I wondered if I'd seen Celeste before I met her, encountering her during my adventures in sleep. She seemed too perfect not to be celestial. She seemed too radiant to be real. When I first laid eyes on her, I actually forgot to breathe.

I still remembered it.

At first, she looked away, unable to meet my gaze. Normally, she was fierce like a lion, looking into my eyes without a hint of fear. But now, she looked down, uncomfortable with the intensity of my gaze.

I didn't want her to look away. If she chose him and I lost her forever, I didn't want to miss a single moment with her. As far as I was concerned, she was mine. She was mine right now. I lifted her chin and forced her to look at me, to make her eyes level with mine.

She cooperated, but her eyes were softer than usual. She was pained in a way I'd never seen before. The look was different. She didn't mirror my appearance or my affection. Something else was on her mind. "What is it, baby?" I pressed my forehead to hers and swayed with her, my hand resting on the prominent curve in the small of her back. Every inch of her body was perfect, beautiful, and sexy. Sometimes she looked airbrushed—even in person.

When her head was pressed to mine, she looked down. But I could feel the change in her breathing as her breaths drifted down my neck. I could feel her rib cage swell as every breath expanded her petite body.

I didn't know if something was wrong or right. But something was different.

She pressed her lips tightly together before she answered. "I love you..."

My feet stopped moving, and my body halted in mid-sway. My hand gripped hers a little more tightly, and just as I'd lost my breath when I first looked at her, it happened again. My chest flattened and my lungs halted. Like a supernatural being, I no longer needed air.

I just needed her.

Those words sank into my skin, entered my bloodstream, and circled to every organ and nerve in my body. Each word was a spike of excitement, a burst of adrenaline. I'd never told her I loved her because I didn't need to. My heart was beating on my sleeve, contracting every time she laid a single finger on me.

But her words were a direct contradiction to her sadness.

"I'm in love with you...but I'm in love with him too."

I didn't want to hear about Henry. Until she stepped on that plane, it was just the two of us. That idiot didn't exist. "You love me more."

She pulled away and looked into my face, her eyes shifting back and forth to look into mine. We were so close together that I was breathing her breaths and she was breathing mine.

"It's been three months, and you're already a part of me. I'm already a part of you. You're my world, the only woman I've ever loved..." I finally told her how I felt, and it felt good to say it. It felt good to actually care about someone, to ignore every other woman on the planet because she was the only one who mattered. My eyes never strayed. My fantasies never shifted from her. Like a confession I'd been meaning to get off my chest, I was relieved I told her the truth. "My family adores you. My friends think the world of you. This is your home now. I'll be your home."

She stared at me, and a thin film of moisture appeared on the surface of her eyes. They weren't tears, just gleams of emotions. A battle carried on behind her eyes, a rage between the two sides of her heart.

I didn't want her to pick me. I needed her to pick me.

"I would do anything in the world to keep you. If my job required me to be away from you, I would quit. I wouldn't desire other women, not when I could have you instead. And I would die at the thought of you being with another man. Real men don't share their women, and I certainly wouldn't share you." I'd just insulted her boyfriend, but I didn't care. He didn't truly love her if he was okay with this upside-down relationship. It wasn't a relationship at all, just a long-lasting fling. She claimed she loved him, but I wasn't sure how that was possible. They may have friendship, have respect. But they certainly didn't have love.

She stared at me with the same expression, her thoughts hidden behind those beautiful eyes.

I started to move with her again, even though the song changed to something else. I brought her into my body so she could rest her face against my chest. My arms circled her waist, and instead of dancing, we just held each other under the shining lights. I felt her breathe, and she felt me.

And we stayed like that for a long time.

I FLICKED MY TONGUE OVER HER NIPPLE, FEELING THE HARD TIP as her tits firmed at my touch. My hands pinned hers back to the mattress, and I sprinkled kisses between her breasts, lapping at the soft skin over her hard sternum.

My mouth migrated down her small abs and the luscious skin around her belly button. I kissed the area, sweeping my tongue over everything I could taste.

She arched and twisted underneath me, her hands squeezing mine as moans escaped her lips.

I kissed both of her hips, loving the way they curved in contrast to her petite waist. I moved farther down until I was between her legs, tasting the pussy my cock was obsessed with. I didn't need to wet her with my mouth because her folds were already soaked. Her entrance was swollen from the blood that burned between her legs. I slipped my tongue inside her wet pussy then circled her clit, applying the perfect amount of pressure to make her knees part even more.

I released her hands and crawled back up her body, a drop of semen sitting at the head of my cock. I wanted to be inside her so much that I quit the foreplay, placed my hips between her thighs, and slid right inside.

Fucking heaven.

She gripped my biceps and inhaled deeply when she felt my big cock stretch her. It was the same reaction she gave every single time, never fully prepared for how well I could stretch her, how I could make her feel like such a woman—completely and utterly.

That other guy had nothing on me.

I rocked into her on my bed, the sheets rustling with our movements. The slick sounds our bodies made were amplified in the bedroom. She was so wet and I was so big that it was natural. It turned me on even more, knowing I could feel how wet she was and listen to it too.

She was the kind of woman who liked to be in control most of the time, so she usually rode me, dropped to her knees and sucked me off, or pushed me onto the bed when she was ready to fuck me.

But she let me do everything tonight. She lay back and enjoyed me, parting her legs and taking all of me. She let me dominate her, let me own her. She didn't have to tell me she loved me for me to be able to see it.

She showed it to me right then.

She pressed her face against mine and panted underneath me. "Deeper..."

I gave her my entire length, shoving it inside that tight little pussy.

"God...yes."

I didn't want to make love to anyone else. How could she not feel the same way? Look at us. We were perfect together. Fucking was hot, but making love like this, nice and slow, was even better.

I buried all of my desire inside her, showing her love in the most physical way possible. My body was streaked with sweat, and when her nails scraped against my skin, she cut me slightly, making the salt from the sweat burn my tiny wounds.

I liked it.

My cock was hard as steel and anxious. I wanted to fill my woman with all of my seed, to give her all of my come and watch it seep from her opening. The orgasm wasn't the best part; claiming her forever was.

But I would let her go first, because I was a gentleman.

She gripped my arms as she came around me, squeezing my cock just as I gripped myself when I jerked off. "Blade...Blade..."

She was hot when she said my name. "I love you, baby." I came before I even finished the words, filling her with as much come as I could stuff into her channel.

She gripped my ass and pulled me deeper inside her. "I love you..."

This was what life was about. Two people in love. Two

people enjoying each other. Two people living in the moment.

Just us.

"She's definitely going to pick you." Ace sat at the picnic table in the backyard with a beer resting in front of him. "If you're dropping the L word, it's a done deal."

"How did you know Amelia was going to pick you?" Cypress asked.

Ace shrugged. "I didn't. I just hoped she would."

"Have you guys...been together since she left Evan?" I asked. So far, Ace was always with us. It didn't seem like he was spending any time with Amelia.

"No," Ace answered. "I know it was hard for her to walk away from Evan. I can tell she's sad and feels guilty about it so I'm giving her some space. She'll come to me when she's ready. She texted me and told me she didn't feel like talking."

"Wow, you have a lot of patience," Cypress said. "I couldn't be that patient for anything."

"Coming from the guy who lived next door to his wife for two years..." It wasn't a jab, but a subtle reminder that Cypress sacrificed just as much to make his relationship work.

Cypress shrugged before he drank his beer.

"I'd rather be with her when she's not thinking about him anyway," Ace said. "Let her accept that her marriage is really over before we start our relationship. I know we're gonna last forever, so I can wait a little longer."

"You're gonna last forever?" I raised an eyebrow because I'd never heard Ace say something like that.

"Whoa," Cypress teased. "I didn't realize you were so romantic."

Ace didn't react or seem even slightly embarrassed. "I love her. So what?"

I shared a look with Cypress, surprised Ace had so blatantly told us his feelings. He normally behaved like a caveman, having very little to say and very little emotion. But he just put his heart on display, totally vulnerable to jokes.

But neither one of us did that.

"Good for you, man," Cypress said. "You guys are both lucky to have each other."

"Thanks," Ace said.

"Yeah," I said in agreement. "That's awesome."

"Hey." Cypress turned to him. "Maybe one day we'll be brothers-in-law."

Ace smiled. "Yeah, true. But we're already brothers, so there won't be a big difference there."

Cypress's eyes softened, and he patted Ace on the back.

I had to admit, I was a little jealous. "I'm a brother too, right...?"

"Obviously," Ace said.

"The little brother we like to pick on," Cypress teased.

"I'm older than both of you," I countered.

"But Ace is bigger than both of us combined," Cypress said.

Good point. "You got me there."

Ace finished his beer then grabbed another from the fridge before he came back. We'd just had pizza like I did with Celeste the other night, and Ace ate a whole one by himself. "So what's next for you and the French babe?"

"I don't know. She's supposed to leave in two weeks." But I hoped she never would.

"When is she supposed to give you her final answer?" Cypress asked.

"She just said at the end of the summer," I said. "So she still has some time."

"She's not gonna go back to the other guy," Ace said as he shook his head. "Wouldn't make any sense. Sounds like there's no passion there. She seems like a woman who wants passion."

"All women do," Cypress said. "They want a man who's obsessed with them to the point of insanity."

I drank my beer. "That's definitely me."

"Why would she go back to being with a guy who likes an open relationship?" Ace asked incredulously. "What kind of relationship is that?"

"A boring one," Cypress said. "And an unhealthy one."

When my friends said these things to me, I was more convinced things were going to work out. "You're probably right...she will pick me."

"The only problem is, she's leaving her country for you," Cypress said. "That might be the difficult part."

"They can always go back and forth," Ace said. "There's five of us, so we can cover for him."

"True," I said. "And if we get married, we can add her bakery to our roster so you guys can take care of it while we're gone."

"See?" Ace said. "It wouldn't be much different from how it is now."

"True." The knot in my stomach loosened further when I considered everything they said. Not only did Celeste and I have a powerful connection, but I was the better man. I was the safe choice. She may have been with him longer, but I really loved her.

So her decision should be easy.

I'D JUST GOTTEN OUT OF THE SHOWER WHEN CELESTE CALLED me. I was about to pick her up and take her to dinner at The Grill, getting both of us out of the house so we would take a break from making love all the time and spend time in public. "Hey, baby."

"Hey..." Her voice was heavy with sadness. I recognized it right away.

"What is it?"

She breathed into the phone before she finally spoke.

I was on edge.

"I talked to Henry last night."

I didn't like where this was going.

"We're always honest with each other, so I told him how I felt about you...that it wasn't just some fling. I told him I'd fallen in love with you...and now I don't know what I want anymore."

This sounded like good news, but I knew there was going to be a twist. She wouldn't be on the verge of crying if this was a good phone call.

"So he got on the first flight he could catch...he's landing within the hour."

Fuck. This was definitely bad news.

"He wants to talk this out. He said he doesn't want to lose me..."

Too fucking bad. "If he didn't want to lose you, he should have kept you close. He shouldn't have fucked other women and let you fuck other men." The muscles in my neck convulsed because I clenched my jaw too tightly. "And you agreed you wouldn't see him until the summer is over."

"I know," she said breathlessly. "But what was I

supposed to do? Tell him not to get on the plane? If he wants to come here, there's nothing I can do to stop him."

I knew she was right. My demands were unrealistic. "He's just going to confuse you, Celeste. You should be with me, and we both know it."

"Either way, I have to talk to him about it."

"Are you going to tell him you want to be with me?" I paused in my bedroom, buck naked and still slightly wet.

Silence.

"Celeste."

She breathed into the phone. "Blade, I don't know. I've never been so confused in my life."

"The choice is obvious, Celeste. Pick me for love. Don't pick him for convenience."

"I never said I didn't love him, Blade."

"But you don't," I pressed. "You would never be with me if you loved him. It's that simple."

Silence again.

Fuck, what should I do? If Henry got into her brain, he could take her back to France tomorrow. "I'm not letting you pick him."

"Blade—"

"I don't accept that. You can't be in love with two people at once. You always love one more than the other."

"You don't understand, Blade. I wish the answer was simple, but nothing is ever that simple."

"What can he offer you that I can't?"

She was quiet.

"Answer the question." I grabbed my jeans and t-shirt from the closet and stayed on the phone while I pulled everything on. I forgot about my boxers, but that didn't matter right now. I was careful with the fly.

"I've known him for a lot longer..."

"And you fell in love with me a lot quicker."

"He's ambitious—"

"I own five restaurants. I have a beautiful house by the beach. You wanna talk ambitious? I'd put that asshole to rest." Spit flew out of my mouth as I spoke because I was so livid. I wanted to punch this guy in the face for coming anywhere near her. She was mine—end of story.

"He'll be a great father—"

"I take care of Lily and Rose all the time. I'll be the best damn father in the world. I want a family—I said that before."

She returned to her silence.

"There's nothing he can offer you that I can't. But there's one thing I can offer that he can't. And you know exactly what that is."

I WENT TO HER HOUSE BECAUSE I HAD TO GET INVOLVED. I WAS already involved the second I laid eyes on her. By coming to the house where he was about to show up, I knew I was interfering when I shouldn't.

But I couldn't let him win.

This was the biggest battle I would ever fight, and I had to be victorious.

I had to keep her.

I knocked on the door, and she opened it with pure shock on her face. "Blade—"

"Is he on his way?"

"Uh...yeah. He's in a cab...what are you doing here?"

"You know what I'm doing here." I felt the anger rise up my throat every time I looked at her. I was pissed at her when I didn't have any right to be. I was just furious I wasn't getting my way. "He needs to know that you're mine."

"Blade, you need to go. I need to talk to him alone."

"No." I welcomed myself inside, the adrenaline pumping through my veins.

"Blade, this isn't a good idea. He's gonna be angry."

"Like I care."

She kept her hand on the door as she stood there. "You're being unreasonable right now."

"Tell me that you're gonna pick me, and I'll go." I walked up to her and looked into her stunning face, at those beautiful lips that kissed me and told me they loved me. "Then I'll give you all the privacy you need."

She held my expression without blinking.

When I didn't hear those words, I was disappointed. I stepped back. "Then, I'm staying."

A cab pulled up to the front of the house, and a muscular man got out of the back seat. Under his sport coat, I could tell he was fit and trim. He had a slender figure similar to mine, full of cut muscles underneath. His short hair was cut close to the scalp, and he had brown eyes. His skin was tanned like he was outside more often than inside.

I didn't like him.

I didn't like that he was tall, handsome, and reeked of wealth.

Fucker.

He grabbed his bag from the trunk then walked to the front of the house.

I walked outside and met him first, not scared to go toe-to-toe with this guy.

He stopped when he spotted me, his eyes narrowing in immediate hostility. He knew exactly who I was. He didn't need to ask for a name. He walked forward again, taking the steps and setting his bag on the stone pathway. He met my look, not blinking the entire time.

I wanted to murder him. I'd never known jealousy like this. I wished he were less attractive, shorter, and less threatening.

Now I had doubts.

Celeste came between us, placing her body in the middle without touching either one of us. "Henry, I told Blade you were coming, and he came over to... He just wants to be here."

He looked down at her and said something quick in French.

She responded in the same tongue.

I knew he spoke English because she just addressed him in that language, so he should have no problem under-standing what I had to say. "You made the mistake of being with other women. You made the mistake of letting her be with other men. You can glare at me all you want, but she's mine now. If that was something you were ever concerned about, you should have done a better job holding on to her."

Henry moved forward like he was going to take a swing.

Celeste pushed him back. "No. There will be no hitting. Only words."

I wished he would take a swing. I would love the oppor-tunity to kick his ass. "I love her." There was no shame or embarrassment in my words. "I love her and I want her. I don't want to share her with anyone else, and I want to take care of her. I want to be the boyfriend that you weren't. I want to be there every single day and be exactly what she deserves. If you think I'm gonna let her go easily, you're wrong. And she loves me too. I see it every time she looks at me. I see it every time I make love to her."

The vein in his temple was about to explode. He shifted

forward like he was going to push Celeste out of the way to get to me.

"If you're a real man, you'll let her go. You don't get to come after her when she finds someone better." I pointed my finger at his chest. "You're the one who fucked up. You're the one who made the mistake. Do the right thing and bow out."

Until that point, he hadn't said a single word. He just stared me down like he despised me. His eyebrows were furrowed, and he clenched his hands until the veins on his knuckles popped. "You screw my woman for a few months, and you think she belongs to you?"

"She obviously doesn't belong to you if she's sleeping with me."

This time, he really did lunge at me, pushing Celeste to the side.

Instead of punching him before he could get to me, I dodged sideways and grabbed Celeste before she toppled over and fell into the bushes. I kept a tight grip on her wrist but pivoted my body toward Henry in preparation for his oncoming blow.

He threw the punch, but I caught it with my bare hand. I twisted his arm down and pushed him back. I wasn't much of a fighter, but growing up with one annoying-ass brother taught me a few things.

"Stop." Celeste righted herself and came between us again. "I mean it. Both of you."

Henry finally backed off.

Celeste sighed in frustration at our pissing contest. "Enough. If anyone makes another move, that's it."

"He pushed you then punched me," I snapped. "In case you forgot what happened ten seconds ago."

She ignored me because she was trying to be neutral, but that neutrality wouldn't last for long. She couldn't be Sweden forever. "Blade, I understand why you're here, and I'm not upset with you for it. But you need to let Henry and me talk."

I gave her a look that said *over my dead body*.

"Henry and I have been together for a very long time. More than being in a relationship—"

"That was not a relationship."

She ignored me and continued on. "And we have a strong friendship and great respect for one another. We need to talk, and it's unreasonable for you to expect me not to." She grew inches in height even though her features didn't change. "You should go, Blade. I'll talk to you tomorrow."

"And he's staying with you?" As in, sleeping there?

"Yes," she said again. "He just flew twelve hours."

"Oh...how sweet."

Celeste disregarded my sarcasm, but her eyes narrowed in irritation. "I'll call you tomorrow."

Just the other night, we were dancing in my backyard, and she told me she loved me. We made love for three days straight. I was inside of her more than outside of her. Now that beautiful relationship had come burning down because this dickhead showed up. But there was nothing I could do. I knew she had to speak to Henry in private. It was unrealistic for her to dump him right there on the spot and just say goodbye. Amelia had been divorced for a year, and she still couldn't do that to Evan.

I had to walk away—as much as it killed me. "Then I'll talk to you tomorrow."

Celeste visibly relaxed when the conversation came to a halt.

I stared at her, waiting for her to kiss me goodbye. I wasn't leaving until she did it.

She knew exactly what I was thinking. A guilty look came over her face before she walked toward me and kissed me on the cheek.

Like the asshole that I was, I turned my face and kissed her right on the mouth.

She kissed me back.

I didn't drag it out, because that was a low blow. I stepped back and walked away, doing my best not to look at her or Henry. I didn't want to think about what they would do in that house tonight while I was home alone. I didn't want to think about him kissing her, fucking her.

But I knew it would happen.

I COULDN'T SLEEP LAST NIGHT.

I tossed and turned until three in the morning before I finally gave up and went downstairs to eat a bowl of cereal and watch TV. I played a few video games, trying to distract myself as much as possible.

Hopefully, Celeste was asleep.

Hopefully, she was sleeping alone.

When the sun came up the next morning, I went to work at the office. Everyone was there, in good moods because the sun had come out. The only person who seemed hollow was Amelia, still upset about ending her marriage for good.

I slumped into my chair and stared out the window.

"Hey." Ace rested his feet on the desk and looked at me. "I got online today and saw you were on your PS4 all night. I thought those days were over now that Celeste is around."

"Well...looks like those days might be back." I rubbed my temple, my eyes exhausted.

"What does that mean?" Cypress asked.

I sighed before I told them the story.

Bree's jaw hit the floor. "No...you can't be serious."

"He slept over?" Amelia asked.

"He's with her right now?" Cypress asked.

I nodded, answering all of their questions simultaneously. "She said she would call me today. It's all I can think about."

"Well, she's gotta end the relationship in person anyway," Cypress said. "So you can't hold that against her. He is her boyfriend."

"You didn't see this guy... He's a good-looking dude. I'm not sure she's gonna pick me." She told me she still loved him. Said it right to my face. It still hurt even though I knew about it beforehand.

"She's gonna pick you," Bree said.

"Yeah," Amelia said. "She'd be stupid not to."

"I don't know..." I dragged my hands down my face. "She told me she loved me...I love her. What does she have to think about?"

"It's more complicated than that," Amelia said. "He deserves an explanation from her. He deserves to know exactly why things are ending. I think they'll talk it out, and then he'll leave."

If that were the case, I'd be the happiest man on the planet. "Fuck, I hope so."

"It'll be alright, man," Cypress said. "The agony is almost over."

"Yeah," Ace said. "You guys were gonna have to confront this in a few weeks anyway. At least you're getting your answer now."

That was only good if it was the answer I wanted to hear.

I'd been waiting all day, constantly looking at my phone to make sure I didn't miss a text message.

It took me a moment to answer, dreading the call as much as I'd been looking forward to it. I answered with silence, unable to speak because there were so many emotions bottled inside me.

She knew I was there. "Blade, it's me..."

The sound of her voice made my chest relax. I loved the sweetness of her tone. I loved it when she said my name when we made love. I loved the way she kissed me with trembling lips. I loved this woman, had loved her since I met her. "Baby."

"I'm standing outside your door right now. I wanted to talk to you..."

That didn't sound good. I hung up the phone without saying goodbye and opened the front door.

She was in a loose gray sweater and dark jeans. A red scarf was around her neck, matching the fall season that was quickly approaching. Her hair was straight today because she didn't seem to care about styling it.

She still looked breathtaking, like always.

I stared at her, my body blocking the doorway. "I hope you're here to tell me one thing. If you aren't, then don't say anything at all."

Her lips didn't move, and she held her hands together at her waist. Her eyes carried heartbreak, and her cheeks were paler than usual. Her response was a long stretch of silence.

The most painful silence I had ever listened to.

She'd picked him.

I stepped back from the doorway because I didn't have enough air. Everything had been stripped from me. My muscled legs no longer felt strong, and my heart felt like it was experiencing its last beats.

I felt like I'd been stabbed in both lungs.

"You said you loved me."

"And I do…"

"But you love him more?" I asked incredulously. "The man who fucks other women when you aren't around?"

She crossed her arms over her chest. "He says he wants to be monogamous now…have me move back to France tomorrow permanently and sell the business."

This guy got to treat her like shit for years, and he still got to keep her? By caving and doing what he should have done from the beginning, he got to have this woman? "And that's enough for you, when I've been willing to give you that from the beginning?"

Her eyes welled up with tears.

"He doesn't love you, Celeste. Not like I do."

"I've been with him for years…"

"What does that matter? I've loved you more in three months than he's loved you in three years."

She blinked quickly, trying to dispel her tears. "I'm sorry…"

"You're sorry?" I stepped toward her, feeling the rage kick in. "Don't feel sorry for anything. You're the one I feel sorry for." I grabbed her chin and forced her to look up at me. "You know why I fell in love with you?"

She held her breath.

"I saw a fearless woman who wasn't afraid of anything. Independent, smart, and beautiful, you could take over the world if you wanted to. But you know what I see now?"

She finally took a breath, the tears starting to fall.

"You're afraid. You're afraid to take a risk on something different. You're afraid to leave something that's comfortable for something new." I dropped my hand, having her full attention. "You're afraid to leave the guarantee of mediocre love for something strong, passionate, and unpredictable. That's not the woman I know...that's not the woman I loved." I stepped back and grabbed the door, prepared to shut it. "Goodbye, Celeste. I hope you find happiness with him—I really do."

19

AMELIA

I knocked on the door and held the casserole dish in my arm. It was baked chicken with rice and broccoli, a home-cooked meal the girls loved. It was still warm against my skin so it probably wouldn't need to be heated up.

Ace opened the door in just his sweatpants. He was shirtless, his tanned skin beautiful and protruding with muscles. He looked at me, his eyes dark and intense—just the way I liked.

I tried not to stare at his powerful chest, wanting to see him for more reasons than just sex. "Are you busy right now?"

"No."

"Can I come in?"

He opened the door and motioned for me to come inside.

I walked in and set the dish on the counter. "I'm sorry I've been absent for so—"

"Don't apologize to me." He pressed his chest against my back, pinning me against the counter. His hands moved either side of me, and he pressed his lips next to my ear. "You know I would have waited a lot longer for you." He brushed his lips against the shell of my ear then released a quiet sigh.

This was what I chose, this powerful connection that vibrated with intensity. I loved the way he made me feel exposed but safe at the same time. I loved the way he acted like a predator and treated me like prey.

His arm circled my waist, and he slowly turned me around until we were face-to-face.

"I made you dinner..."

"I saw that." He eyed my mouth.

"I haven't been a great girlfriend lately..."

"You're my girlfriend. You don't need to worry about being great."

My girlfriend. I loved hearing that. "Bree and Cypress are watching the girls tonight. I thought we could have dinner and...spend time alone time together."

"That sounds nice."

"To make up for this past week..."

He grabbed my chin and adjusted my face so I was looking right at him. "I understand, Amelia. I'm glad you took your time. Your absence didn't make your loyalty to me any less strong. You picked me." He cupped my face and leaned into me before he brushed his full lips against mine. "I understand that."

Ace was so sweet to me, undeniably patient. I wasn't sure what I'd done to deserve him. I wasn't sure what I'd done to deserve the beautiful love of a beautiful man. "In that case... you want me to warm this up and make you dinner?"

"No." His eyes burned into mine. "You don't need to take care of me, Amelia. I'm a grown-ass man who's gonna take care of you. Let's skip the dinner and go straight to dessert."

He lifted me onto the counter and pulled his boxers and sweatpants down, revealing the enormous cock that had rocked my world more times than I could count.

I stared at it, licking my lips automatically.

"You know how many times I've jerked off to you in this house?"

How many?

He heard my unspoken question. "A lot." He picked me up off the counter and carried me to the couch in the living room. "This is where I sit with my bottle of lotion and a box of tissues." He laid me down and yanked off my jeans.

The idea of him touching himself and thinking of me made my entire body contract with desire. "Yeah?"

His eyes were connected to mine. "Yeah." He lifted up my shirt and yanked it over my head before he unclasped my bra with a single hand. He worked fluidly, his experience with all the women before me turning him into a pro.

But now I got to enjoy him.

He separated my thighs with his narrow hips and placed his heavy body on top of mine. It was like lying underneath a mountain. His muscles shifted against my skin every time he made a slight move. His face was pressed to mine, and he got a hold of my hair like a master held on to his sub. He adjusted my head until my neck was exposed, and he placed a soft kiss right against my pulse.

I closed my eyes and explored his back with my hands, feeling the tight muscles and the strong tendons that connected everything together. His back was an inverted triangle of muscle, just unbridled power.

He moved his hips and slid inside me, pushing through my tight opening and sliding down my even tighter channel. His cock made a home there, knowing every single inch like the back of his hand. He pressed his forehead to mine and released a satisfied moan when he was fully buried inside me.

It felt incredible. "Ace..."

He released his grip on my hair so I could move my face toward his. "This pussy is mine now."

He hadn't asked a question, but I felt obligated to agree with him. "Yes..."

He thrust inside me, moving slowly like he had the rest of time to make love to me. "And you're mine."

"Yes...all yours."

HE SAT ACROSS FROM ME AT THE TABLE IN JUST HIS SEXY boxers. Bare-chested and barefoot, he was like having a sexy caveman in the house. His skin was tanned, and his chest was free of hair. Only a slim happy trail existed between his hips.

He ate the dinner I'd brought over in silence, his eyes always on me and never on his food. We'd made love on the couch three times before we finally broke apart. Now that a table was between us, we were separated, but the way he maintained eye contact with me made me feel like I was sitting right in his lap.

I wondered if he was like this with the others, with Lady, this intense and profound. I could feel him in a room without even looking at him. Evan and I had a strong relationship, but it wasn't quite like this.

He drank his water, watching me as his masculine throat shifted to take down the liquid. When he finished, he licked his lips then set the glass on the table. "You want to talk about it?"

I'd told Bree exactly how I felt about my conversation

with Evan, but I'd never mentioned it to Ace. Seemed like something he wouldn't want to listen to. "We don't have to. I'm sure you never want me to say his name in front of you."

"You picked me over him," he said. "The man you were married to. I'm not the least bit threatened by him. I'm not insecure. I'm not jealous." He stabbed a piece of broccoli with his fork and placed it in his mouth. "And we're friends, Amelia. We talk about things—all things."

I wasn't sure if I would be so understanding if he wanted to talk about Lady. I was jealous anytime I saw him with another woman—even if they were just friends.

"I know Evan is going to be around a lot, and he and I will have to learn to get along. I don't want him to feel like he can't see his kids because of me. I don't want him to think I'm trying to replace him. The girls need him."

If all men were like Ace, the world would be a better place. "Thanks for being so easygoing about it..."

"You and I are gonna be a family someday, and Evan is already a part of your family. In a way...he and I are gonna be family too. If we have the right attitude about it, we should all get along and respect each other. I can't speak for him, but I'd like to think we can be friends."

"I think he'll get there...eventually. Right now, he's just upset."

"I understand. I'd feel the same way." He kept eating, his muscular jaw working to chew his food.

"I know I made the right decision. I just wish I didn't have to hurt him in the process."

"He'll find someone else and move on someday. Don't beat yourself up over it. And don't forget all of this happened because of him. The second he was tempted to be with another woman, he should have told you about it and worked something out. You could have gone to marriage counseling or something. But he didn't fight for your marriage. He just walked away."

I knew Ace would never do the same thing Evan did. His loyalty to me was unshakeable. If we ever ran into a problem, he would be honest with me. He would give me the respect every partner deserved. Trust would never be an issue for us. "I know…"

"Do you feel better now?"

I nodded.

"Good." He returned to staring at me intently.

"Can I ask you something?"

"Anything."

"Did you stop seeing Lady because of me?" I thought that was the case, but when I'd asked him about it, he said no. Maybe he was lying.

After taking a long time to chew his food, he finally nodded. "Yes."

"Because you thought you wanted to be with me?"

He shrugged. "I didn't know what was going to happen between us. I didn't know what I was doing most of the time. I just knew I wanted to be with you and not her. It didn't feel right."

"So did that mean you were with other people…?"

"No. I wasn't with anyone since I ended things between us. Just alone with my hand…and thoughts of you."

If we hadn't done it so many times, I would probably be aroused again.

"Now that we're doing this, should we talk about our business? Some ground rules if we…you know."

"We aren't going to break up." He spoke with more confidence than I'd ever heard him produce. "We don't need to waste time talking about a possibility that will never happen."

"Why are you so sure?" I didn't challenge him, just expressed my curiosity.

"You just know," he said. "I've been with tons of women that were beautiful and smart... I had a great time. But I didn't feel the excitement that I do with you, the comfort of being with a friend. When I'm with you, I don't want anything else. I'm happy. I'm satisfied. I don't need anything else. That's how I know."

If I hadn't thought this would last forever, I wouldn't have picked Ace. I would have stuck to Evan, something that was guaranteed to work. I shared the exact same thoughts, but for slightly different reasons. "Then we don't need to talk about it."

He gave a slight smile from across the table, his rugged handsomeness melting into a boyish charm. "No. We don't need to talk about it."

Evan didn't come back to the house until a week after our last conversation. I didn't get a phone call or a text from him. Eventually, the girls started to ask about him.

"Where's Daddy?" Lily asked at the dinner table.

Ace was there, eating the dinner I'd made. He was great with the girls, being a role model and a parenting figure. He didn't struggle to keep his authority, but he never crossed a line, and he left the punishments to me.

"Yeah?" Rose asked. "Where'd he go?"

I didn't bother Evan because I knew he needed space, but I hoped he would come back soon. He needed to understand he was always welcome here—that this was his home.

A knock sounded on the door, and we all turned our heads to the entryway.

I immediately assumed it was Evan, but he probably wouldn't drop by unannounced, not when things were so tense.

I went to the door and answered it, expecting to see my sister.

But it was Evan.

With his hands in his pockets and a dark hoodie on his torso, he looked the same as he did before—but without those naturally bright eyes. No, they were somber and matte, not glossy and full of life. He looked at me like the sight of me pained him. "Hey..."

"Hi." I smiled when I looked at him, happy to see him. "Thanks for coming by." I moved into his chest and hugged him.

He hugged me back, his grip tight.

"The girls are asking for you."

"They are?" he whispered.

"They miss you."

"I miss them too. I missed them a lot this week..." He pulled away, a full beard on his face.

"You're always welcome to take them for the weekend, even the week if you want."

"I'll move in to a house first. The apartment is pretty small. It's a one-bedroom."

I stepped back and ushered him inside. "Have dinner with us."

He walked in but stopped when he saw Ace sitting at the table. He didn't even look at the girls.

Ace met his look before he got up from the table and walked over. He stepped up to Evan, his expression warm instead of cold.

Evan was the first one to raise his hand for a handshake.

But Ace ignored it. Instead, he walked into his chest and hugged him. He gave him a pat on the back.

Evan hesitated before he reciprocated the affection.

Ace pulled away then slapped him on the arm. "It's good to see you, man. I'm glad you're here."

Evan continued to stare at him in surprise.

I was grateful Ace was doing the best he could to make Evan feel welcome. He would definitely get a blow job later tonight.

Evan cleared his throat. "Yeah...it's good to see you too."

"The girls were just talking about you." Ace stepped aside and turned to the table. "Get up and give your father a hug. Come on."

Both of the girls hopped out of their chairs and ran into Evan. They bumped into his waist and nearly made him stumble over because they charged so fast.

Evan chuckled before he wrapped his arms around them. "Did you guys miss me?"

"Yes!" Lily squeezed his waist. "You haven't been at our tea parties, Daddy."

"Yeah," Rose said. "It's not as fun without you."

Evan's eyes filled with affection as he stared at the two beautiful beings we'd made together. "Then let's play after dinner."

"Yay," Lily said.

Rose hugged him again.

Evan kneeled on the stone floor and wrapped his arms around both of them. He closed his eyes as he treasured our daughters, the angels we created together. Our marriage didn't work out and we would live our lives separately, but we would always be connected. We would never regret what we'd had, not when something so wonderful came out of it.

Ace came to my side and placed his hand on the small of my back. He rubbed me gently, a knowing smile on his face.

I smiled back, happy with everything I had. I had the greatest memories of being married to Evan and being a family of four. But being a family of five was just a great, just as beautiful.

Because we all loved each other.

20

BLADE

I didn't go to work the next day. I texted Ace and told him I was sick.

Celeste had already left. Like a pathetic loser, I walked by her house and saw how empty it was. She and Henry had already hopped on the plane and headed back to France. I walked back home and finally went to sleep.

Since I hadn't slept in thirty-six hours.

When I woke up, it was four in the afternoon. I didn't shower or change my clothes, and I immediately went downstairs and turned on my PS4. I drowned out my mind with video game violence and aliens.

I didn't think about anything.

I hadn't eaten anything in a long time, but I still didn't have an appetite.

I chose to be numb.

I chose to be hollow.

A knock sounded on my door, but I didn't have the energy to answer it. "It's open..." I didn't care who walked inside. If it was a high school girl selling cookies, she could take my wallet and leave.

But it was the gang—every single one of them.

Bree was in the front with two pizza boxes in her hands. Cypress came next with a six-pack. Ace walked toward me at the couch with a sympathetic expression he never showed outside the five of us. Amelia gripped my shoulder, saying more with the touch than she could express with her mouth.

They all knew.

When I didn't go to work, they knew why I didn't show up. They knew me so well it was impossible for me to hide anything. "She went back to France with him yesterday...or today...at some point." I wondered if she would be back to sell the house and her business. I doubt she would contact me if she did.

It suddenly hit me that I would never see her again.

Ever.

Fuck, that hurt.

I swallowed, feeling the muscles of my throat tense and shift.

Amelia sat beside me and wrapped her arm around my shoulder. She pulled me close to her and held me like a sister.

Bree set the pizzas down and rubbed my back.

Cypress was the first one to say anything. "Sorry, man. All of us are."

"I know." I rubbed my jaw, my muscles tense.

"You want to talk about it?" Ace sat on the other couch, downplaying his happiness with Amelia just for me.

"There's nothing to say," I whispered. "I told her I loved her and asked her to pick me...but she wanted him." After everything we'd been through, she still wanted him. "He said he wanted to be monogamous now...but he shouldn't have taken so long to figure that out."

"She'll regret her decision," Bree said. "Give it six months."

"I don't want her to regret it. I'm not gonna wait around for her. She picked him. End of story. If she comes back to me, it'll only make me sad."

"You'll find someone better," Ace said. "You'll find the one someday."

She was the one.

"You want to head to the beach?" Cypress asked. "Play football?"

"No." I didn't want to do anything.

"How about some pizza?" Bree asked.

I appreciated their company, but I didn't have an appetite. "No thanks."

"How about we play a board game?" Cypress asked.

"I don't want to do anything..." I didn't want to be harsh when they were only trying to help.

"Well, that's too bad," Ace said. "We aren't leaving your side. Make the best of it."

———

THE NEXT DAY, WE ALL TOOK THE DAY OFF AND WENT HIKING in Point Lobos. It was less than two miles away and a short drive, and we spent the whole day there. We packed a lunch and ate on top of one of the cliffs that overlooked the water.

It was nice to get out of the house and directly under the sunshine. The air was clean, much better than my stuffy house. I was tired because I was oversleeping, having no reason to get up in the morning anymore.

Bree made sandwiches, and we enjoyed them while we listened to the waves.

"These are great, sweetheart," Cypress said as he chewed.

"Thanks," Bree said with a smile.

Sometimes I forgot I was with two couples because it didn't feel that way. It always felt like five friends hanging out, not me as the awkward fifth wheel. "It is good..." I'd been a dick for the past few days, and I knew I needed to lighten up. They would only tolerate my bad attitude for so long.

"Thanks," Bree said.

I stared out at the ocean, and my mind wandered back to Celeste. I wondered what she was doing in Paris, if she thought about me as often as I thought about her. Did Henry quit his job? Was she happy?

Ace knew my thoughts drifted away and tapped me on the arm. "Look, there's dolphins."

I saw them swimming at the edge of the cliff face, jumping and splashing around. I saw dolphins so often that it wasn't novel anymore. I nodded then took another bite of my sandwich. "Cool..."

"You won't always feel this way." Amelia spoke from her place in the circle, sitting on a towel with her water bottle in front of her. "I've been through a lot...as you know. I can promise you it gets better, Blade. At the time, we all think heartbreak will kill us...but we survive."

"Thanks, Amy," I whispered. If I didn't have them, I would have suffered a million times worse. In my darkest hour, I counted my blessings. "Thanks for everything, guys. I know you have other stuff to do, but you stay with me... I appreciate it."

"You know we love you," Bree said.

"Yeah, man," Ace said. "You're our brother."

I forced a smile, but it was partially genuine. "I know. I love you too..."

ACE PULLED UP IN HIS RANGE ROVER AND STOPPED IN FRONT of my house.

I opened the door and hopped out, and that's when I noticed Celeste sitting on my porch.

With two suitcases.

"Oh, shit..." Ace whispered.

"She came back!" Bree squealed from the back seat.

"Shh," Cypress hissed. "Ace, drive off."

"Oh yeah." I heard the door slam as Ace hit the gas and drove up the street.

I didn't look at the car because I was too absorbed in the sight right in front of me. Celeste was here, sitting on my porch and looking at me. She wore no makeup, and she was in jeans and a t-shirt, her most casual appearance.

It took me a second to understand this was real. I wasn't making it up or having a dream.

She was really standing in front of my door.

I slowly walked forward and took the steps until I reached the walkaway.

She looked at me with an expression of uncertainty, obviously unsure if she would be greeted with open arms. She did pick him. She did leave with him. That was her choice.

But she also chose to come back.

I stared down at her, unable to form words with my mouth.

She stood up and looked me in the eye, her face pale

and her eyes dead inside. She looked like she was on the verge of crying, tears ready to escape like water bursting from a dam. "When we got to France, I stayed there for a day. I went back to my apartment where all my things are... I told him we would make it work. But it didn't feel like home. It didn't feel right. It didn't... I should have stayed with you."

My chest rose and fell heavily as the truth sank into me. This wasn't a mirage. I was really looking at the ocean, not a desert.

"I'm sorry I hurt you," she said with a strained voice. "I'm sorry I left. I just hope...you love me enough to take me back."

I didn't think before I spoke. The words left my mouth all on their own. "You already know I do."

The tears broke through and streaked down her face. She moved into my body and wrapped her arms around my neck, crying into my chest.

I turned into my protective lover mode, wrapping my entire body around her to make her feel safe. I let her cry into my chest, and I consoled her at the same time. My woman was back, my lady. I loved her so damn much. My chest ached just thinking about it. "Don't ever leave again—unless I come with you."

"I promise." Her tears clung to my neck and slipped underneath my shirt. She pulled her face away and kissed me on the mouth, her soft lips feeling incredible against mine. My tongue detected the salt from her tears, and that made me need to possess her even more.

I never wanted her to cry again.

I would never make her cry again.

"Blade, I love you... I love you more than I could understand."

My hand cupped her cheek, and I forced her gaze on me.

"I was scared...just like you said."

"Are you scared now?" I whispered.

"No. Never again."

I finally kissed her, knowing this woman was now a part of me. She was beautiful, strong, and passionate. She was my other half, and I never thought my other half could be so magnificent. I would love her every day for the rest of my life.

And make her a part of my family.

21

BREE

"Have you heard from Blade?" I grabbed the ball off the sand and threw it as hard as I could. Dino was so fast that it wasn't worth his time to go short distances. He would just be back with the ball in two seconds. So I had to launch it far and into the edge of the water so he had to combat the waves to get his toy.

It kept him in shape.

"No," Cypress said. "He hasn't been at work all day, so I assume he's getting laid—a lot."

"Ooh...he's living the dream."

"Yep. We would know." Cypress walked beside me and displayed a handsome grin. The sun was hitting his face perfectly, showing off his tanned skin and chiseled face. He'd just shaved, so more of his beautiful skin was visible.

"True."

Dino was back in a heartbeat and dropped the ball at my feet. "Geez, he's too fast. It's like he's still a puppy."

Cypress snatched the ball and threw it farther than I did, getting some distance so Dino would tire out. "It'll be years before he slows down. By then, we'll have kids. So the timing will be good."

When he spoke of the future in that context, it didn't bother me anymore. Having a son who shared his likeness would make me happy. Starting a family and letting our love grow like flowers in a garden was a dream come true. "Yeah..." Cypress and I had a routine for our daily lives, but its predictability was wonderful. I loved waking up to his face in the morning, making love when we were still half asleep, and then heading off to the business we both owned. After work, we took turns making dinner then we spent the evening in front of the fire, talking or watching TV. At night, we made love again then went straight to sleep.

To some people, it might seem boring.

But I loved it.

Dino was back once again.

Cypress threw the ball. "That dog is buff."

"I couldn't run like that if I tried."

"That's not true. You ran that marathon."

"But I didn't sprint it," I countered.

Cypress chuckled then grabbed my hand. Like some of the other couples along the beach, we strolled along like two people in love and enjoying the sunset. When we reached the far right of the beach, the sun was just about to dip behind the ocean. Watching the sun disappear over the horizon was something I would never get tired of. It was a wonderful sight, witnessing the change of daylight to evening.

Dino came back with the ball and dropped it at our feet. But he took a seat, his tongue hanging out as he caught his breath.

I crossed my arms over my chest as I watched the

refracted light meet my eyes. The sun was gone, but the rays still penetrated across the sky. "Isn't that amazing?"

Cypress was silent.

He wasn't standing beside me, so I turned around, expecting him to tower over me with his extra foot in height.

But he was on one knee.

With an open box in his hand.

`Along with a diamond ring.

My eyes started at the glorious diamond, and I lost my breath. All logical thought died inside my brain. I stared at the man I loved as he kneeled before me, asking me to marry him even though he'd already asked me this once before. "Cypress..."

"Marry me."

I cupped my mouth as the tears started. They dripped down my face and stuck to my hand. "Oh my god."

He grabbed my elbow and dragged my left hand down so he could slide the ring onto my finger. It was a princess-cut diamond, and it was more beautiful than anything I ever could have imagined. "How much longer are you going to make me wait?"

"Yes!" I charged into his body and fell to the sand so I could wrap my arms around him. I ended up knocking him over, but he laughed so I knew it was okay. He took the hit as we fell, and he rolled over onto his back so I could be on top of his chest. When he looked up at me, he didn't just wear an expression of love. It was joy mixed with relief, and I knew exactly why.

"Thanks for marrying me—again."

"Thanks for asking—again."

He cupped my face and kissed me. "I'd ask you as many times as you wanted—if you always said yes."

WE SKIPPED OUR DINNER RESERVATIONS AND WENT STRAIGHT home, no longer hungry because we were both high on joy. We kept Dino downstairs and headed to our bedroom. Piece by piece, our clothes slipped off and fell to the floor. When I only wore my ring, we were both in bed, our naked bodies tangled together.

Cypress's heavy mass sank me into the mattress, and he pressed his hips between my thighs, forcing them to fall open as he pressed his cock against my folds. His length rubbed against me, feeling the slick stickiness that my body produced en masse.

My hands explored his chest as I looked directly into his face, seeing the masculine tension in his corded neck. His blue eyes were hypnotic but also hard as a glacier of ice. His look was hot enough to burn me, make me melt quicker than a pat of butter on the stove top.

His black ring sat on his left hand, the place where it belonged and never left. Since he'd moved in, I'd never seen him remove it. When he went to bed, he didn't put it on his nightstand. When he took a shower, it was still on his finger. Now he wore it as he held himself on top of me, the metal touching the skin along my rib cage.

He grabbed the base of his cock and guided the head inside me, meeting my soaking wet pussy and sliding inside.

I was so wet. At least I didn't have to be embarrassed since this was my husband.

He slid entirely inside and absorbed my tightness with a gentle moan.

"Cypress..." I just fell in love with him more. My hands gripped his back, and I felt the metal of my band dig into his skin. It was the same ring I'd worn for years, but now it felt old and new at the exact same time.

"Wife." He pressed his face to mine and rocked into me. "Husband..."

He moaned at the sound of the title, the use of the word turning him on. He rocked the bed harder, crashing my metal headboard into the wall. He picked up speed and moved faster, fucking me hard before he fucked me slow.

Our lips moved together, and our breaths were synced. When he moaned, I did too. When the sweat collected on his body, it collected on mine. We grabbed each other, our lips breaking apart and then coming together again. I could feel his definitive hardness as he swelled inside me, ready to give me his seed the second I was ready to collect it.

My tits shook up and down with his movements, my nipples hard and rubbing against his body. My legs were wide apart, and I shifted them wider still, wanting all of that cock—balls deep.

Cypress folded my body so he could get deeper, wanting to plunge his desire inside me fully. He pushed through my slick tightness, stretching me wide open and making me feel full like every husband should make his wife feel.

I pressed my face against his chest and saw my diamond catch the light, watch it glitter in the minimal light. It was more than just a pretty ring, but the sign of our eternal commitment. I just wished I'd worn it as long as he wore his.

I didn't want to come right away, but I couldn't fight it anymore. I breathed into his face and let out a scream that shook the walls. "Oh god...Cypress."

He pumped into me harder, grinding his body against my clit and making me writhe until my orgasm hit its peak then began to pass. Our bodies smacked together as we moved, and the slick sounds our wet bodies made heightened the sex.

I wanted him to keep pleasing me, but I wanted to please my husband. "I want you to come inside me. Give it to me."

He moaned before he released, giving me all of his come —mounds of it.

My nails dug into his arms, and I locked my ankles around his waist, keeping him sheathed inside me so I could absorb all of his come. It felt so good to have his seed inside, heavy and warm.

Cypress caught his breath when he finished but didn't pull out of me.

"How much come can you stuff inside me tonight?" My hands moved up his chest and to his shoulders.

"We're about to find out."

WHEN I OPENED MY EYES THE NEXT MORNING, I WAS ALONE.

It was just me and Dino.

Cypress was nowhere to be seen. When I touched his side of the bed, the sheets were cold, so he'd been gone for a while. I sat up in bed, and Dino's eyes perked at the shift in the mattress. "Cypress?" If he were downstairs, he would hear me.

No response.

I reached for my phone on the nightstand to call him but saw a note instead.

It was from him.

SWEETHEART,

Put on your wedding dress and meet me at the Perry House at
5. I'll be waiting for you.
Happy Anniversary.
Love,
Your Husband

I READ THE NOTE AGAIN AND REALIZED IT WAS HALLOWEEN.
How could I have forgotten? I jumped out of bed and found
my wedding dress hanging in the center of the closet. It had
just been pressed because it didn't have a single wrinkle.
The bottom was absent of dirt too, which told me someone
had dry-cleaned it.

"Oh my god…" I was getting married today.

It was my wedding day.

The front door opened and closed downstairs. I could
hear it because the acoustics were crazy in this house.
"Cypress?"

"No." My sister's voice reached me from downstairs. Her
feet tapped against the hardwood floor as she made her way
up to me. "It's me." She stepped inside, in a purple gown
with her hair pulled back. "You got his note."

"I did…" I looked her up and down. "You look beautiful.
Is that—"

"Yep. It's the bridesmaid dress you picked out."

"You still have it?"

"Like I'd ever throw this away." She extended her arms
to me and hugged me. "I'm so excited for you, Bree."

"That means there's gonna be a wedding?"

"Yeah." Amelia pulled away and looked at me with tears
in her eyes. "Cypress and the rest of us started planning a
long time ago. I've invited everyone that came to the
wedding last time. All of your bridesmaids are here, the

food is exactly the same, the flowers are the same…everything is the same."

Speechless, all I could do was cry. The tears started immediately and streaked down my face like rain on a windowpane. "That's…I can't even…"

"If you still have doubts about Cypress, you need to forget them."

"I don't."

She held up my hand and looked at the ring. "Still as beautiful as I remember…"

"It's gorgeous. I love it."

"Cypress did a good job, but I helped him pick it out."

"It all makes sense…"

"Well, you need to start getting ready. We've gotta do your hair, your makeup, and you've got to eat something."

"Do I need to help with anything—"

"We've got it covered, alright? You just worry about enjoying the happiest day of your life."

———

ALL OF MY GIRLS WERE THERE, FRIENDS FROM HIGH SCHOOL and college. They didn't ask about my memory issue, obviously caught up and aware of the whole thing. Lily and Rose were the flower girls, and Blade looked handsome in his suit and purple tie. He was one of my bridesmaids, along with the rest of my girls.

I hadn't seen Cypress yet, and my heart was doing somersaults. I wanted the wedding to start as soon as possible so I could see him. It had only been a day since I was in his arms, but I missed him.

I missed him like crazy.

My distant relatives, friends, and family were all there.

His parents were there too, and I met them for the first time when I was getting ready. But they didn't greet me like a stranger. They greeted me like I was already their daughter.

Amelia grabbed me after I said hello to a few other friends and pulled me to the side. "The photographer is ready for your first look. Cypress is there."

I remembered the story he'd told me, but I'd just assumed I would see him after I walked down the aisle. But seeing him alone made sense, in front of the brown door with the beautiful ivy hanging down.

The moment was finally here.

Amelia guided me outside, and a few of the wedding guests spotted me, all waving and smiling. We walked up the street and turned the corner, and fifty feet away stood Cypress. His back was turned to me, his shoulders broad and powerful in his navy blue suit. His hands were held at his sides, and he stared farther up the road.

Both photographers were there, waiting to snap our pictures.

Amelia dropped her hand from my shoulder. "Walk up behind him and tap him on the shoulder when you're ready."

"Okay..."

Amelia smiled before she walked away.

Now it was just Cypress and me. The photographers were ready, but I didn't notice them off to the side. They blended in with the road, unseen. I slid my hands down the front of my dress, suddenly unable to breathe. The fabric was restricting because the panic was rising. I looked down at myself, tested my heels, and then walked forward.

The hill had a slight include, so I picked up my dress and walked twenty feet until I was close to him. When I got there, the tears started to fall. I'd experienced this moment before, years ago. All of this had already happened. I wore this dress, and he wore that suit. The sun was out and the sky was clear; the breeze smelled the same.

I couldn't believe he'd done this for me.

I stopped because I needed to get a hold of myself. I didn't want him to look at my red and blotchy face. I wanted him to see a beautiful bride. I grounded myself and forced myself to stop crying, to just feel happiness.

I stepped forward when I had pulled myself together.

But then I started to cry again.

Forget it.

I came closer to him until I stood right behind him. I knew he could hear me because I was making such noise with my shoes and tears. I stared at the center of his back, watching it rise and fall with his deep breaths. He seemed to be calm, while I was nothing but a mess.

I finally pressed my face to his back and rested my hand on his shoulder.

He paused for an instant before he turned around.

Tears were in his eyes and flowed down his cheeks. Once he looked at me, his bottom lip quivered slightly. There wasn't just happiness in his eyes, but overwhelming love and affection. He looked at me like I was the only woman in the world, the one person he'd been waiting for his entire life.

I cried harder.

My arms moved around his waist just as he brought me close to him.

That's when I noticed the stain on the front of his suit. It was tan, the same color as my foundation.

He watched my gaze. "That's your makeup...from our wedding. We were standing right here when you did it. You hugged me and cried, and that's when you marked it. You loved it so much you asked me to never wash it...and I haven't."

My fingertips felt the material, noticing how dry it was because it had happened so long ago. "Cypress..."

He brought me into his chest and buried his face in my neck. He breathed hard with me, the emotion overcoming him just the way it did with me. I had always hoped my husband would cry on our wedding day—and he did.

"I love you," I whispered.

"I love you more," he said back.

We held each other until we both stopped crying. Cypress meant the world to me because he'd never given up on me. He was always committed to me, always the best husband in the world. He could have walked away from me a long time ago, but he never did.

He was fully exonerated in my eyes.

"Thank you for giving this to me," I whispered. "For letting me experience everything that I lost."

"I promised I would help you remember. And I keep my promises."

I moved my face in front of his so I could look him in the eye, moisture pooling on the surface just like mine. "You never gave up on me..."

His fingers moved underneath my chin so he could keep my gaze locked on him. "Till death do us part."

A smile crept onto my lips even though my eyes were still damp with tears. My mascara was running, and I got another blot of foundation on the front of his suit. My fingers felt the stain, the foundation sticking to my fingertips. There were so many things I wanted to say that I couldn't get past my lips. How could I express everything that I felt in such a short amount of time? All I knew was we were in this together—forever. "Till death do us part."

EPILOGUE

BREE

I walked downstairs and found Dino's leash in a drawer. "I'm gonna take Dino on a walk. He's been restless today."

Cypress was sitting on the couch playing a video game. His headset was on because he was playing with Blade online. "I'll be right back." He pulled the headset off and paused the game. "You're going now?"

"Yeah."

When Dino saw the leash, he started spinning in circles, excited as he wagged his tail.

This was our life now, a kind of boringness that was exciting every single day. I loved coming home at the same time and still being together all the time. We never got sick of each other. I even missed him when I took a long shower.

"I'll come along," he said.

"You can finish your game. I don't mind."

"Nah. I'd rather spend time with you." He smiled as he walked toward me, six foot three of all man.

I smiled back, more in love with him than I ever thought possible. "Alright. Let's get going before it gets dark."

I walked outside with Dino while Cypress grabbed his sweater. Dino didn't even need a leash, but I liked to put it on him just to be sure. I had just straightened out the leash when Dino spotted a squirrel and sprinted.

"Dino!"

He ran right into the street where he knew he wasn't supposed to go. Thankfully, there wasn't a car in sight, but that didn't matter.

"Dino!" I walked down the steps, slipped on the stone, and fell back. My head collided with the step behind me.

And then everything turned black.

"Fuck." Cypress's deep voice filled the room.

"Cypress." Amelia's soft voice came to my ear. "It'll be alright. The doctor said she's gonna be fine."

"What if she goes back?" he asked frantically. "What if she forgets everything that happened in the past six months? What if she forgets me...?"

"Before we assume the worst, let's wait until she wakes up," Blade said. "Cypress, calm down."

"You calm down," Cypress hissed. "This is my wife. I just got her back..." His voice broke. "I can't lose her again. I can't do it."

"Dude, it's gonna be okay," Ace said. "When we know more about the situation, then we can panic."

They finally went quiet.

I was aware of the IV in my arm, of the catheter between my legs, and the beep of the monitor. My eyes were still closed, but I knew I was in a hospital room.

Why?

Why was I here?

I forced my body to open my eyes, and they fluttered open until I could take in my surroundings. All the walls were white, and a blue curtain blocked the open door. My sister was there, along with all of my friends.

Cypress was there too.

He sat in a chair and leaned forward, his elbows resting on his knees while his head was bowed. A black ring sat on his left hand.

I stared at everyone, feeling the blood pressure cuff tighten on my arm.

Amelia was the first one to notice my eyes were open. "Bree?"

Cypress's head snapped up, and he stared at me. His eyes narrowed, and the emotion immediately leapt into his look. He rose to his feet but didn't come close to me.

"Bree, it's me." Amelia came to my side and rested her hand on my arm. "Your sister."

Blade stood up and was on my other side. "Hey, how are you feeling?"

"What year is it?" Ace asked.

"Give her a second," Amelia hissed.

I blinked my eyes again and looked at Cypress.

Cypress stepped back and angled his head, his chest rising and falling heavily. "She doesn't remember me..." The tears burned in his eyes and reflected the fluorescent lights. "She doesn't..."

I blinked again, realizing I'd hit my head on the stairs. I remembered Dino running out into the street. I remembered Cypress yelling behind me. I remembered coming up behind him and tapping him on the shoulder on our wedding day.

But I also remembered so many other things.

I remembered the day he came to my house a year after

we broke up. I remembered him apologizing and asking for another chance. I turned him down and ignored him, but he showed up at the café every single day for lunch and didn't stop until I agreed to go out with him. Then we had dinner at Olives, and we split a plate of hummus.

Then my memories shifted to all of my friends being angry that I was seeing Cypress again. Amelia was more pissed than everyone else. I kept sleeping with Cypress anyway until I couldn't lie about it anymore...

And then we fell in love.

He earned my trust back.

We were together for a year before we moved in together to my grandmother's house.

And then he proposed...

And then we were married.

I remembered all of it. I remembered realizing he was my next-door neighbor, only to find out about my accident that ruined my memory. When I hit my head again, it was fixed.

But now I remembered everything like I'd never hit my head at all.

I remembered everything. "Cypress..."

He stood with his hands on his hips, eyeing me with uncertainty. He slowly walked toward me, his shoes tapping against the tile floor. He stopped when he was right beside the bed, looking terrified of whatever I might say next.

My hand reached for his, and I felt his wedding ring. "I remember..."

He took a breath so deep it could have broken both of his lungs.

"But I remember everything else...I remember our wedding day. I remember when you proposed to me. I remember when you moved in for the first time. I remember when you asked me to forgive you."

Everyone exchanged looks, confused by what I was saying.

"Wait...you remember everything that happened the first time?" Cypress whispered.

I nodded then sat up in bed, tugging on the IV slightly. "I remember you made me fall in love with you...and then you did it again." My eyes watered when I looked at my husband, the man I'd loved for the last four years. I had him back. I had all of my memories back.

I had my soul mate back.

That's when I started to sob. "I remember..."

Cypress sat at the edge of the bed and hugged me. "Oh my god..."

"I remember everything." I squeezed him hard and sobbed into his chest. "I remember..."

Cypress cried with me, his chest heaving and falling. "Sweetheart...I don't think I've ever been so happy."

"I don't think I have either." I pulled away and looked him in the eye, seeing the tears match my own. "You stayed... You could have left, but you stayed."

"I would never leave you," he whispered. "No matter what."

I wiped away my tears and sniffed. "You knew I would come back to you."

He nodded slightly. "And even if you didn't...it wouldn't change anything."

I cupped his face and kissed him, kissing the man I loved more than anything else in this world. Not only did I get him back...I got myself back as well. I remembered Rose's fourth birthday party. I remembered our honeymoon. I remembered the first day we got Dino as a puppy. "I love you, Cypress. So much…"

He squeezed me against him. "I love you too, sweetheart."

Amelia sniffled as she stood beside the bed. Blade sat on the other side and rested his hand on my back. Ace came next to Amelia and rested his arm on Cypress's shoulder.

"Let's give them some privacy," Amelia whispered.

"No." I pulled away from Cypress and looked at all of them. "I missed you…I missed you all so much."

We came together for a group hug, all of us trying to fit on the bed at the same time.

I hadn't felt this much love and this much happiness at one time. I was unlucky enough to lose years of my life, but I was even more blessed to get all those years back, to get my family back. Now I had everything…everything I had lost.

I had it all.

AFTERWORD

Dear Reader,

Thank you for reading 218 First Hugs. I hope you enjoyed reading it as much as I enjoyed writing it. If you could leave a short review, it would help me so much! Those reviews are the best kind of support you can give an author. Thank you!

Wishing you love,

E. L. Todd

ABOUT THE AUTHOR

Subscribe to my newsletter for updates on new releases, giveaways, and for my comical monthly newsletter. You'll get all the dirt you need to know. Sign up today.

www.eltoddbooks.com

Facebook:

https://www.facebook.com/ELTodd42

Twitter:
@E_L_Todd